Angelwalk
&
Stedfast

Roger Elwood

ELM HILL BOOKS
A Division of Thomas Nelson Publishers
Since 1798

www.thomasnelson.com

To Dorothy Elwood
—and her wisdom that
I should return to my destiny

Angelwalk & Stedfast ISBN: 1-4041-8572-0

For additions, deletions, corrections or clarifications in future editions of this text, please contact Paul Shepherd, Editor in Chief for Elm Hill Books. Email pshepherd@elmhillbooks.com

This is a work of fiction. The characters, incidents, and dialogues are products of the author's imagination and are not to be construed as real. Any resemblance to actual events or persons, living or dead, is entirely coincidental.

Products from Elm Hill Books may be purchased in bulk for educational, business, fundraising, or sales promotional use. For information, please email SpecialMarkets@ThomasNelson.com.

Cover design: Margaret Pesek
Interior design: Mark Ross / MJ Ross Design

Printed in the United States of America

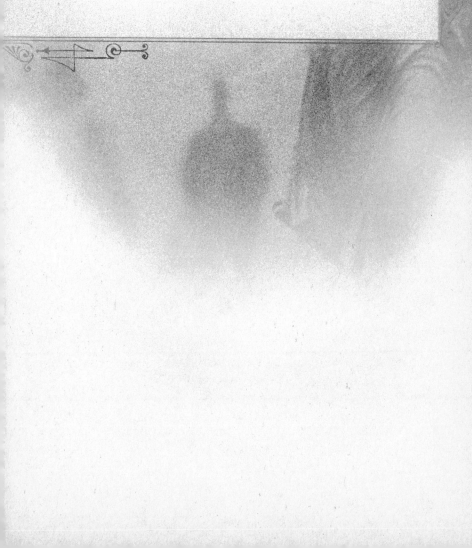

ANGELWALK

One

I CANNOT AGE, BUT I DO FEEL somehow old as I sit here, on a mountaintop overlooking the plain where the last great battle of Mankind has taken place. The bodies number into the thousands, and blood collects everywhere—giant, deep pools like a titanic wave over the ground, submerging it. It is possible to drown in blood down there . . .

I momentarily turn away; the odor so strong that it ascends the mountain. I try to close my ears because the cries of the dying are loud enough to form a crescendo that also reaches me—but there is no escaping the panorama below; either in its sights or its sounds.

I decide to leave the mountain and go down to the plain where the old prophecies always had been pointing with devastating clarity.

Some of the dying have had the flesh literally seared from their bones, and they have only seconds left, those that survived at all. They see me, of course—the living do not—but those nearly dead, suspended, in a sense, between two kinds of life indeed, see, reach out, beg.

"Please help me, sir," I am asked again and again.

"The pain . . ."

"I know I've been blinded, now; yet I see you anyway I see—"

Ahead, standing as though on an island uplifted in the midst of a blood red sea, are several hundred soldiers, but no longer with weapons, their former bodily shells lying at their feet.

I approach them.

"We could not continue," one of them tells me. "All of us asked for God's forgiveness through Jesus the Christ."

"There is no doubt that many of our comrades are doomed," another adds, "because of their allegiance to the Devil. We bid them good-bye . . ."

One by one they ascend. The final soldier turns to me, smiles, says, "We did the right thing."

I nod.

. . . we did the right thing.

Yes, they did—all of them—that one group of hundreds out of countless thousands.

They refused the Antichrist. And he had them slaughtered as a result, threatening to do just that once again to any others who might decide to rebel.

And now—

Not one of them bore the scars of how they died—no bayonet wounds, no bullet holes. In their resurrection they had been healed, given the bodies that would be theirs throughout eternity.

But the others share not at all the same end. Every few seconds, more are dying. Bodies piled upon bodies, visible where the blood is not quite deep enough to hide them. I look about, and see hands raised against the sky, like stalks of marsh grass in a bloody inlet. For an instant only. Then cut down.

They also see me. They surround me as I go past, trying not to look at them, their eyes haunted where they yet have eyes. Some do not, seared away; only the empty sockets remain. But they see me just the same. And all turn away; knowing they will spend eternity like that—in agony; flames searing them but never fully consuming.

The scene oppresses. I cannot stand it any longer. I leave, not sure of where to go. I have time at my disposal. I can do whatever I want with it, yes, even choose to stay where I am—in this time and place— or retreat through the centuries, their contents disgorged at my very feet.

And yet, in a way that is beyond mere loneliness—oh, how wonderful if it were but a question of being merely lonely—I have nowhere to go. An irony that presses me down inflicts on me a weariness that is so pervasive it is as though all of history has become a singular weight from which it is well-nigh impossible to extricate myself. And I think, in tremulous recollection, of all that preceded this moment, this literal battlefield on which I find myself.

Lord, I whisper with prayerful intent against the dissipating sounds of the vanquished. My dear, dear Lord.

~◦~

The beginning.

We are sitting by a crystal lake. A hint of violets surrounds us with its gentle scent.

"Do you know what I used to feel really guilty about on earth?"

The question is asked by a man who had been a show business agent during his mortal life.

"I would be interested in learning about it," I tell him with full sincerity;

He smiles as he says, "When I worked with clients on Broadway; I met plenty of angels, but they weren't like you at all."

We both enjoy the humor of that and then he adds, "My conscience hit me hard, in those days, for two reasons: One, the type of individual with whom I often had to work. I remember the guy who headed one of the studios. One day, he invited me to a party given by a producer. I went, against my better judgment. What I encountered was loathsome—open perverted activity, the consumption of illegal drugs, blasphemous jokes, and much more. Many of the offenders were extremely influential in the entertainment business. They had a stranglehold on what the public saw in theatres and on television.

"The second area of difficulty was when I had to pass judgment on people, when I had to decide who was or wasn't worth. Now I know that all of us are worthwhile in the sight of God, that He is concerned about every creation of His, whether a sparrow in the field or a jet pilot or even an agent. But in those days I earned my living in an environment that paid lip service to values and honor and integrity and self-image but in the end created the conditions for the destruction of each of those.

"So there I was, looking at this actor or that one, and I would have to say that one would make it big in the profession, and another might as well quit early. Again and again I played a kind of god game with those kids.

"Actually most took it well, better than I would have, while others did not—but then something happened that changed the whole rat race for me."

"What was that?" I ask.

"I met this exceptionally handsome young actor—tall, attractive and, yes, extremely talented. He was a real contender for the starring role in a potent new TV series. Then someone else came by and he seemed just right also. I had to choose between them."

"So what was the difference between that incident and any of the others?"

"I had to turn down the first young man. He took it hard, so hard in fact that he shot himself to death less than a week later. He left a suicide note that read, 'I have no worth as a human being. I have nothing. I am nothing. I return to nothing.'

"I was never the same after that. About a month later I accepted Christ as Savior and Lord because I realized that I felt very, very worthless at that point, that the only redemption for me was that which the Lord purchased with His shed blood at Calvary."

He pauses, looking at the lake, its surface sparkling like the diamonds described by poets.

"I will never again have to judge another human being. And I myself have been judged and found acceptable in the sight of Almighty God."

He stands, smiling.

"I've just arrived, and would like to experience more of what I could only dream about back on Earth. Would you excuse me, Darien? That is your name, isn't it?"

"Yes," I say simply.

He walks off, cherubs dancing at his feet.

I wish . . .

The words are unspoken, thought only.

I turn and go in another direction. Soon I am talking to people born mentally retarded who now have minds like Augustine or Luther. And the parents who deeply loved them, who stayed with them, who shared the anguish because of their steadfast faith that "all things work together for good"—these parents have been repaid a thousand times, for what carnal life denied them is fully realized in Heaven; children with whole minds and bodies, children who can converse properly and walk without assistance.

I wish I could accept . . .

"If Heaven offered only that," one mother tells me, "it would be worth everything."

Those born without limbs or those who lost arms or legs or hands through accidents are now restored. They have been "repaired." One woman who had never had any limbs at all and who remained a human oddity all her life can now walk about, jumping, running, and shaking hands with everyone, her face aglow.

Those once blind can see and stroll through the parks and gardens, looking with astonishment; those once deaf just sit and listen; those born mute gather in little groups and chatter away.

I wish I could accept all this without . . .

I meet a man known informally as "the Intellectual." He greets me with abundant enthusiasm.

"There was a time when I. would have labeled all this as abject nonsense," he admits. "Strolling through Heaven! Saying hello to an angel! There was a time when I would have—"

He interrupts himself, saying, "I looked at life as a uniformity of natural causes in a closed system. How could God, if He existed, which, of course, wasn't the case . . . how could God suddenly reach down into that system anytime He desired, and bring about the Incarnation, the parting of the Red Sea, the healing of lepers? No! I said to myself and to others. A thousand times no! Any thought of the supernatural was sheer idiocy and I would have no part of it.

"I lived in a kind of cocoon, refusing to acknowledge that anything at all existed outside it. What I couldn't see, feel, hold, or reason out didn't exist as far as I was concerned.

"And God as a concept simply failed to compute, as I said back on Earth. He threw my entire equation out, and since that was the case, I ended up throwing Him out because that equation and the scientific concepts from which it originated were my life's foundation. That was what I worshipped, not pie-in-the-sky puffery."

"What changed you?" I ask.

"It was the strangest moment, frankly. I owned a private plane. I was out in it one day; alone. Something malfunctioned in the motor. I saw smoke. The plane nosedived. There was no possibility; considering the elevation and how fast it was falling, that I would survive.

"I prayed then. I know, in looking back, how extraordinary that was. Me, the atheist—I prayed! I had heard all about so-called foxhole Christians and I had scorned their weakness, their instability; yes, their hypocrisy. And yet I was doing the same thing.

"Well, I survived, sustaining remarkably few injuries, certainly nothing serious. As I climbed out of the wreckage of that plane, my first thought was about how little pain I felt! I had some cuts, some bruises, but nothing else.

"I was, of course, glad to be alive. But the fact that I was alive stunned me. I examined all my safe, scientific theories, computed in my mind the logical possibility that I would be alive, and yet nothing supported the reality I was experiencing at that moment which was, simply; my survival.

"I remembered that quick, strangely instinctive prayer: Nothing else could have explained what had happened. God had stepped into my closed world, penetrated my humanistic cocoon—and given me a life that, according to the proper computerized readout, should have been wiped out.

"But you know; that wasn't all. I learned something else. I learned the meaning of His forgiveness, the validity of it, the depth of it. I had spent much of my adult life trying to convince others that He was simply a myth and that Karl Marx had had it right when he called religion an opiate for the masses. I destroyed the faith of thousands, you know. And yet God chose to forgive me. I was driven to tears as I understood the significance of that. I closed myself off from everyone for weeks. When I emerged from that self-imposed solitude, I became like Saul of Tarsus. The new me was St. Paul, dedicated to the Kingdom, not bent on causing it to crumble."

We talk a bit more, and then he goes off. Isaac Newton is waiting for him . . .

I wish I could accept all this without the questions, one after the other.

Now I am standing beside a golden sea. The waters are pure, clear; birds swoop overhead. No longer is it necessary for them to kill in order to survive. One of them lands next to me, and walks up to me. I run my hand down its back; it chatters contentedly, and then takes off again.

Earlier, I watched as lions played with lambs. (A lamb hid behind a tree and as a lion was walking past, jumped out at it. The king of beasts yelped in mock surprise, and was about to pretend to run when it discovered the identity of the culprit. No roar escaped its jaws; instead it licked the lamb on the forehead, and the two walked off together, the lion wagging its tail, the lamb trying to wag what little it had for a tail.)

I wish I could accept all this without the questions, one after the other, that keep hammering at me . . .

I think back to when they first started. It was soon after my friend Lucifer was forced to leave Heaven, taking with him a third of all of the angels.

And the great dragon was cast out, that old serpent, called the Devil, which deceiveth the whole world: he was cast out into the earth, and his angels were cast out with him . . . And his tail drew the third part of the stars of heaven, and did cast them to the earth.

Those who remained were told that he had exalted himself too highly, that he proposed to be on a level with God and, in fact, eventually to assume His very throne.

How art thou fallen from heaven, O Lucifer, son of the morning! How art thou cut down to the ground, who didst weaken the nations! For thou hast said in thine heart, I will . . . exalt my throne above the stars of God . . . I will ascend above the heights of the clouds, I will be like the Most High.

I never was able to converse with him about this. The Casting Out happened so quickly. And since then I have asked myself, again and again, one singular question: What was the whole story?

As I remember the moments I did spend with Lucifer, I can see some elements of ego in him, some hint that he was different from the rest of us.

Different . . .

Indeed that was the case—the most glorious of all—with a countenance second only to the Trinity's. A majestic bearing, a power that made him truly stand out.

Others gathered around him. We all listened to his ideas. But as for myself I really never had anything to be discontented about. I yet recall my first moment of existence—from nothingness to awareness, looking up into the very face of God, knowing that though He had created ten thousand upon ten thousand of us, each was special to Him, each as though the only one. God reached down and took my wings and breathed into me the power of life, of flight, the reality of immortality. He first created my very self, and then He gave that self life everlasting.

I was grateful to Him. I came into existence in the midst of a place so beautiful, so good in every way that I had no reason to be discontent. When there is perfection, what could be better?

But Lucifer, I do admit, was not the same at all. Does this mean that God made a mistake? No, He created us—He never dominates us. We are His servants but not His slaves.

Yet was what Lucifer had done so serious, so pervasive that a loving, forgiving Creator could not forgive him? And yet later the Father sent His Son to die so that forgiveness was purchased for the rest of time. How could the same God not also forgive Lucifer and give His finest creation another chance, a chance to change, to—?

Always the same doubt—from just after the Casting Out to the birth of Christ as God Incarnate to His death, burial and resurrection and beyond, to the present. Doubt unchallenged, becoming ever more compelling . . .

Ultimately I decide I cannot endure my inner turmoil any longer. I shudder contemplating what I am about to do . . .

~✺~

"Are you going to see Him now?" my friend and fellow angel Stedfast asks.

"Yes, I have requested a meeting and He has agreed."

"Do you think, really; that is wise, Darien? Why not just accept, and trust?"

"Can you . . . do that?"

"Oh, yes, Darien," Stedfast replies without hesitation. "It is not difficult for me. I see all that has been, and all that is, and what the prophecies promise will be, and I know that acceptance and trust are right and, yes, deserved by God as our response to all that He has done."

"I wish I could accept without question," I say; "as you are doing. I did once, before the Casting Out, but now—"

"Earth, my friend Darien, is where doubts grow. Heaven is where they are put to rest, forever."

Our conversation ends only because it is time for the meeting that will determine my destiny.

In an instant I am with Almighty God, alone, no one to interrupt us. He knew, totally, of my concerns. His plan had been set, I suspect, ever since the Casting Out, He waited only for me to ask . . .

"All around us is warfare, Darien. My prophet Daniel spoke of a ministering angel being late because of having to do battle in the heavenly realm. Satan tries to cause havoc whenever and wherever he can."

I had never been on the front lines myself. Suddenly the stranger. is of that fact hits me hard. It is as though God knew I would not be a committed warrior but instead something of a pacifist, not at all certain of the enemy. Yet I had heard, in any event, stories about Lucifer, whispers from the battlefield about a shadowy; almost mythical figure—or at least that was what he had become over the ages as memories of him firsthand faded. The Lucifer I knew had a rich baritone voice and he used it to good effect as he persuaded angel after angel, but certainly he was not a loathsome adversary as would be told by returning warriors, with their tales of contending over the spirits of saints, awful encounters between demonic creatures and the heavenly defenders. I recall in particular an alleged foiling of a plan to storm the gates of Heaven itself; yes, it had brought chills to my very being, and yet I could never decide how much was battlefield bravado and how much was factual.

"I need you with me in this battle, Darien. But I cannot have you halfway. I must have your totality of commitment. You cannot fight an enemy whom you find appealing or whom you think is being dealt with unjustly."

God gives me a choice then: Indeed, I can go to Earth for as long as needed. Since time is not an actuality but merely a contrivance for the convenience of Man, I would be given the ability to go anywhere or any "time" I want. If I felt, at the conclusion, that Lucifer had been dealt with improperly or that perhaps he had reformed, then God would allow Lucifer back into Heaven, along with the others. If, however, the evidence supported the verdict, the justice of Lucifer's exile, then I would in fact return, alone, without so much as a whimper, and in the process forever abandon any notion of following in Lucifer's footsteps.

"Yours is a terrible responsibility, Darien. Your findings will affect all of us forever."

I leave God's immediate presence to ponder just a bit more what should be my course of action. Before that decision is made, I meet with several more of those in Heaven who had spent their mortal lives on earth.

One man tells me of being in an airplane, relaxing, when suddenly a bomb explodes. Directly ahead of him a six-year-old child is torn out of her mother's arms and sucked through a gaping hole in the side of the craft. An elderly woman has the fingers of one hand ripped off on jagged pieces of metal. The man chronicling this dies as he goes through a secondary hole that is just barely wide enough for him; he can feel flesh catching on the twisted metal and his lungs collapsing as the pressure changes drastically.

"It is violent down there," the man says but without fear any longer. After all, he is in Heaven where there is no fear, no sorrow.

I next meet a woman.

"I was attacked and killed while walking home," she says calmly. "It was at night. Perhaps I should have been more careful. But I tended to trust people, to think the best of them while not taking into consideration the sin nature that is part of every human being on the face of the earth.

"And, you know what, no one came to help me. I sensed there were people around, people who heard me scream, people who even could see what was going on, but they were afraid for themselves."

No bitterness exists—such would be out of place in Heaven. She is merely recalling the events. If anything, there was pity for the ones who stood by and did nothing, her dying agony buried in the corridors of their minds perhaps for the rest of their lives, like a haunting cloud always on the horizon.

"I left behind two sons and a daughter as well as my dear husband. I am so grateful that all of them do know Christ as Savior and Lord and they will be here, with me, eventually, and then there won't be any separations again, ever."

She is now smiling, a radiant look indeed.

I talk with others, find out more about life on Earth than I ever imagined could have been true, primarily because I had never asked questions before. My concerns, my doubts are spurring me on. Surely the picture being painted must be distorted in some way. How could it be entirely attributed to Lucifer? How could it be that Lucifer is guilty of stirring up such evil?

"Lord, I will go," I say finally.

He looks at me with an expression unfathomable but not unkind. My Lord could never be that.

"You go with the prayers of Heaven behind you," He says with great tenderness.

And then it happens. One minute I am in Heaven, the next, my odyssey has begun . . . .

Two

THERE IS NO TRANSITION PERIOD.

It is like stepping from one room to another. I go through an invisible door, and, suddenly, I am on Earth. I have experienced no bursts of light, no swirling gasses, no rolling thunder. I have instantaneously negotiated the void that must be faced by every human being, whether on the way to Heaven or to Hell; whatever the direction it is a journey, yea, destiny inescapable, profoundly inescapable. But I have simply gone in the opposite direction . . . .

It starts out well, this journey, for me. The day is Sunday. I hear the sound of hymns. I am out in the country. The sun is directly overhead, the air bright, clear. Flowers are blooming. I walk beside a busy road, automobiles passing by at a steady, fast clip. I begin to feel very good indeed. This is the way I pictured the world. Perhaps there are unpleasant things, things that should never be, and yet not to the extent we all had supposed. Those who went off to fight spiritual battles in heavenly places dealt with the extremes, the fallen angels who had gone over the edge and could never be redeemed. But they are the exceptions— all the old stories of corruption upon corruption simply cannot be true, I tell myself. Nothing could be as bad, as decadent, as pervasive as that.

And this Sunday, this cheerful, clear, mellow Sunday, goes a long way toward bearing out my notions. I see many people dressed well, smiling, walking up a pathway to the front door of a country church. It is a white building, made principally of wood, not a garish structure at all, but obviously one made with respect and love, for those who would worship inside and for the beloved God toward whom they would direct that worship.

I join the congregation. The hymn has ended, and there is now a sermon being delivered. The pastor is in his mid-fifties, tall, fine-looking, his voice commanding, encouraging at times, reprimanding at others, filled with the sort of wisdom that can come only from being based in the Word of God. It is a powerful sermon—yes, it talks of sin, it warns of becoming prisoners of the sin nature in each and every human being in that building—but it is a message of hope as well, hope that is the whole foundation beneath the death of Christ at Calvary. Otherwise, that death was wholly in vain, mocking His suffering.

The pastor finishes, another hymn is sung, and then everyone starts to leave. My attention focuses on one family in particular.

The father is still young, in his mid-forties, the mother in her late thirties; they have two children, a teenage daughter and a son in his very early twenties.

Happy.

That strikes me immediately. A solid, happy family. I join them as they drive home. I stay with them as they share a Sunday dinner of roast beef, natural dark gravy, French fried potatoes, green beans, and apple pie. (I almost wish I could know hunger so that such a meal could satisfy me.)

They talk quite a bit—I enjoy the sound of their voices. I enjoy seeing them laugh and hug one another, seeing them express what is wonderful, what is beautiful indeed about humanness. There is a bit of sadness in me as I see but do not participate, as I watch them sharing but must be set apart myself, with them but not of them.

Much time passes. For me, in Heaven, there was no such thing, of course. Time is nonexistent there—that which is forever cannot be measured by seconds or minutes or even millennia.

And yet I am in a world that exists on time, that can be tyrannized by it, that at the very least cannot escape it, all the smashed clocks, all the rundown batteries, all the rusty or clogged or spent movements notwithstanding. It is a world where the greatest of rulers, where the most powerful of nations, no matter what the circumstance, all are captive to time.

I shake myself from my musings. This family's day is ending but mine cannot. They sleep, but I am unable to do so. I spend my first night literally not knowing what to do. Others in Heaven, the humans who come in a steady stream, have talked of no longer needing sleep. For many sleeplessness had been a problem. They wanted to sleep, grabbing it in troubled scraps of minutes or hours but not enjoying the refreshment of, as they say, "a good night's sleep." Now, in Heaven, they do not have it at all

and they do not need it. That seemed to be one of the more astonishing realities for so many.

While the family sleeps, I sit and ponder. They talked of pain, yes: an elderly family member is ill, in fact may be dying in a nearby hospital. The son is upset about his grades at college, from which he is home on vacation. The mother is concerned about her husband working overtime too much, exhausting himself. He himself seems to dislike one of his bosses but does not know what to do about it. The daughter is worried about a relationship with a boy at school.

But these are human problems. After Eden they became regular components of the human experience. They are everyday commonplace, scarcely of significant trauma. The health of the grandmother seems the most urgent matter.

And they cope. They face everything with a spirit that enables them not to be unduly concerned, not to be paranoid, a word I have heard before, as I met with some in Heaven who were relieved that they no longer have any fears, anything to fear, their minds clear, free, soaring to the fullest imaginable potential.

I find myself becoming very close to this family, and it is odd that this is the case because whereas I can see them, they cannot see me; there is no interplay between us. As far as they are concerned, I do not exist. While they believe in my kind, they do not know about me.

So I am not prepared for the events to follow, events that will send me from that family out into a world I now wish I would never have confronted . . . .

Within one week of the first time I encounter this family, they all are "dead." It is hard for me to think in those terms, for they are not now dead at all; and their present state of being provides that opportunity which could not have occurred in "life," that is, for us to meet at last. For that I rejoice. The wall finally has been broken down and—

But the way it occurred, the circumstances that took their earthly presence from them, translating them into spirit, as I am spirit . . .

That way is what appalls me as I think back upon it, as I remember being there and not able to do anything to help, an observer of human pain, trauma, looking and feeling but not—

During that week, wonderful, revealing, reassuring, I am constantly amazed by humanness. There is much, I suspect, that is unfortunately embodied in that word "humanness," but what I am seeing is a measure of what God meant from the beginning—love; patience, joy, a strength together that only the family unit can manage.

Moments of touching kindness . . . .

The son, Jon Erik, asks if he can do the lawn for his father who has come home from his business especially weary, and really needing to spend the weekend resting.

"Hey, Dad, you look tired," Jon Erik remarks. "Take it easy for a change. Okay?"

The father, Gordon, smiles, nods, thanks his son.

Moments of a special kind of sharing between mother and daughter . . .

The daughter, Rebecca, is telling her mother about love, this young man at school whom she thinks she does indeed love.

The mother, Lillian, reminisces about her first date with Gordon. They laugh together, Rebecca wondering if her friend is the one with whom she will spend the rest of her own life.

Moments cut short . . .

It happens as all four of them are coming home from a basketball game. Wesley, Rebecca's special one, played as part of the home team.

He follows them in his car.

Night-time. . .

Another car speeds through a stop sign, hits the one carrying the family. It is spun around twice, then flips once and smashes into a telephone pole.

Instantly there are flames.

All of them but Jon Erik die upon impact. He manages to stumble from the wreckage, his body afire, his screams heard for some distance, I am sure.

Then he falls just inches from where I am standing. Scarcely a second later his spirit leaves his body. His mother, his father, his sister join him. They look at me, not knowing who I am.

"Can you help us?" the father asks. "We're very confused."

"Wesley!" Rebecca then asks. "Mom—what's happened to Wesley?"

It is then that they look upward. There is a light on them, engulfing them. Their concerns drain away. And then they are—gone.

Wesley tries to enter the flaming wreckage, but bystanders restrain him. He then falls into the arms of a stranger, sobbing.

Why?

They were Christians, they lived imperfect lives, but they tried very hard to please God. Everyone left behind who knew them would be asking the same question, and others related to it, over and over until the shock eases, and even the sad pull of this tragedy on their emotions disappears, and their own lives go on.

Wesley, as devoted as he was, as loyal and loving, and ready to spend the rest of his life with Rebecca, does recover. Not without struggle. Not without tossing in bed many nights afterward. Not without being so overcome with grief at the funeral that he has to be led away by his own family, for he cannot leave the cemetery of his own accord—there is, momentarily, no strength left in him.

He will think about Rebecca for a long time, perhaps to a greater or lesser extent for the rest of his life. He will think about her when he marries another, and they have children, and he wonders what the children of Rebecca and himself would have been like.

But someone else will pay, in a sense, a far worse price: the teenage boy, his system loaded up with drugs, who caused the accident.

He will be committed to an institution, and while there he will be gang-raped, and afterwards he will take his own life . . .

Three

A LITTLE MORE OF THE WORLD to which I have confined myself unfolds. With my human friends, with this family of whom I grew so fond, admiring them for their humanity, it seemed, at first, not so bad. Life for them had its sins, yes—impatience, anger, the threatening thread of lust between Rebecca and Wesley, moments that arose as a result of the warfare between flesh and spirit, and not to be excused, not to be brushed aside as acceptable because these were indeed human. All this, yes, but none so bad, it seems to me, as the blood on the hands of that teenage boy who killed them all.

I go to be alone, in a place away from humanity. I do not really know where it is. I think it might be a park. There is a pond in the middle, with goldfish swimming around in it, and a tall, carved-stone fountain and some pennies hopeful people have thrown there while making their wishes.

I am absolutely alone. It is early as yet, but the fact remains that I have seen none of what used to be my kind, none of those cast out onto Earth.

Where are you? I ask wordlessly. I want to see you, to talk, to learn.

Nothing.

Only the fish. Two robins and a sparrow on the grass. A squirrel scampering up a nearby tree. The sun is setting, darkness coming slowly, preceded by a golden light that reminds me just a bit of Heaven but then is gone, and just the artificial light of street lamps remaining.

I stay there—how can I judge the length of time when I have not as yet judged, really, truly, what time is?—and then leave, walking the night, not knowing where to go . . .

❧

It is cold that evening. I see people—with their scarves and ear muffs and hats—grimacing as they walk. I pass a theatre with questionable photographs displayed outside. Next to it is what the sign outside proclaims to be an adult book store.

I go inside.

I see the pornographic magazines and books, as well as the so-called "marital aids." In the back are booths. And inside are men watching XXX-rated images . . . .

I feel like shouting to them about their sin. I feel like grabbing them and shaking them, so repulsed am I by the very idea that a private act between husband and wife should be so degraded.

Am I upset over something minor? Am I overreacting to sexually starved individuals getting release?

No, no, a thousand nos if need be. Because I have been in Heaven. I have seen "life"—the only life, ultimately, that is life, not the temporary action of heart beating, lungs functioning, not that life which must end after a short time compared to eternity—life lived without lust, life that is pure, life in harmony with God's will.

I run from that place, its awful sounds, stale odors, and ugly yet pitiful sights.

I am shivering as I reach the outside. My whole self is shaking. And not just because of what is on sale inside the shop.

The implications . . .

Yes, the implications that spread far, far beyond that place on that street that cold winter evening.

~∾~

It is morning.

If I were of flesh and blood, I could say perhaps that I had not slept all night. But not being such, I search for a spiritual equivalent, and find none except to realize that I feel something akin to tiredness. The shock of the events since I came to Earth is having its impact upon me without question.

A police car is stopped in front of a restaurant. There is some shouting.

A man comes running outside. Two officers pursue him. They chase him for quite a distance on foot. Passersby jump to one side or the other. One is knocked down. Finally the officers corner the fugitive in an alley. He raises both hands over his head. I see them talking to the man.

"You realize that you have the right to remain silent," one officer says.

My attention wanders to the second officer. He is more distressed than the other.

"You are scum," he shouts. "How many kids have you destroyed because of the drugs you've sold them?"

"Hey, man, I gotta make a buck," the man says as he spits on the asphalt.

The second officer lunges at him and has to be restrained by his partner.

They take the man back to their car. I go with them, though, of course, they are unaware of this. The man is booked, as the expression goes, and put in jail.

I find out why the one officer is so disturbed. His son is in a hospital nearby, confined there because of a drug overdose. I listen as the officer and his partner are having coffee in a diner across the street from the police station.

"Tommy was going to be a computer programmer."

"You refer to him past tense. Is there something you haven't told me?"

"Yes, Dave, this morning—"

He breaks off the sentence, his face going red.

The other officer is quiet, waiting patiently.

Then . . .

"Tommy really had the ability to go all the way to the top—be another Bill Gates, the guy at Microsoft, who's become a millionaire several times over. Or that Steven Jobs at Apple. Tommy had their brains, once. But not any longer. It'll be a miracle if he can use an adding machine from now on."

"That bad?"

"Worse. His mind's nearly gone. As careful as Lisa was! Giving up the cigarettes and drinking while she carried him, not even taking aspirin! And that was before all the reports proving the effect of that stuff on the unborn.

We just used common sense. And Tommy was real, real healthy when he was born. A big baby! He weighed more than ten pounds. He felt so heavy to Lisa that we half thought there might be twins in her stomach.

"But now, oh, he'll 'recover.' He won't be a vegetable. But he also isn't going to be anywhere near what he could have been if that lousy—"

He bangs a fist on the countertop.

"I hate that guy and his kind so much I—I hope I can control myself when we come up against the next one. I just hope I don't go over the edge."

His partner pats him on the back, and they leave the diner.

Later, the officer—I find his name to be Henry—and his wife Lisa visit their son.

"Mom! Dad!" the teenager says as he greets them in his room at the hospital.

Lisa and Henry embrace him.

Later, the extent of the damage he has suffered is obvious. His words slur a number of times. He seems nervous, his cheeks twitching sporadically. And Tommy forgets a great deal—what day it is, the fact that his sister is due home from college soon, and he does not remember that the new hard disk drive for his computer had come in the mail, though his parents told him only the day before. And there is the frustration that gradually builds up, apparent in his manner, the quivering of his voice, the expression on his face.

Lisa and Henry know a truth that they have not as yet admitted to their son.

It will never be any different for him . . . .

He is going to be the way he is for as long as he is alive, paying for his drugs for a lifetime. And his frustration will continue to build until, one day, he attempts suicide. He survives that attempt, but it is only symptomatic of other aspects of his drug involvement, aspects that will worsen as he gets older until, eventually, he goes on a rampage and kills a dozen people in a quick-food outlet.

Many squad cars are dispatched to the place. Tommy surrenders without a fight. One of the arresting officers is his own father.

Lisa and Henry say good-bye, not knowing, not having the slightest hint of what lies in store, and I am alone with Tommy. He paces the floor, anxiety causing him to perspire excessively, his hospital garb sticking to him. And then he lies down on the bed in his room, and starts weeping. Soon he falls into a fitful sleep, but even then there is no peace for him as a nightmare fills his mind with terrors that are not very far from the reality already experienced, and which will be repeated, even months later, as he endures the first of a series of drug related "flash-backs."

At the age of twenty-six, Tommy will die in the electric chair. Not all the legal maneuvering conceivable—even considering the matter of drug damage—will do him any good. Only the date of execution is delayed, in fact prolonging his anguish. He spends more than four years in prison before that final day.

Time which does not exist is no hindrance to me and so I am there, in that chamber with him. The current is sent through him. His body jolts once, twice, then slumps forward. Tommy's spirit leaves that fleshly temple.

"You saw me die?" he asks as he sees me.

"Yes, Tommy, I did."

"Where am I going now?"

In the distance, or so it seems, I hear an eerie sound, like the gnashing of teeth.

Tommy hears it, too.

"I wish—" he starts to say, then is gone.

I feel, for a moment, a singular burst of heat.

And then an hysterical mother's cry that will never, never be forgotten . . .

Four

I NOTICE SOMETHING the corner of a building.

A shape.

Familiar. It's—

Another angel!

I am unable to move at first. He sees me, disappears. I go after him. Down an alley. Across a street. And—

He slows, stops, turns, smiles.

D'Seaver!

A friend . . .

"Darien," he says, looking a little embarrassed.

"I thought I was the only one," I say honestly.

"You have just arrived?"

"Only a little while ago, really."

"What do you think of Earth?"

I fall silent.

"It is a shock, is it not?"

"Let me show you a few, well, sights."

I agree to go with him.

First stop is a place with darkened corridors bordered by tiny rooms, each with a single cot. And in the walls between each room are holes.

"What is this, D'Seaver?" I ask.

Most of the doors are closed.

I hear sounds.

Groanings.

A whimper occasionally. Someone cries out rather loudly.

There is a whiff of a chemical-like odor:

One of the doors is slightly ajar. I see a man with his body pressed up against a wall. His head is rolling from side to side. He is naked.

Corridor after corridor: Men with towels wrapped around them but nothing else. Two in a whirlpool tub, holding one another.

The lighting is almost nonexistent.

And in one room there is none at all.

It is much bigger than the others. Several men are inside. They—

"D'Seaver, why are we here?"

"I wanted to show you."

"Show me what?"

"What is going on. To actually see and—"

"We must leave."

"But—"

"Now, D'Seaver, Now!"

We are gone, It is not difficult to leave. We just will ourselves to do so. We have no bodily substance as such. We can be anywhere we want, as soon as we want.

And we are in the midst of a cemetery.

"All of them will end up here so much sooner than necessary," I say. "Then, for all eternity, they will cry and scream in pain. They will plead for it to end, but it will not. And it will get worse. Every fear they ever had will be fulfilled. Every suffering they ever knew will be revisited upon them tenfold."

D'Seaver, only half-listening, points to something partially buried in the grass near one of the tombstones.

"That is a bottle of amyl nitrate."

"What is that?"

"They sniff it—the heart beats faster and faster—and enormous sexual desire is aroused."

"Why here?"

"I viewed the funeral. Most of the participants had brought such bottles with them. Two or three were talking about opening the coffin and making love, as they call it, to the corpse."

I can scarcely believe what I am being told.

"It is Sunday, according to Man's calendar, Darien. We should go to church."

I agree that we should. Not too far away is a modernistic-looking building. It seems to be constructed entirely of glass, almost in a pyramid shape except that the pinnacle is nearly flat. The sun shining off it makes the glass sparkle in a dozen different colors. People are lined up, waiting to be seated. Altogether there will be thousands inside by the time everyone sits down.

The interior is no less spectacular, with round metal beams crisscrossing the ceiling. Each pew is cushioned with a velvety material. In the middle of the altar area at the front is a huge cross, probably twenty feet tall. At the base, grouped around it, are bright red flowers. The altar seems to have been laid of marble, light-colored, with darker tan veins running through it.

All this is indeed impressive. Choral sounds come from the front, and a hundred men, women, and children sing as they file out and take their places.

Immediately I start to feel refreshed, as though I am about to take a bath to cleanse myself.

We stay in the back of the church. Minutes pass—it is indeed awkward for me to use such a term, awkward to think of anything at all like time.

The choir has finished. There are some announcements. My whole self rises in anticipation. I need this very much. I remember that first service, the family, all the rest.

The minister comes to the pulpit, smiles as he surveys the congregation.

"And, now, everybody turn and shake the hand of someone near you."

The people do this. A feeling of warmth diffuses throughout the hall.

The minister continues, "I want to introduce to you someone all of you have seen on television and in films."

A man with curly hair and a rather rugged face joins the minister:

He talks about treating people properly, talks about caring for starving children, talks about being honest at income tax time.

A chill begins to nip me around the edges.

Finally the actor steps down, I think with considerable relief.

The minister beams at the congregation as he says, "There are good people in this world. They think in positive terms. They don't make negativity their god. They can control their own lives and make of those lives what they want. I think that's wonderful."

He pauses, then asks, "How many of you agree?"

Everyone claps. I do not. I turn to D'Seaver. He is clapping.

That chill is growing . . . .

"And now—"

He holds up a porcelain angel. A nearby television camera zooms in on it.

"This is a gift to anyone who writes and sends in a love offering," he continues. "It is made of the finest porcelain, molded and painted by hand."

Then a collection is taken up. The minister leaves the pulpit. A black man comes out and begins to sing. He seems a little uncomfortable. And not because he is black. But he does well, with more than a hint of real feeling as he sings, "My Tribute: To God Be the Glory"

I hear someone in front of me whisper, "That's a little heavy, isn't it."

Why? I want to shout. Why is singing about the shed blood of Christ so "heavy" for church? Why—?

Several minutes later, the minister returns and begins his sermon.

I listen, with growing alarm, that chill totally enveloping me.

"The epidemic has been described by some as punishment from God. We all know that a loving God would not do that. We all know that that sort of Victorian thinking belongs with all that fire-and-brimstone talk with which some men of the cloth try to frighten the rest of us into submission."

He takes off his glasses, his expression serious.

"We make our own Hell right here on earth. We make life hellish when we forget the principles of upbeat thinking, when we allow negativism to crowd out the positive, the cheerful. And what is Hell but the most negative concept of all."

I can remain no longer.

"We must not stay," I say to D'Seaver without turning to look at him. "We must—"

"Stop it, Darien. This man is good. He is just right, in fact."

"Right about what?"

The minister continues: "My new book, which is an international best-seller, is entitled A POSITIVE REBIRTH, it has been made available in the church bookstore for just $12.95, which is $2.00 discounted off the retail. It tackles what has been wrong with the church ever since Billy Sunday and Dwight L. Moody and others of that ilk thundered their protestations of perdition."

He moves with great flair, throwing his hands about, arching his back, his face a mask of exaggerated expressions. His voice raises or lowers with just the right emphasis.

"The time is here for a positive rebirth. Away with the gloom and doom!"

He holds up his book, waves it a couple of times before the television cameras.

"Place this book beside your Bible. Read them together. And you will receive a blessing beyond your wildest dreams. You will find your finances impacted very favorably. You can do better with God's Plan for Financial Enrichment than in any bank."

He takes some money from his pocket, shows it to everyone.

"Give to Him ten percent or more of all that you earn, and He will return it severalfold. God is the best investment you can make. He does not want any of us to be poor. Remember that, my friends. And grab a little of the green for yourself!"

I remember a missionary I had met in Heaven. She had been quite poor during her final years of service. Gradually her support was being reduced by significant percentages. She went back to the United States, leaving the mission field forever. Her husband had died months before, and she was no longer able to handle the strain of the work alone. She got back to her hometown on a Saturday, stayed at a friend's house that night, and drove to church with her the next morning. As they walked up to the entrance, the missionary saw the minister park his car and then go inside the church. He had a new luxury model that cost nearly $25,000. She pulled her worn coat around her, asked the Lord to forgive her, turned around and never went inside that church again. In less than a month she was dead. The congregation sent some funeral flowers. But no one attended. There was a picnic that day by the Ladies Auxiliary, a fund-raiser to send the minister and his wife to Hawaii for a week.

No more, I say to myself. No more in this place . . .

"Now, D'Seaver, we go!" I say firmly, turning to face him.

It is no longer the D'Seaver that I had known. Something different . . . something different.

Demonic.

All pretense is over. No more posing as an angel of light . . .

Instantly D'Seaver and I are outside.

"Lucifer cannot know about you," I say, repulsed by him, barely able to look at what he has become.

His laughter is coarse.

He pounds his feet on the ground, cloven hooves moving with anger.

"You utter fool!" he shouts, slobber dripping out the corners of his mouth. "You act so surprised. You thought I took you to that place, with those men, to lament what they were doing. That is The Plan, Darien, they are part of it. So is that pompous fool. If he were any more transparent, he would not even be there!

"That parade. The riot. More that you may stumble upon while you are here, Darien. It is a real-life script. And it is being played out exactly as it should."

I turn and go. Behind me I hear the sound of shrieking laughter . . . .

Five

I GO BACKWARD IN TIME, at first enjoying this ability as though it is a kind of toy, something for amusement. And that it is initially. To be able to see the building of the Pyramids! To be there at the American Revolution. To be present with the ancient Aztecs as their civilization was thriving, something that would have been highly coveted by modern archaeologists if it had been possible for them. It was a civilization filled with the worship of false gods, encrusted with heathen practices but undeniably grand in the sense of the knowledge possessed by the Aztecs, knowledge that amazed even twentieth-century scientists. So it was, as well, with the Incas and the Mayans, but even great knowledge, great power lasts, really, for just a season—whatever they knew, these brilliant peoples, more or less died with them, overgrown by the jungles out of which they had carved their cities. The kings and warriors worshipped and feared centuries ago now left only a legacy of ruins and the fascination of those entranced by questions probably unresolvable.

Backward in time, forward as well, through events and places that comprised the history of the Human Race, for good or naught. From the days of dinosaurs to the birth of the Industrial Age, to—

The Holocaust.

I am standing in the midst of Dachau, the German concentration camp.

The sky is overcast, at least that is what I assume until I see the sooty clouds of smoke coming from a giant stack not far away. Floating through the air, dropping down in patches here and there, are specks, thin, like burnt paper, settling on the ground, grey-white.

I walk down one "avenue" between two rows of buildings. Ahead a line of soldiers is standing single file. In front of them is a ditch, and standing just at the edge are a score or more of naked, emaciated men, their faces pale, gaunt.

The soldiers aim rifles, fire, and the men collapse into the ditch. Their bodies join others. This day is apparently being devoted to "thinning" the population of the camp.

"Garbage collection," I hear one of the soldiers say to another, his laughter hoarse, cold.

I want to reach out and throw him in the ditch with his victims. I want to call down all the wrath of Heaven and give him pain and suffering for eternity. And then I realize that that is exactly what he will have. That he and others like him as well as the ones issuing the orders will indeed have punishment never ending—it might not come in a year or even a decade, but it would come, inexorably,

I turn from that spot, toward the ovens. I see men and women tied, gagged, being put inside. I hear their terror, I feel their pain as flesh is seared by heat, seconds seeming endless and then—

Later, the ovens are emptied, bones not quite powdered put into bags and taken elsewhere. And then more bodies. An endless procession of bodies.

I enter one of the laboratories. A little boy, naked, is strapped to an operating table. A man, mustached, dressed in a white smock, is cutting him open! No painkiller used—no gas to knock him out—nothing but the "live" operation, whatever it is, for whatever insane purpose.

Afterwards, I hear the "surgeon" talking to an assistant. This is all part of an experiment to see how much pain a human being can take before losing consciousness or dying. They do it again and again, to the young, the older, the elderly; some of the old ones take it longer than do the young, but most die on the tables—there are a dozen or more of these in other rooms in that same building. A few, a bare handful, survive: some blinded when acid is poured into their pupils, missing arms, legs, parts of their bodies paralyzed because of their brains being poked around in, surviving, yes, surviving those moments of horror and, later, the continuing rigors of the rest of Dachau's daily routine, surviving to the moment of liberation by the Allies and beyond, to live the years left, few or many, in periodic anguish, the residue of being treated as they were . . . then death comes, an anticlimax for many, for they had "died" a long, long time before.

The ovens, the ditches, the "operating rooms" are part of what assaults me in an engulfing torrent. Many others die of disease or malnutrition, many commit suicide, some live with minds that have snapped so that, for them, there is never to be liberation, at least not on Earth.

I visit another camp, this one called Auschwitz. A woman is being brutalized by her "doctor." She falls into a heap on the floor. Her life is almost over. Her murderer stands over her, and she looks up at him, and whispers, "I forgive you . . . may God show you The Way," just before he slashes her throat.

In the blinking of an eye, her spirit has risen from her battered, torn body. She sees me, smiles.

"It is right, what I said?"

I nod.

"Good," she replies. "Is time for me There?"

I rejoice as I tell her that it is.

She is gone . . . .

～◦～

I go back to Dachau. Many years have passed. It is filled with well-dressed people. There are memorial plaques, with names listed on them. The tourists come and go. I wish I could shout to them, about all that had gone on before, a few decades earlier, the buildings, the ovens, the laboratories fairly ringing with the cries of the tormented, the dying.

I see a field next to the camp. It is lush, the grass brilliantly green, the soil dark, rich-looking, flowers vibrantly colored, trees healthy.

I wonder why. The rest of the area is so bleak. And then I comprehend through a veil of revulsion that that healthy, colorful field, so serene on the surface, is where countless numbers of bodies had been buried, human fertilizer nourishing the growth of nature.

But cruelty was never confined to the Germans, I discover. The Japanese had their part in it: the relentless Bataan Death March was just one example. For the veterans who survived, it remains a harsh, awful memory. For me, back in time, it is current, palpable, a living reality.

Thousands are sick, wounded. They walk through mud. In other spots dust is so thick it clogs their nostrils and they cough, deep coughs that, for many, force open further already festering holes, cuts.

I see a soldier drive a bayonet through one of the prisoners, and then two other soldiers join him because the American is not as yet dead, and the three of them stick him again and again with sharp steel, laughing maniacally.

Some men die from previous wounds or malaria or other diseases, their bodies left by the road. (How many would be recovered, and shipped back home eventually? Not a large number, I suppose. They would simply rot where they fell.)

And once again I see something beautiful in the midst of it all, the march of horror that claimed so many lives. I see a man who is a chaplain on his knees, praying, as one of the soldiers hits him across the back of the head with a rifle butt. The chaplain falls but is not quite unconscious. This infuriates the soldier, and he is about to hit the man again, helpless in the mud. The chaplain looks up at him, smiles, and says, "Do what you must. I still will not hate you." And I see something utterly, literally incredible. (It is a word I hear often during my journeys, spouted carelessly, a word robbed of any real impact by its cavalier overuse but the only one that does apply, the only one to describe what I see.)

The Japanese soldier seems to understand what the chaplain has said. He hesitates, pulls back the rifle. And immediately I see a fallen angel beside him, whispering something into his ear: The soldier still resists. I recognize my former comrade to be D'Filer. I see D'Filer go to another soldier, and then this second soldier approaches the first. They get into a fight. The first soldier accidentally is run through by the bayonet as they struggle. He falls, clutching his stomach, just a few feet from the chaplain. The American crawls toward him. The second soldier orders him to stop. The chaplain refuses. The soldier aims his rifle. The chaplain reaches the body of the other soldier, puts his arm around it just as his head is blown open by the force, the nearness of the rifle that has been fired.

D'Filer is not pleased, he knows what has happened. He is infuriated by forgiveness. This is contrary to everything he wanted. There are two deaths, yes, but the result is forgiveness. He cannot stand that. He goes up and down the long line of American prisoners, driving the Japanese to outbursts of anger in order to vent his own. Prisoners are kicked, spat upon, clubbed with rifle butts, forced to walk faster when they can hardly walk at all . . . .

It is now decades later, that same road, a monument being dedicated beside one section. There are scores of Americans and Japanese. Some look warily at one another. But one American extends his hand to his Japanese counterpart. They shake, smile. The American takes something out of his pants pocket. So does the other. They laugh at this. One has a small Bible, so does the other.

"When?" the American asks.

"On my knees a year after Hiroshima. My wife and two children were caught up in the blast. They did not die immediately. They lingered for months. When I saw them, they were almost gone. They had been burned badly, their bodies flaking flesh. My children were both blind. They could hardly talk. I could not even hold them.

"I wanted to kill every American I saw, I wanted to destroy the entire country. And then I remembered Bataan, and the American chaplain I murdered, the dozens of other Americans I killed, beat, spat on, even starved. I remembered that that chaplain may have had a family also. And later, God opened my heart to be forgiven as well as to forgive. If I had never seen that chaplain, never saw him put his arm around Tanaka, and—and—"

He holds up the Bible as he wipes some tears from his eyes.

"This was the chaplain's. It is with me always."

～～

A strange world, largely a kingdom of darkness, a place filled with the ranting and raving excesses of demonic hordes, former angels transplanted to a former Eden, cutting across it a swath of atrocity. And yet a world with such triumph as I had seen, such goodness as I had witnessed, such purity rising regenerated from a giant morass of murder, rape, unfettered passion, unmitigated depravity.

Being filled with all unrighteousness, fornication, wickedness, covetousness, maliciousness, full of envy, murder, debate, deceit, malignity, whisperers, backbiters, haters of God, despiteful, proud, boasters, inventors of evil things . . . Who knowing the judgment of God, that they which commit such things are worthy of death, not only do the same, but have pleasure in them that do them.

And still I could not find Lucifer. Had he been surrounded by a mutiny, and cast off ship, so to speak? If so, where was he? Where was the creature because of whom I had begun my quest in the first place?

Six

I APPROACH A SO-CALLED REST HOME for the elderly. It might better be called a dumping ground for rejects, mothers and fathers left there, like so much worn, excess baggage, to be cared for by hired professionals.

An attempt has been made to present the circumstances as cheerfully as possible, but for many it is a hopeless charade. Only one thing will lift the burden—the love of families that seem instead to have rejected them. This is the end of the road for the bulk of the people inside, a final prison, and a death sentence.

From the wonder of birth to the passion of youth, on to the achievement of middle age, and then the wrenching, awful waste of years spent as those in the rest home are spending theirs—a game of cards, an evening in front of a television and, occasionally, a letter from the family but coming like a single drop of water to someone in the midst of a desert, a walk on the grounds, a smile from a nurse, some food three times a day, and then to bed, the routine repeated and repeated and repeated until the monotony becomes a noose from which they feel their life is being choked out of them.

I see two women whose circumstances are as different from one another as could be imagined. Millie seems quite dynamic, spending much of her time helping the nurses with the other residents.

"They're my family," she says happily.

It turns out that they indeed are the only family she has. Her husband died of a heart attack a year or so before. Her daughter, son-in-law, and two grandchildren all perished in a plane crash months later.

"I was so alone it was ridiculous," she tells a new nurse. "But then I figured I had a Friend who would never let me down."

"Who was that?" the nurse asks.

"The Lord Jesus Christ. He's promised never to leave me nor forsake me. Though the whole world reject me, He never will. I have taken all my many burdens and put them at His feet. And I am now serving Him more completely than ever before in my life."

She lives her faith, helping to feed Alzheimer's sufferers, those with senility dementia, those so crippled by arthritis that their hands seem more like twisted claws, the pain well-nigh unbearable.

"I can hardly think straight it's so bad, Millie," says one of them.

"Then I'll think for you," she says, smiling. "Let me start right now, dear one . . ."

So it goes, entering the lives of the others, laughing with them, getting them to laugh when instead just a bit earlier they had been crying, introducing the lonely to Christ.

And then there is Charlotte. Charlotte sits in her room most of the day, either in bed, or in a chair next to it. She eats a little, cries a lot, refuses to join with anyone in anything.

"Let me alone!" she screams. "Just get out of here. Let me alone to die."

Millie has tried to talk to her about Christ, but Charlotte refuses. Her room is a grave to her, she has already died and been buried in it. Death itself will seem at once anticlimactic to her. As far as she is concerned, life is over.

Two women: one with Christ, one without Him. One lonely, saddened, filled with self-pity, angry and bitter—the other vibrant, contributing, joyful.

"I wish I could do something to reach her," Millie says to a friend.

"Some people are happy in their misery," the other replies. "You are light, she is darkness. You draw people to you, she sends them away. That's just how it is, Millie. Thank God for those like you."

Millie smiles on the last day of her earthly life. I am by her side when her flesh-and-blood body becomes quiet, the heart and lungs still, the brain finally—

"Are you—?" she asks excitedly.

"Yes, Millie, I am."

"Am I in Heaven now? What about—?"

She smiles as she looks upward.

"Oh my!" she says an instant before she is gone.

I am at Millie's funeral. It is attended by a hundred or more men, women, and children. Many of those present had once stayed at the rest home, but Millie had revived their spirits so completely that the physical part of them also improved, and they could leave.

The children had been brought to see grandmothers and grandfathers confined to the home, and Millie had mightily touched their lives as well. There are doctors attending, nurses, more. Millie's legacy of love would be remembered for a long time.

I return to the home. Charlotte is standing in the doorway to her room.

She is holding a sheet of paper in her left hand, a note that reads: "I'm going to be with my Savior this day, dear Charlotte. Won't you take Him into your life before it is too late? Let me have the privilege of welcoming you into His Kingdom someday. I love you, dear one . . ."

Charlotte begins screaming, "How can she say she loves me? Nobody loves a mean old hag. Nobody!"

She starts toward Millie's room, sees the empty bed, the vacant closet, the dresser drawers all cleaned out, no toothbrushes in the bathroom, no—

"Millie!" she yells. "Oh, Millie!"

She falls onto the bed, sobbing. But she keeps the note clutched tightly in her hand. Opened on the bed, next to her, is Millie's Bible. She picks it up and starts reading a particularly pertinent verse.

If we confess our sins, He is faithful and just to forgive us our sins, and to cleanse us from all unrighteousness . . . .

She apparently had been harboring a whole catalogue of sins, letting her guilt over these eat away at her, turning her bitter, the bitterness manifested in angry and resentful behavior toward others.

She reads other verses dealing with the reality of God's forgiveness and cleansing. A few hours later she gets down on her knees and asks Christ to enter her very being and fill the void in her life.

In less than a week Charlotte will die also. But before that happens, she will have gone to everyone at the home and asked them to forgive her in much the same way as she had asked the Lord.

Everyone is amazed at the difference in her.

Charlotte dies quietly. There is little pain. The peace of her death contrasts with the anger and the upset of much of the latter part of her life.

She closes her eyes, and stops breathing. In an instant, Charlotte's spirit, the real Charlotte, of course, sees me.

"Charlotte!" We both hear that voice as though across eternity itself.

"Yes, yes, I'll be right there, Millie."

She turns, winks at me.

"I'll never be rejected or alone again . . . will I?"

"Never."

"Forgiveness for all the meanness?"

"Yes."

She looks serene, a smile lighting up her face.

"Millie's got somebody standing by her side, His hand outstretched. Is that—?"

I need not answer.

As she goes, I hear, for a fleeting instant, the familiar sound of angels rejoicing . . . .

Seven

SINGER HAS MADE MILLIONS OF dollars. He is the star of the year, with deals pouring in for all kinds of tie-ins—TV specials, film roles, posters, a dizzying montage, one after the other.

But he cannot sleep at night—because a certain nightmare assaults, tearing open the darkness in bursts of wrenching anguish.

In the dream he is singing before a packed auditorium. The crowd has paid a total of $400,000 to see and hear him. He is at the top of his form, with lyrics that speak of a life of easy sex and growing demonic worship.

Drink the blood of the saints . . .

The words ride on electronic waves into the minds of the young.

Curse the god of your fathers, bow before the New Age Christ . . . They hear, to leave that dark place and emulate in the soon-spent vigor of their youth, until madness comes on feet of crystal.

Stick your obscene finger into the face of the Almighty . . .

But something else happens in Singer's nightmare, altering in fantasy the outcome of reality. He hears a rattling sound throughout that place, louder, louder, drowning out his music. He stops, peers through the clouds of maryjane and hash, and sees light reflecting off an audience of skeletons. Some have flesh hanging like tom garments from rib cages, others have skulls cracked open, and a few, just a few, show stomachs with the tiny hands of babies grabbing bones like death row prison bars, yelling, yelling, yelling.

He turns to run, screaming, and is confronted by two skeletons backstage, bending over a mirror, using rolled dollar bills to try and snort up the white powder in rows before them, but they cannot because they have no lungs, no nasal passages, no—

Where am I to go? he asks himself in terror. Where—?

Behind him the audience is on bony feet, climbing up on the stage. In an instant he is surrounded, the foul odor of decay sweeping over him as—

Awake!

As before. Always the same. Turning on the light. A bodyguard rushing in. Sweat in buckets from head to foot.

And he will fall back to dream again, to scream awake as eventually the night is gone.

Over and over until—

He disappears one afternoon. No notes. No clues. Just gone.

Singer is found one month later, in a distant forest camp, tied to stakes in the ground, heavy ropes on his arms and legs. He has been partially dismembered. Nearby are his heart and his intestines on two altars of still-burning coals.

A diary is discovered, it has been mostly destroyed by flames.

One passage reads:

I found this group today. They seem so wonderful. They hate the whole lousy world as much as I do. Lucifer is their friend, and so am I . . .

He saw me, Singer did, as, earlier, his murderers carved him apart amid his unheeded pleas.

"I die from my own legacy," he said, "my lyrics my eulogy, is that it?"

"Yes, Singer, that is it."

There is a place for you, for me, where the neon emperor flashes his commands, and innocent blood is the wine of perdition . . .

As Hell sucked him in, across time and eternity, he sang, for an instant, of amazing grace too late . . . too dimly remembered from times of innocence since lost on compact discs and Dolby . . . before the encompassing abyss unending.

Eight

THE WANDERING ANGEL IS ALONE, on a vast plain. He stops briefly, looking up at the sky, sighing. To go back there, he says to himself, silent to the nothingness, shrugging wearily.

To go back—

He interrupts himself, a wave of laughter causing him to double over and fall to the parched earth, but with no reaction to his presence, nor would there be throughout the journey, indeed from the beginning of time, a mortal chill perhaps, a whisper of something there, then embarrassed silence, unbelief his scalpel.

How ironic, he remarks, again to himself. I yearn to return to a place that I have spent all of history trying to convince the Human Race is indeed the stuff of myth, a phantom longing, somewhere that is nowhere because it does not exist.

He recalls the arguments, so profound, the thoughts planted as seeds, nourished and allowed to spring full-bloom, wreaking the havoc that atheism has been causing over the centuries.

The uniformity of natural causes in a closed system . . .

He repeats the concept with relish, savoring those words as though they were a gourmet meal perpetually spread before him, and he is being sustained by their nutrients.

A man is sitting in a chair in the middle of a room. He is alone. The chair is his point of integration in a world that is only the room around him. There is nothing beyond that room. There is no God, nothing but the three elements—the man, his chair, and that sparse, limited, very cold world.

"But there is more, of course," the angel says aloud to the desert and the sky and the distant horizon. "I fooled millions, yea, hundreds of millions. You all have labored your pathetic lifetimes not knowing that that is but one room in a vast universe of rooms and over it all is—"

He stops, looking around, shivering despite the noonday heat of that baked, arid place.

"Who am I?" you have asked in your agony. "You are machines, I say in return. You live in a barren world, beyond which there is nothing— just machines, that is all. You die as they do, turning to rust and decay and then utter, utter nothingness. The system is closed. God will not reach down into it, ever, because He is just a figment of your cowardly inability to face the reality of your despair. "

Then he recalls the students.

"You were ripe fruit ready to pluck from life's tree. I put into your institutions of higher learning professors committed to humanism and nihilism and atheism. They took your minds as potter's clay, remolding and reshaping.

"I went into your churches and your museums and sang the melody of despair. Sometimes I disguised it with god words and sometimes I wrapped it in canvasses of Picasso and Gauguin and Cezanne and others, but it was there, sugarcoated as humanism and existentialism and situationalism. How words fooled you—how they midwifed your doom."

The angel sees the skeleton of a man, studies it for a moment, then goes past. Behind him there is no trail, no cloven hoof prints, the sand as ever.

"And this is your handiwork?" I say as we meet, again, an eternity after Heaven.

"Oh, yes, it is," he replies. "Hear the wind—it cries questions without answer. Look at the sand—hope and faith crumbled, through which we walk, undetected."

He casts a glance over the endless miles, parched, with skulls turning to powder, stirred up in patchy little clouds by not-distant cries in the air, wind from the forlorn lost.

"Man," he says without a smile.

"What you have made of him."

"Yes . . ."

And the wandering angel continues on, unable to turn back, past half-buried monuments, with rusty plaques of commemoration, and weapons of war now silent, the bloody stains wafted away, the sun mocking their decay. Toward the lake at the far horizon, its flames rising high.

Nine

I DECIDE TO SOAR. MY KIND HAS HAD that ability since the beginning. There was a time, before the Casting Out, that no limitations existed on our travels. We could go throughout the whole of what was, boundless distances, unimpeded, exploring the wonders of creation.

Oh, what a glorious period that was—Earth had not been created as yet. We soared from one end of the rest of creation to the other, saw the beginnings of life, saw so much that was thrilling and invigorating and—

And then a third of us were uprooted. One after the other left. We were given an explanation and everyone seemed to accept it but me, of course—and now here I am, soaring alone, above a world in the throes of such awful pain, pain of the mind, body, and spirit so intense that it still seems almost unfathomable to me.

I see the millions in famine. I see babies with bellies bloated obscenely, the rest of their bodies bone-thin. They try to get nourishing milk from their mothers' breasts, but there is so little of that. And then they die, though not suddenly, not quickly at all, tiny rattling sounds of agony inside them, some twitching of the muscles, eyes rolling back, breathing in ragged gasps—for hours it is like this, not even to mention the slow draining away that precedes these final moments, a gradual death, worse than drowning, worse than a knife in the heart though, figuratively speaking, it is that as well.

And then the mother, in each case, holds her child, not willing to admit that her flesh and blood is gone. Her womb, a world in itself, protected him for nine months, but the outside world destroyed him.

I see one mother yet carrying a still, limp body hours after the child died—this one was three or four years old—and that body has become hard, one arm frozen in an extended gesture, the fingers stiff, wide apart. Eventually it is taken from her because already, in a desert land, it has begun to smell.

And then I stop in Alexandria, Egypt . . . .

It is dirty there. Alexander the Great would be shocked by the place. Dirty is really too polite a word. Filthy comes closer, even though that seems still a bit mild somehow.

Yet I see many, many mothers in Alexandria who are apparently quite happy, tending to their children, feeding them, laughing with them, washing their faces, being with them in the time-honored way of mothers. The striking thing is that since they have known poverty all their lives they have adjusted to it, and they are somehow content to a degree, literally because they have never known anything else.

Children come up to well-dressed and groomed foreigners, tugging at their sleeves, begging for money, smiling but not in a phony way, not in a flagrant sense of trying to generate pity or compassion, not as a turned-on/turned-off kind of thing, ready at a moment's notice.

They are covered with dirt smudges, their clothes ragged, few with shoes on their feet, and yet a pittance together with a smile, a shake of the hand, a pat on the head makes them nearly ecstatic with joy.

I am now sitting at the base of the Great Pyramid just outside Cairo, on one of the giant blocks, waiting until sunrise. The scene is like the interior of a cocoon, dormant, quiet, only the snorting of an occasional camel discernible, the air rich with the pungent odors of a long-dead antiquity.

The sunrise is rose-red, a flicker, then more, expanding light, the ancient city of Cairo first darkly outlined, then aglow with light, then awash with it.

I see children again. This time they are with their mothers, occasionally with their fathers as well, walking, packs of what-ever on their backs. Their bare feet stir up clouds of dust with a reddish tinge, a texture like clay or chalk, and the odor of tombs.

And I see a man with an old camel. They, too, work the roads, confronting tourists eager to gain a little more atmosphere. It is obvious, as I watch, that the man loves this beast. They have been together many, many years. I sense that neither has a home, they live in the open, as countless numbers have done in Egypt ever since the days of the pharaohs, except perhaps for a small tent to help against the sweltering oven in which they find themselves during the noon hours of each day.

Undoubtedly, I imagine to myself, the man will die before the camel does. The animal will probably stand by his body, nudging him without comprehension. Someone else would take it on, and it might outlive the newer owner. But eventually, after decades of wandering, commanded by this man or that one, learning to depend upon each one, even to love each one after a fashion, it, too, would go to its knees one final time, as it did to receive a rider, grunting, and turn over, never arising again.

I cried because I had no shoes.

Until I saw the man who had no feet.

I see such among the poor there in Egypt. I see a mother with no feet, she has her baby in some sort of bag hanging from around her neck, another child holds her hand as she alternately hops or crawls along. There is no man with her. She provides their only hope, they provide her only love, the center of her world. Though the poverty is there, suffocatingly, though often all she can give her baby is the milk from her breasts, she accepts, she goes on, she keeps that family of three together, with no washing machines to lighten her load, no hair dryers, no remote controlled garage door openers, no one-a-day vitamins or nail polish or other "necessities." For her, tomorrow will be another day just the same as today. She and they will survive until the day afterwards, perhaps another week or month or whatever the remaining span, not knowing what the day is or the week or the year, knowing nothing in fact but hunger and dirt and looking up at a stranger for a little spare change until—until the end comes, as it surely will soon, malnutrition and disease reaping a common tragedy.

I get the feeling, as the expression goes, that so long as they die together, so long as the mother can have her little ones around her, their bodies pressed to hers, so long as she does not have to worry about their love, unlike, ironically, mothers else-where, insulated from dirt and hunger and disease, cocooned in a world beyond the imagination of that trio on the outskirts of Cairo, who do not know whether their sons or daughters are alive or dead or dying, shot full of drugs, riddled with sexually transmitted diseases, crying out, alone, in some abandoned, ramshackle place, unlike such mothers, unlike such children, these three may die together as they live, with no one else but themselves, even humming some kind of tune to one another. I hear it from them now, mournful yet lyrical, made up as they go, music created from the very core of their beings—their voices a mutual melody of comfort until one by one the sounds die to a whisper and then silence altogether, except for the cries of the baby, until even that plaintive sound in the darkness, quickly dissipating, is gone, and the world goes on, ignorant of them ever . . . .

There is hunger and disease elsewhere, stalking. On the fringes, laughing, I can see the figures of former comrades, gloating as the hungry occasionally resort to cannibalism. How could they? I must ask. How could they, knowing what goes down their throat, knowing what their teeth are tearing, their tongues are tasting?

It has happened before, I know. In my travels through time, I learned, earlier, of the Donner Pass incident, a group of men, women and children, without food, freezing, taking this ghastly step to survive. Or that plane crash in the Andes Mountains, the survivors forced into the same grisly act of desperation.

This is a world once Eden. This is a United States once Puritan. This is a humanity once pure. No place is free of sin. It is only a matter of degrees. And who has committed the greater sin? Those who eat the flesh of others? Or those whose compassion has shrivelled and shrunken, a near-blasphemous mockery of charity, a selfish egocentricity like a wall around their hearts, causing the problem in the first place?

. . . only a matter of degrees.

The sin of no charity. The sin of cannibalism. Joined by a vast ency-clopedic gathering of others. Sin in rampant poverty. Sin in pillowed, perfumed, pampered luxury. The same, a thread drawn through the gut of each living human being.

Many worship unreal gods, they do despicable things, their practices sicken one's very being. And yet they are ignorant. They have grown up in societies that know nothing else. I think of the Eskimos, they wor-ship survival, it is their god, they worship It in the midst of the worst winters on Planet Earth. And when they live through another one, they feel that their prayers have been answered. The feeble old have no place, they cannot carry their own weight and do not contribute, so they are al-lowed to leave, no one stopping them, and they go out into the awful blizzards, and die.

The ancient Incas, Aztecs, and Mayans all had sacrifices of their infants, to appease their own gods. Some tribes in Africa consider can-nibalism a "holy" honor. And many more, in the past and the present, in isolated places and savage societies committing atrocity upon atroc-ity, but with ignorance, with no idea whatever that that which they do is a stench in the nostrils of a triune God.

How much worse for those aware? How much worse for the chick-enhawk, as he is called, who picks up a teenage boy and they go to a motel room and the man gets his pleasure by forcing the boy to abuse him through countless demonic perversions? And demonic it is. Hovering grotesque beings—my former friends, my former fellow wondrous creations of a God capable of creating the majesty of what they once were, these very ones—I know their names, I came into being the same instant they did!—now propelling His other creation to abominable acts.

How much worse, I shout to the sky and the air and the ground beneath me, to others once like me but now laughing at my shock, my outrage, counting my loathing as pleasure because they exist on such emotions, pain their love, hatred their ecstasy, things whispered in darkness their beacon of light, blinding them, funerals their celebrations, death their domain, Hell their Mecca, and yet they are not satiated, their gluttonous appetites incapable of fulfillment, bloated though they are with the carrion of their vile imaginings . . .how much worse, I say, regaining my composure, for those who allow what they know to be so foul that the stench of it gags and sickens and makes anyone with even a thread, a thin, thin thread of righteousness vomit it up in gushers of revulsion.

Ten

I AM AWAY FROM THE CITIES NOW, the soaring, the wars, the poverty. I am in the midst of a forest. I stand and smell the air. I listen to the sounds of life in trees, bushes, a nearby lake. I feel somewhat refreshed, and I wait, relaxing, getting my thoughts together.

Nowhere have I seen Lucifer. Only those who claim to follow him. Only those who claim that he dominates them so strongly, so inescapably, that they are bereft of a will of their own, submitting to him in everything.

If that is indeed the case, then how different from those who follow God, who have accepted His Son into their lives as Savior and Lord. Lucifer's followers, if they are to be believed, are automatons. But with Him, it is free will only, not an enslavement but a dedication, not an obsession but a devotion.

What an answer to the age old question of why God allows certain things to happen. If Lucifer's fallen angels are to be—.

If?

That question nags at me. Can the leader be blamed totally for what those with him do? What if all this is without his knowledge? If he has confidence in those who serve him, does he need to check their every move, approve each plan, detail? Perhaps his not doing so, if those in whom he has placed trust betray him, is cause for questioning his judgment in that very area of having chosen them in the first place. But that is another kind of weakness—hardly the same as Mifult overseeing the death of millions of helpless babies, the infamy of those perpetrating the Holocaust. Or—

My musings are interrupted by something carried on the air, it would seem.

The sound, far away, of a piccolo.

I stand, listening more closely.

Yes!

Rather like some of the music heard in Heaven . . .

But where?

I am attracted to it. Enchanted by the gentleness of the notes.

I find the player.

An old man, possibly well into his eighties. He is sitting on a flat rock beside a stream, the sound of the water a faint back-drop to the melody of his instrument.

I stand there, listening, awed by what I hear.

"Well, say something," he says, startling me.

"I—well—I mean—how—?" I stutter embarrassingly.

"You are not very secretive, you know. But then you proba-bly thought you did not have to be. Is that it?"

"Yes, I suppose—"

He chuckles.

"I remember you from the old days. Kind of naive. A little gullible. But good-natured. A dreamer perhaps. But not foolishly so."

"Please, how can you—?"

"See you?"

"Yes? Tell me how."

"Because I came along with them, for the ride. I am the only one who did, of course. The others were quite zealous from the beginning. For me, it was just a matter of curiosity, Though I, too, was cast out, guilt by association, I guess you might say, I have never really joined the others. I have remained uncommitted to their atrocities. But I can never return, either, to the way it once was. God asked for a choice. I made mine, however half-heartedly, and with motives that were substantially different, but it was made just the same. And I am stuck with the consequences, unfortunately."

There is a note of wistfulness in the way he speaks.

Underlined by a profound sadness.

"I have counterparts among the human beings of this world, you know. People who want to go along for the ride, who are faintly attract-ed by the bravado of many of their contemporar-ies, but tom by the knowledge that they cannot serve two masters—allowing themselves to be beckoned by the one, they end up rejecting the other."

I stand there, still amazed.

"But that old man's body which you inhabit? How?"

"He is the same way. He is unaware, of course, that we are here. He will die soon, and then I must find someone else. It is the same with the others, at least the ones who have been as-signed the possessions—they work from within while the rest wreak havoc from without, oppressing with equal vengeance."

"You have been in—inside others?"

"When I choose to be. I have not succumbed to any orders by any-one. I do as I wish."

He pauses, very briefly, then talks with affection about the old hands that are writing down his thoughts, hands mottled with the spots of a liver in distress, varicose veins apparent, nails turning faint yellow.

"I started a journal some time ago. Here it is. See, he's writing in it now."

"And it will be passed on to someone else when you move on?"

"Exactly. There will be new editions when each of the old starts to crumble."

"But why?"

"I am known as Observer. It is what I do."

"But who is going to read it?"

"Those who play host to me. They read it. But they see it only as a collection of myths. They read, oh, yes, they do that, but their under-standing is darkened—and, eventually, each will put it aside."

I am eager to know the contents of that book.

"It is to be read only when it is to be read," Observer says ambiguously." It is a perpetual legacy, left behind by a wandering spirit hoping that, someday, those who have it will indeed comprehend."

I want to pursue this matter further with him, but I know that I will not be at all successful. Instead I content myself with the bits and pieces told to me by Observer as we sit there by that stream, the sun poking through overhead branches, and glistening off the rippling water.

"I have seen The Fall and The Flood. I have been with John on Patmos, at the French Revolution, the Civil War, the two World Wars—from the ancient days to the computer age. And, you know, even I feel something akin to weariness."

He hesitates, then: "You have been around also, have you not?"

I nod.

"But there is a difference between us, my former fellow inhabitant of Heaven. You have sampled history, I have been through it. You have dabbled here and there—I have experienced centuries as centuries. In Heaven, time was an impossibility. For Man, it is a necessity. And to a great extent we—the others and I—are entrapped by many of the constraints, the conventions, the limitations of the very creature they—not me, please understand, never me—would like to destroy, would like to snatch from the loving arms of a kind and generous Creator."

He begins to sob then.

"I do this often. These are not tears, of course—we are beings of spirit, not tear ducts and blood and nerve endings. But we cry spiritually. We cry with emotion and depth even more profoundly than this old man who wept many years ago over the death of his wife."

Observer old man stands, walks to a deeper, broader part of the stream, points to some fish there.

"Many will not make it, you know. They will die in that stream or be hooked by fishermen and fried in a skillet and eaten with delight. But they do not know the future. The others and I do. That is why they are so frenzied. That future is always closer, never forestalled. For these fish, it may be the frying pan—for us, it is the fire."

He shakes himself with great weariness.

"I cry because I know I am doomed. I know what is in store. I will be there in the lake of torment with all the rest. It is the choice each being makes—of spirit or of flesh—and there by it he must abide for all eternity, in pain or—or in peace."

He turns, sits down again, age readily apparent.

"My host is dying," Observer says simply, "He will see us soon."

The pen drops from the old man's hand as he clutches his chest. The ancient book falls to the ground, amongst some autumn leaves. Lips issue a single cry and then are frozen together, eyelids closed, head bent to one side.

First it is Observer as spirit en toto who leaves that body, and I see an angel much like myself but also very different, wings at half-mast, face pale, the glow of Heaven gone, his lostness apparent in the tragedy of separation from God mirrored in his eyes, the forlornness of his very countenance. And then the old man's spirit, that which is him in actuality, not the disposable cloak soon to rot away, also leaves that fleshly shell.

"You've been with me many years, have you not?" he asks, looking at Observer.

Observer agrees that this has been so.

"I was a good man, kind, charitable."

Observer nods.

"I never engaged in adultery, I lied little."

"That is correct."

"I never cursed any man. I never stole money, I am good, am I not?"

"Yes, you are."

He smiles, but it fades as quickly,

"But why are they waiting for me?"

In the surrounding forest are a dozen fallen angels. The sight of them is chilling.

"I have helped the homeless, fed the starving, comforted the dying."

The dozen shapes are beckoning, cloven feet stamping the ground.

"I have served on church committees, raised money for missionaries. I have also planned picnics for the elderly and—and—"

The shapes move from the trees into the clearing.

"Must they have me? Must all my good be as nothing?"

They grab him and take him away, his screams filling the air. One turns, smiles momentarily at Observer. And then is gone with the others.

Observer is shaken.

"I must wait here until the body is found," Observer notes, his voice trembling. "It may not be long. It will be found, along with the book, and I will go along until it passes into the hands of someone else like me, and whoever that is will provide me with pen, ink, and a hand to write. I am called Observer, yes, but I have felt that another appellation was perhaps a trifle more accurate."

"And what would that be?"

He grimaces with centuries of awareness, centuries that weigh upon him like some kind of boulder, pressing him down, sapping away his vitality.

I can scarcely hear him at first, and tell him so. Then he speaks louder as he says, "TuMasters, that is what it should be, would you not agree?" Mifult. D'Seaver. D'Filer. And now TuMasters. What a motley crew, the bane of humanity. And yet there are more, of course, out there among the masses, planting, nurturing, reaping.

"I live under a delusion, you know, as all of us do. Many of the others abort, rape, slaughter. I seem so bland in comparison. I seem to do nothing but observe, hence my title. And that is the appalling reality of my existence. I look, I write down my useless insights through my hapless hosts, but that is all. I interfere not. I stay within a limited circle, insulated, my hosts and I. And we let the world collapse around us."

He has been looking up at the sky, which has but a lone cloud at that time and place.

"When you get back, please, please, please tell Him how very sorry I am."

I start to speak, to say something very evangelical, if you will, to tell him it is not too late.

But he has turned his back on me, and he is sitting by that old, old book, the piccolo lying nearby, and the moment of regret has passed, the door to himself is closed, and Observer will do as he has always done . . .

Eleven

THE KITTEN IS MEWING.

It cannot be more than a few weeks old, the fur still tufted with something like fuzz. A man in a white smock is holding it in his right hand. With his left he is putting little beads of fluid from a dropper into each of its eyes.

The kitten cries louder. The man puts it in a cage with another of its kind, then leaves.

The first kitten cannot stand. Little knives of agony slice continually from its eyes into its brain and then throughout its tiny body. It tries to wash the awfulness away by licking its paw and then rubbing that paw over its left eye, and next the other paw over the right eye. Yet this is to no avail. The pain continues. In fact, it is getting worse.

The kitten starts to vomit, what little food was held in its young stomach spewing onto the newspaper underneath, onto its own fur, and that of its companion.

The kitten can no longer see, its blindness caused by an acid-based dye that has literally eaten away much of the soft material of its eyeballs.

Its body shakes once, twice, its limbs extended out straight as though frozen in that position. Then it gasps up some blood. And dies.

Its companion walks hesitantly over to the still form, not aware of what has happened, and lies next to it, hoping to comfort what is now beyond that.

A short while later the man in the white smock returns, finds the lifeless body, dumps it into a nearby wastebasket, takes the second kitten, and another dropper with a different solution inside and—

Madison Avenue.

Product marketing meeting.

A tall man, his shirt sleeves rolled up, shows a chart to others in the room, "It's a great new color," he beams. "I'm calling it luminescent pearl. The women will love it."

The chimpanzee cannot stop scratching its head. It has been doing so for nearly an hour. Its fingertips are bloody, pieces of skin hanging from—

"Last year our best shade was sunset orange," the man continues.

The chimp has blood all over its head, but still it keeps scratching. It does not know what else to do.

"How many units do we expect to sell?" He repeats the question that has just been asked.

He inputs some figures on a calculator in front of him and gives the result to those in the conference room with him.

"That's pretty good, if it's accurate," someone speaks up.

There is general agreement that the outlook certainly is appealing, the more dollars the better.

The chimp is covered with his own blood, for it has continued to scratch itself tearing more and more flesh. Now too weak to do anything else, it slumps back across one side of the cage.

"How about the testing?" a little man on the left side of the oak conference room asks. "What about the safety factor?"

"No problem at all," the main speaker replies. "We're finalizing the results now. You know what I always say? Better to kill a chimp than to harm one single hair on a single customer's head. We can always find another chimp, but finding customers isn't always easy."

It moans with enormous anguish several times, then is silent altogether, its eyes rolling upward in its sockets, slobber dripping out of its mouth and down its chin, hanging like dewdrops from the black hairs. And then it dies.

Everyone claps. The mood is buoyant. They have a new color. And sales have never been better.

~⊘~

I am privy to more in other panelled conference rooms in tall buildings along that avenue. Other products are being generated. More dollars coveted. More suffering generated for animals at the mercy of those whose highest ambition, whose most compelling ideal, is additional profit for their companies.

"Who cares if they need it?"

"That's right. We'll create the desire and masquerade it as need."

All the demographics are there. All the convincing marketing research designed to lull the public into an acceptance of whatever the manufacturers care to purvey.

This is not America, I cry out to unheeding ears. It is not the vision of the Pilgrims or the Puritans. They left one kind of domination but not to sow the seeds of another in its place.

And flashing across my vision is a montage of faces, the faces of mothers whose babies are deformed because of cigarettes. Or alcohol. Or drugs innocently taken in trust of a doctor's prescription, only to see a pitiful, twisted little shape coming from the womb, and turning for solace only to hear the shouts of "Abort! Abort! Abort!" all around. You should have killed the thing. You should have—

They are out there in the cities, the towns, the villages. Pumping poison into their systems, through mouths and skin pores and into veins. Poison over the counter, in the midst of shopping malls. Or in a secluded place from a man who profits, chuckling at his fruits. Poison into the temple made by God, graffiti of the spirit, but far more deadly than initials or obscenities or protests on an outdoor wall.

Poison, yes, packaged and labelled and advertised. Poison to color the hair. Poison to prolong the "freshness" of food. Poison to move the bowels. Tested, oh, yes, they test all of it. They reap their profits on the backs of God's helpless ones, the dogs and cats and birds and mice and monkeys and other creatures who wait in their cages for the inevitable, condemned not for crime but commerce.

Present your bodies a living sacrifice . . . .

But is a body riddled with the residue of mindless consumption,

consumption ignorant of the content of what is being consumed, dictated even among His chosen ones by the latest "discovery" to retard aging, change hair color, take away bad breath, ban body odor, bring on sleep, calm frazzled nerves during the day, give a reason for smiling, is such a body cosmeticized, aromatized, plasticized, artificialized for profit and not a dedication to the betterment of the Human Race, is such a body traumatized by the media, pummelled by sensation at every turn, is such a body indeed truly, truly, truly a living sacrifice or rather a kind of mannequin, dressed up, prettied up, propped up by the merchandising to which it has succumbed? Is there not in that Scriptural admonition at least the implication that those bodies are to be worthy as well as living? Is a gift to a charity of a suit with holes and patches and loose threads and stains and rips in fact a gift? Or, dare I say, an insult instead? Too often, as I have seen in my travels across Earth, a gift is not actually that but instead more like a spent whore, riddled with disease, crippled by exhausted inner drives, drained of energy, worthless in her profession, lying down before God and saying, "Here I am, Lord." That body of that whore has already been sacrificed, but not to God. When a celebrity leaves the glittery world of show business and professes salvation by faith in Christ, is it plus nothing and is it worthy? Or has an illusion been created, the formula now salvation by faith in Christ plus transcendent media attention that revives a slumping career?

But this is the world. The domain of the flesh. What about the get-rich-quick minister steering his congregation on the road to prosperity? Offering them keys to a generously filled bank vault instead of Heaven? The healer on television who claims the name of Christ and then makes a sideshow of purported healing that even the most naive, the most gullible find patently absurd? What about the "Jesus loves me" Ping-Pong paddle peddlers? Those who take sacred verses dealing with Christ being the Light of the World and make that Scriptural truth instead a Jesus nightlight to be used in bedrooms everywhere? What about all the rest of holy hardwaredom? Pens and bracelets and bookends and handkerchiefs and endless other products made "righteous" by the name of Christ?

Oh, God, I say, and not in vain—I could never use my Creator's name in vain—this is what has become of America, the world? This is His creation, now, a little higher than the angels? This is Earth, once Eden? If I had a stomach, if there were bowels within me, I would be in great distress. I would vomit up the sickness that grips me, the slop from within like that which I see without, nauseating and vile.

∽◉◦

And even now, yet another wretched truth unraveling, I still see not the creature accused of it all, only those called demons, spirits of the hideous and profane, things that bump in the night, and—

Lucifer.

Emissaries aplenty, but not Lucifer, my former fellow inhabitant of heavenly places.

Where are you, son of the morning?

WHERE AM I TO GO?

I cannot be seen except by dying human beings on the way to Heaven or Hell. I am as close to desperation as I can possibly be, my inner turmoil so strong that I feel moved to petition to Him to let me back, that I do not really need to find out the truth about Satan because I perceive the truth about the world to which he has been confined for so long. But I suspect God would not allow me to return to His Kingdom under such conditions because, in His wisdom, He knows the old doubts would crop up again later, and—

An idea springs into my mind. If I can just not give up in trying to locate Lucifer, perhaps, upon doing so, I could alert him to what is going on, and together we could make things right. What a triumph that would be! And the return of the highest archangel to Heaven would surely be an event of rejoicing without precedent. If we all used to celebrate over the salvation of one sinning human being, what would it be like if Lucifer returned in contrition and with the banishment of all the evil in the world as his legacy?

The possibilities overwhelm me. And I become more deeply committed than ever to the goal of finding Lucifer, for the new reason makes a pygmy of my previous one. Lucifer and I allies! Banishing the perversion, the drugs, the pornography, banishing all the other corruptions that have swept over Earth like the most epochal tidal wave of history.

I ask fallen angel after fallen angel. As before, it is not difficult to find them. A whole horde are at a heavy metal rock concert, infiltrating the audience, backstage with the strange—garbed musicians, and—

No one will tell me. The most I can get out of them is that Lucifer will find me, not the other way around, when he wishes to do so.

I discover my former comrades at a television station during a debate between a minister who claims that the Bible contains God's truth, and another who protests that the Bible is His truth, from cover to cover. And they also are in the newscaster's booth as he tells a "neutral" story about the Communist takeover of another country in Central America. And they are there as commercials are being telecast, commercials that appeal to the vanity of millions of viewers. They are everywhere at that station, in every department, because this is where their lies, their distortions can be disseminated to a wider number than even they could reach otherwise. But all profess ignorance about where Lucifer is, although at the very mention of his name, they become exceedingly nervous, paranoid.

One in particular seems more upset than the others. His name is Nufears.

"Why do you want to meet Lucifer?" he asks. "Why would anyone?" He looks from side to side, apprehension growing.

"He is not what you may be expecting."

"But I have to see for myself."

"I must tell you that he—"

He disappears, suddenly, without explanation.

I stand there in a corridor, rock music and interviews and newscasts being spun out all around me. And I am just as puzzled as ever.

Twelve

More time passes. At different places. In that city. And in others. And I am now in a place where it could be expected that I would find the highest concentration of fallen angels anywhere in America, surpassing even the number in Hollywood.

The President is dying. Gathered around him are his family, two physicians, and three Cabinet members. The rigors of office have taken their toll on the oldest President in the history of the United States.

"He should rest now," a doctor says softly, and they all leave the room.

The First Lady, as though sensing that he will be gone when she returns, whispers, "Good-bye, my love . . . ."

The President knows of my presence, so close to death is he by then, and seems not startled by it.

"Almost the moment?" he asks, his voice hardly audible.

"Yes, Mr. President, it is."

"Oh, how I rejoice over that. How I indeed rejoice."

"You have done well these seven years."

"I tried very hard, you know, I witnessed to as many members of Congress, foreign heads of state, and whoever else I could. Many paid no heed, but I hope I managed to reach a few."

"In Heaven there is great anticipation over your imminent arrival."

"Is that really, really the case, my new angel friend?"

"Oh, yes. The President who tried to govern in the right way even though that did not guarantee how correct he was from a political point of view. You put God first always, and nothing else matters in the long run."

"And I know how much of a miracle it was that I was re-elected!"

He coughs, then says: "I once heard a joke. St. Peter welcomes a minister and a politician through the so-called pearly gates. The former is assigned a very nice place to live in for eternity but not especially elaborate. The latter is given a palace, a stunning residence indeed. The politician is appreciative but puzzled. He asks St. Peter, 'But why am I being blessed so mightily while a man of the cloth is treated so humbly?' St. Peter replies, 'It is not uncommon for ministers to come here and stay forever. But it is a momentous event indeed when that happens to a politician!'"

I laugh at the joke, then say, "You must have been perplexed by a great deal of what you have seen, here, over the years."

"Oh, a considerable amount has been ghastly. If ever there was a capital as much for the Devil as for the nation, then Washington, D. C., is it, I am afraid to say."

"Terribly frustrating for you, Mr. President?"

"More than anyone except God Himself will ever know. For example, If I could have established an AIDS quarantine, I would have. It seems suicidal not to have done so. In virtually all other periods of epidemic throughout history, from ancient times to the modern, quarantines have been accepted as a necessity, and this one has perhaps the most devastating potential of all. But certain segments of our society got wind of it, labeled it as a transgression against their civil rights, and, well, as it turned out, they enlisted their cohorts in the media and in the judicial system and I soon had the columnists, the commentators, the judges, and the ACLU against me from the beginning. How blind we have become in this generation. Civil rights my foot! It's a matter of morality and the public health!"

"They would find Heaven a very quarantined place, in one sense," I say in agreement. "No one is an idolater, effeminate, whoremonger, sorcerer . . . ."

"How well I know that verse, how much it and others like it have guided me over the past seven years. The threats I received, many of them in the most obscene terms! That kind of reaction only strength-ened my determination, I can assure you.

"In addition, I wanted to get prayer back in schools, but I was ridiculed as a religious fanatic. I wanted to help decent people in other lands to throw off the heavy rule of communism. And I was labeled a McCarthyite because of my opposition to that atheistic government. But the facts are there—persecution of Jews and Christians alike, intol-erable conditions for any and all political prisoners. I—"

He interrupts himself, coughing more severely this time, and then continues, "Do you think God, in His infinite mercy, would introduce me to any of the Pilgrims and Puritans in Heaven?"

"I am sure He would be pleased to do so, Mr. President."

"How grand that would be. I want so much to tell them what I tried to do, to rekindle a little of the spirit of what they intended when they landed on these shores. And how ashamed I am of what the nation they died to create has become. Our air poisoned, our morality shriv-elling up, an ugly distortion of their ideal, this land with more places of sin than there are churches.

"You know, good angel, I will enjoy eternity for many reasons, of course, but for one in particular."

"What would that be, Mr. President?"

"That I won't have to talk myself hoarse, that I won't have to fight yet day after day, week after week, month after month, year after year for what is good and decent and Christ-honoring. My spirit isn't weary, you must understand, but my mind, my body, there isn't any strength left."

He dies then, this President of the United States, as I stand by his body, and welcome the spirit that arises from it.

"No pain," he says with wonderment.

I nod.

"How old, how very old my body looks. It is true that the Presidency hastens age more than any other job in the world."

"But no longer," I say. "All that is over now. You will not have to pre-
pare for any further battles with Congress, Mr. President."

"Angel?"

"Yes?"

"I hear some music."

And I do as well.

"Oh my . . ."

Against the background melody of an old Thanksgiving hymn, the
President of the United States meets his first Pilgrim . . .

~⚬~

Washington, D. C., reacts with official mourning. Heads of government from all over the world come in under tight security. And yet
even so a terrorist incident at Dulles International Airport shows that
almost nothing is sacred in the atmosphere of this insane world.

A little girl is standing alone near the front entrance to the airline
building where a delegation from England is scheduled to arrive.

Dressed in clothes that make her seem a harmless doll, she is holding a rather large handbag. Every so often she looks up at a passerby
and smiles.

At the opposite side of the building, a British Airways plane lands. A
total of twenty members of Parliament disembark. The Prime Minister
and her husband are also on board, but she has had a slight case of air-
sickness. The others wait at the gate.

"She is supposed to be made of iron," whispers one of them.

"Please, Harold, do not be sarcastic," an associate responds. "You try
to hide how much you really do admire the lady, but despite yourself,
you cannot."

The other man is silent.

In a few minutes the couple joins them, and surrounded by security
guards they head toward the entrance. The Prime Minister seems quite
recovered, walking with a sure step.

As the party approaches, the little girl runs up to the first member of the delegation, and gives him the handbag. She is smiling with the sweetness, the innocence of the very young.

"Please, mister, my mommy—!"

She is unable to finish.

An explosion demolishes a large portion of the building, pieces of it scattering for nearly a mile. Most of those directly inside are killed—as well as many more on the outside, bodies flung in a dozen directions.

Several times the number of those dead are injured, blinded by shards of glass, flesh torn by metal, limbs severed, bones broken.

"A war zone!" says the U.S. government official observing the scene.

And that it appears to be. The terminal is in ruins, girders twisted like a toy erector set abused by a very angry child.

Shattered glass is so deep in some spots that—

Cries fill the air. Sirens form a continuous orchestration.

The Prime Minister has survived, but her husband is dead. She is asked by a member of the Joint Chiefs of Staff who has hurried to the airport if she would rather not attend the President's funeral but instead go directly to her hotel.

"Thank you, sir, but the First Lady needs me at this hour," she replies.

As she walks toward an awaiting limousine, she notices a tiny blood-stained dress, red with white lace at the edges, the body it once covered now in scattered pieces.

"Would that be—?" the Prime Minister starts to ask.

"Yes, madam, it is, I'm afraid," the general replies with ill-concealed reluctance.

"Please, sir, would you take my hand? I feel very weak now,"

Reports have spread throughout Washington, D.C., with startling rapidity. Some discussion is given to delaying the President's funeral for a day. But that would create more massive security problems than it would resolve.

The First Lady is there. As are the members of Congress. Even the President's political enemies give him praise. One of them, a senior Senator responsible for defeating some of the President's most cherished programs, begins his speech but cannot continue, his grief beyond suppression.

Hundreds attend from scores of countries. The Russians. The Chinese. The French. The Italians. One nation after another, some for the diplomatic necessity of it, others out of a genuine regard for this man, and out of awareness for the fact that life is tenuous, whether it ends "naturally" or through the act of a terrorist group willing to use a child no one would suspect.

The Prime Minister of England now ascends the podium in front of the White House.

"When I left my native land, I had a husband," she says. "When the plane landed just two hours ago, he and I were planning to spend as much time with the First Lady as we could, given the affairs of state back home. Now, in the midst of this nightmare day, she and I both need to comfort one another.

"Life begins with a miracle bestowed by the hand of God. It ends as we take His hand and He helps us from this mortal body. My husband died in my arms, but he died triumphantly, for his last words were, 'Dear, dear wife, the Savior is waiting, now, for me. An angel attends my way. You must leave me and hurry on, my dearest love.'

"That is in part why I have the strength to come before you now. But it is just a part, however important it is. The other lies in words spoken to me by your President less than a week before his illness claimed him. The words may be familiar to some of you. They are from the Book of Revelation:

"'And he shewed me a pure river of water of life, clear as crystal, proceeding out of the throne of God and of the Lamb. In the midst of the street of it, and on either side of the river, was there the tree of life, which bare twelve manner of fruits, and yielded her fruit every month:

·and the leaves of the tree were for the healing of nations . . . And there shall be no night there, and they need no candle, neither light of the sun, for the Lord God giveth them light: and they shall reign forever and ever.'

"That is the future, ladies and gentlemen, the only one that matters. Right now, as I speak, the President of the United States and my minister-husband are where no bombs can touch them, no lies can hurt them, no pain can sap their strength."

Tears trickle down the sides of her cheek.

"Forgive me," she says as she collapses into the arms of the First Lady.

The next morning, the Prime Minister of England boards a plane with the body of the man she loved for thirty-five years . . .

Thirteen

Even so, government continues on as always, for the better as well as for the worse . . .

I find prayer breakfasts and an organization called Congresswomen for Christ and other such-wonderful to see, encouraging, of course, but along with them, and in greater abundance are the lobbyists for the various industries whose products have caused a great deal of the pain of the world: the liquor lobbyists, the American Tobacco Institute lobbyists, the ones pushing legalization of marijuana, those who favor making prostitution legal. On and on—a veritable sea of them, foaming with the poisons inflicted by their own "doctrines" in opposition to those of Almighty God.

Does it stun me to find the American Tobacco Institute swarming with demonic activity—no real possession, actually, but slavering hordes of oppressors? I overhear several of them discussing a game plan.

"No one can easily make the case that tobacco in itself is evil."

"That may be true, for the moment, but I would not be excessively confident."

"You are too easily upset. The fact is that we have an ideal environment here that has been working out nicely for years."

"Yes, make smoking socially acceptable. Make it commercially profitable. And help form an organization funded to make it respectable, and keep it that way."

"Marvelous! But that has been only the beginning. The pain we can inflict, the suffering!"

This one demon is fairly ecstatic with enthusiasm.

"I thought I had died and gone to Heaven—well, you know what I mean—when I saw that chap coughing his life away from emphysema," he continues. "It was wonderful, I tell you. The blood and phlegm and other stuff gushing out of his mouth. And the suffocation he was feeling because of the damage to his lungs. I was delirious for a long time after that, my thoughts jumping ahead decades to encompass all the possibilities."

Says another: "And the retarded children! Wow! What we fail to abort, we can cripple, we can retard, we can do so much else!"

One demon seems to glow as he adds, "And then we zap them with euthanasia. I do not know about the rest of you, but I want to be there when they kill the first mongoloid idiot legally!"

They are gleeful, planning a whole monstrous tapestry of mischief to be inflicted during the weeks, months, years ahead.

I visit other organizations, each dedicated to spreading its own "doctrine." My next stop is one dealing with freedom of speech and the press.

I encounter a variety of discussions there, in offices, and behind conference room doors. A man who publishes pornography is discussing his chain of adult bookstores. The lobbyists are nodding in agreement.

"It's a free country, you know," the pornographer is saying. "If I want to show some skin, that's exactly what I'll do. This ain't Russia after all, you know. People get their jollies from the stuff in my stores, you know."

"Exactly," a lobbyist agreed out loud.

"Why, you know, I've doubled the number of private booths. I'm providing a real service, you know. I've even had a special deodorizing system so that the places won't smell, you know, like those gay bathhouses. I've got the best line of plastic toys in the industry. And, you know, the aromatics—just great—a cheap high—and my films and books, you know. What more could the stupid public ask for?"

"Yes, yes, absolutely," a Greek chorus responds.

He opens up an attaché case and takes out a pile of magazines.

"These are what America is all about," he says.

"I should say so," one of the lobbyists agrees as he leafs through a copy.

"Just good clean sex," the man says, licking his lips.

"I mean, where would, you know, that guy from Lynchburg be, you know, without sex?"

Everyone bursts into laughter.

"Look at those," he says, pointing to a centerfold. "Lust, you know, good old lust. That's what makes this world, you know, go around, guys."

I leave though I would rather have disputed everything he said. I would rather have given him the volumes of police reports that indicated that the majority of all violent crime resulting in death had a sexual base. Not to mention the epidemic of sexually transmitted diseases—the disintegration of families—just the kinds of byproducts that his "good old lust" propagated.

Freedom of speech was never meant to bring about the license to engage in any type of lustful, degrading, demoralizing enterprises, allowed to spread their poison because trying to stop this would be "unAmerican." I can say that from having visited only a little while ago the men who created the Constitution, spending time by their side and hearing all the reasons behind what they would write, what they would desire for the nation.

And further back, hundreds of years, I was with the Pilgrims and Puritans. I heard the essence of what their vision for America was. A country free of persecution but also a country founded on the premise of a new Israel, a land devoted to God, a land that would be free but a freedom with different connotations than the word bruited about in modern times. It was not freedom, they would have said, looking at the United States of the current day for men and women to be enslaved to promiscuous sex, to violence, to drugs. A law abiding country was not one in which countless numbers broke moral laws, laws handed down by the Creator. There was never to have been that kind of freedom or license. In the days of the Pilgrims and Puritans, anyone caught in the sin of adultery or homosexuality would have been dealt with in exceedingly harsh terms. Too harsh, it might be asked? Too unloving? Too judgmental? That which is clearly stated in God's Word, that which is without equivocation branded intolerable should not be overlooked, should not be permitted by those who claim the name of His Son, under the guise of not wanting to be judgmental. Oh, what cancers are allowed to run unchecked in the name of nonjudgmentalism!

～◎～

I visit other organizations set up to serve the elderly, the poor, the homeless. Most are strapped for cash, most have almost to beg for the dollars they need. Yet the tobacco lobby, the alcohol lobby, those with secret bank accounts that benefit terrorists worldwide, others of that ilk seem to have no problem finding dollars, for their money is carried to them in sacks on the backs of those dying of lung cancer, and those who are retarded, and those who head for X-rated films instead of being with their families. In a world of evil triumphant, a world of too few good men and women doing too little to stem the tide, to dam it up so that it cannot spread any further, in such a world, the Washington, D. C., lobbyists, sustained by those profiting from the moral degradation, are always going to be ahead, running around like termites eating into the very structure of society, and helped by armies of workers, with banks of computers and millions of brochures and press releases, and unlimited media access, media controlled by those of like mind and spirit.

And where are the Christians? I ask myself, reflecting on that first, fine family at the outset of my sojourn on Earth. Where is the salt of the earth? Salt is supposed to prevent spoiling. Without the salt, there is decay.

I visit some Christian lobbyists who are having money problems, but some others are not, at least not as severe. They are good at raising money. They are good at spending it. And then the other lobbyists, the unsaved ones who would like to see the hastened disintegration of Christian influence in the United States and elsewhere, take the weapon that has been handed to them, the weapon of financial accountability, and fling it back into the heart of Christianity, and those thus wounded cry and scream and raise a fist at the evil world around them.

I stand, amazed, at one ministry in particular. The head of it lives in a home worth $600,000, he has parties in a houseboat valued at $100,000, his wife has a diamond ring worth $20,000, and he just spent $1,000,000 on designing and building a cafeteria so that, to use his words, "my people can eat in style."

That ministry is located not very far from Washington, D.C. Of course, when you are an angel, distance is of no consequence, but I suppose some of the habits, the conventions about time and such that the human beings around me have, are beginning to affect my own thinking.

In any event, I visit the headquarters of that ministry. I see a fleet of limousines carrying guests about.

"They were donated," someone says in response to another's question, the very question I would have raised if I could have done so. But the money was still spent, I would retort, it could have been used to buy less luxurious transportation, and the difference used to support more missionaries or feed more of the poor or given to other needful ministries—the fact that the limousines were donated is irrelevant under the circumstances. (Was the $20,000 diamond ring donated also? I wonder.)

I see the building designed to house visitors, the hanging crystal chandeliers in the lobby, the plush carpeting, the leather-covered sofas and chairs, the imported marble, the hand-carved statues.

"It was bought and paid for through a special fund donated by our supporters," I hear. Same special reasoning millions of dollars siphoned away from the mission field, the stomachs of hungry children, the ministries barely able to pay their heating bills.

And I see one little woman, probably in her late-seventies, wandering around, astonished by what she sees, appalled by it as well. She goes into a jewelry store on the premises, sees a particularly fine-looking diamond ring, and finds out that it had just been traded in by the founder's wife who wanted something a bit more elaborate.

She leaves that store, that building. She walks to a bench in a shaded grove nearby, she bows her head, and prays aloud, "Father, take me from this place."

But the vast majority of those present seem joyous. A group of them is singing a hymn back in the lobby. Others are eating a buffet lunch. A mother is holding her daughter, both of them well-dressed. A brass-plated piano is played by someone in a tuxedo.

Getting up to speak is a member of the hierarchy, a vice president of the ministry, who tells of the need for sacrifice, enabling the Lord's work to continue—while not letting you know that his salary is $200,000 a year, and there are others being paid higher sums than that! How much of an abomination this must be in the eyes of God is not lost on me. Many people are indeed sacrificing to keep that ministry going. But just that vice president's salary alone requires a donation of $100 annually from each of two thousand elderly supporters. He lives in a large $250,000 house, so add another twenty-five hundred to that number. And he has an expense account greater than the income of thousands of the Christians giving to the ministry. How pathetic! I scream, realizing that I know those figures because the man had told them, earlier, to a visitor-friend, not braggingly, no, not that, but matter-of-factly, which may have been worse actually. Thousands of men and women faithfully giving of their earnings or their retirement incomes, thinking that all this is going for the support of missionaries, for example, and not knowing what is really happening.

Next, there is entertainment. The founder and his wife appear on a stagelike area in the midst of the lobby. Other lights darken, and a spotlight is turned on the two of them. Both are wearing hand-tailored clothes. The founder's wife has more jewelry than just that one large diamond ring, her necklace, bracelets, earrings—all are glittering.

"Everybody enjoying themselves?" she asks.

A roar of affirmation is heard.

Virtually all of those present are caught up in the atmosphere that is, yes, deliberately constructed, a kind of retreat from the outside world.

A truth dawns on me. That is the problem. It is a cocoon of crushed velour and leather and crystal and diamonds and hand-tailored tweed and brass and so much else. But the cocoon is not eternal, it is transitory, from it they must emerge, after a week, even a month, to face that very world from which they have retreated.

"It's a ministry," a guide, beaming, tells one of the visitors.

But to whom? A dying mother from the streets of Alexandria, Egypt—a starving child from the sands of Ethiopia? A missionary from Calcutta, India? And how is it to minister? As an example of what is in store for every Christian? Eating in style in a million-dollar cafeteria? Dressing in style? Living in style? Driving in style? Partying in style? The byproducts of . . . faith?

And what of the times when none of this shields, none of this is there to cling to, to look at, in a sense to hug around the body and the spirit like some gigantic blanket? If this is what faith brings, where is faith when donations drop, when bills cannot be paid, when the diamond ring seems more like a finger raised in a gesture of obscenity?

I leave that ministry sadly. For I sense among those present a kind of substitute for true spirituality. Oh, they are saved, yes, a fact about which I have little question, at least in most of the instances I see, their love of Him obvious. And perhaps this is what really counts, and count it does, but there is more, of course, going beyond the trappings of luxury, that image the world around sees, an image of extravagance, of a Christianity as much based upon the externals of affluence as the internals of salvation, regeneration. Take away the former and there is still the latter, without question, but then it boils down to the quality of life. And how high will be that quality if the externals are eventually gone, replaced by the more mundane, yes indeed, the more typical world known by many more Americans?

I journey on to Atlantic City, a place of glitter in the midst of continuing decay and moral corruption . . .

The man seems old, but he probably is not. His face is so wrinkled that it gives nearly an ancient impression, his hair is straggly, not a great deal of it left. His eyes are bloodshot; his hand trembles as he lifts a soup spoon to his lips. Someone to his right coughs and he mutters something about spreading germs. Finally he finishes the chicken noodle soup and leans back on the folding metal chair, waiting for the rest of the meal. He wipes some specks off slacks that are worn bare at the knees and torn loose from the stitches on the sides. His shoes have served him countless miles of pavement and asphalt pounding, but they will not last much longer. He has twenty cents in his pocket.

The director and his staff do the best they can, but the load is enormous. Each year there is a deficit, each year anxious moments are experienced, each year, the transient population grows, swelling larger and larger, bloated by drug addicts, alcoholics, and those addicted to another pursuit: gambling.

Row after row of cots take up all the space in several rooms. Each one is occupied. A waiting list haunts the director and the other workers.

"We trust the Lord for everything," he says simply to a visitor from out of town, someone interested in helping to support the mission.

The director shows the visitor, a businessman in his midforties, around the premises. The work is orderly, effective, but certainly not showy.

"We make the dollars go as far as we can," the director comments. "There is no fat here."

The businessman is impressed. After spending several hours at the mission, he leaves to return home in another state. A short time later, he commits to a regular schedule of donations.

But others, as I find out, are attracted to the glamour of the other ministry and ones like it, caught up in the aura of prospering, and put off by the more basic work of that rescue mission and ones elsewhere across the land.

One man is shaking violently, vomiting over the male staff member trying to help him. The director is called in, decides that they need a doctor for the man. The latter has stopped heaving, at least for the moment. He looks up at the staff member, covered with slop, and at the director and says, his voice hoarse, barely audible, "God does love me even now, doesn't He?" The director replies, "Even as we do."

A doctor comes, gives the man a sedative. In the meantime, the staff member has changed clothes, and the three of them sit in the director's office.

"I don't know how you take all this," the doctor says to the two of them.

"We do it because God wants us to reach out to these men," the staffer replies. "We might want to give up sometimes. Throwing in the towel would be easier than cleaning off the stuff somebody has thrown up all over you. But the alternative is to abandon them, and none of us here could live with ourselves if we did that."

The director is obviously, and rightly, pleased at what his staffer has said. He adds only this: "These men have burdens the rest of us will never have to carry. The pain in their eyes is so overpowering with most of them that, well, anyone who is unmoved must be a statue made of stone."

He rubs his chin, an ironic smile on his face as he says, "Periodically the gambling interests offer to help fund the work. From the beginning we have turned them down. Gambling and allied problems are behind what we are seeing here. We can't accept help from those responsible in the first place."

I leave them, and go outside. It is near dusk in Atlantic City. A line of transients is waiting to get into the mission.

But, I say in words unheard by any of them, where are the diamonds?

⁓◉⁓

I feel utterly alone. I have been alone, of course, from the very begin-ning, at least in the sense of not being joined by others like me, angels who chose not to follow a new leader. But somehow, now, the loneliness is more pervasive, a mournful dirge all about me, the music that of pros-

titutes soliciting customers on Atlantic Avenue, of chickenhawks cruising near the Boardwalk, of high-rollers screaming as they lose thousands of dollars, of gangsters in dark comers fixing deals, of the elderly walking the streets because they can no longer afford rents boosted higher and higher by greedy new apartment building owners, of this, and of that, and so much else, a dirge reaching up, I am sure, to Heaven itself.

Fourteen

PHILOSOPHER IS DYING.

I hear them talking about that fact. But he himself is smiling, counterpointing their sad expressions.

"I go to be with Him," Philosopher says simply.

Several minutes later, he is "on stage" for his last public appearance, this one in a large college auditorium that has virtually no seats empty, for Philosopher's fame is great. No one in the audience realizes how close to death he is. Only the members of his family and his physicians and his pastor are aware. They had vigorously protested any expenditure of strength on another public meeting, but Philosopher was unyielding.

"There may be one more human being out there whom the Lord wants me to be His instrument in reaching," he told them. "I cannot disappoint my Savior."

And so he sits, in a softly padded chair, looking at the three thousand students, faculty members, and parents waiting to hear him speak.

"I am honored that you are willing to sit and listen to the ramblings of an old man," he says, his voice normally rather thin, and the loudspeaker system has to be adjusted so he can be heard by everyone.

"I want to present only what God allows me to say. I now await His leading."

He bows his head for a moment, and the audience waits patiently.

Philosopher finally looks up again, tears trickling down his cheeks.

"When I was the age of most of you, I did not know what to believe. How could I look at that which was so apparently real and physical, with form and substance, so that whatever it was could be touched and held, and say that a white-haired old man somewhere in the sky created it all by just waving his hands a few times?

"I could not accept any of that, for it seemed to me the stuff of delusion, and I had managed to convince myself that I was smarter than most people, and, as a consequence, certainly less gullible than the 'religious.'

"I started early with this attitude, I must admit. Usually it hits young people later, in college, as some of you can verify, when they are away from the influence of parents."

And he tells them about the years of agnosticism that plagued him, years of careless living, rather like a prodigal squandering everything in rebellion against his father, except in this instance, he did not even believe that he had such a father.

"And then I stood by my flesh-and-blood father's bedside. He had been praying for me all those years. I held his hand, and remember to this day how very cold it was.

"'Son,' he said to me. 'I have always been truthful with you, have I not?' I agreed that he had. No matter how much I disagreed with my father, I knew he was incapable of lying. 'Will you believe me if I tell you that there is a God and that, right now, my hand is in His, just as my other is in yours?' My whole sense of rationalism rejected what he was telling me. 'Son,' my father continued, 'why have you kept your Bible if you feel that it is nothing but a collection of myths and legends?' I was stunned. How could he have known that? He might reasonably have assumed that I had thrown it away. 'Son, you marked one passage in particular—Revelation 21:4—why?' I could not answer him at first. Who had told my father? A student at college? A professor? But how could anybody have found out, for one thing? No one had access to that Bible except me, because I kept it locked away.

"My father had been crying until then. Yet even as I looked at him, the tears were disappearing, almost as though Someone were wiping them away. He reached up his left hand, and I took it in mine. 'I love you, son,' he said, his voice getting weaker and weaker. He had been in a lot of pain over the month or so prior to that. And a few hours earlier, he had tossed and turned, little cries escaping his lips. But during those present moments, he seemed stronger. His hand gripped mine firmly, resolutely. His eyes sparkled. 'Dad,' I asked gently, 'how did you know?' He replied, 'I didn't.' Then he closed his eyes and never opened them again."

Philosopher stops briefly, the memories still poignant, his own tears glistening under the glare of overhead spotlights.

"As many of you know, that passage of Scripture is as follows: 'And God shall wipe away all tears from their eyes, and there shall be no more death, neither sorrow, nor crying, neither shall there be any more pain: for the former things are passed away'

"I wanted to tell myself that it was a kind of delusion, that some special mixture of adrenaline and the medicine had revived him temporarily, and the drying of the tears was quite natural. But that still did not explain how my father knew about that Bible and that passage. I had marked it only a few weeks before, long after he had been confined to bed, as a futile hope—at least that is what I considered it to be, an exercise, really—that when my father died, it would not be in a moment of pain, that he would go quietly. We often argued—perhaps debated is a better word—about matters of the spirit, but I loved him deeply, and to have him slip away on a bed of agony would have been intolerable for me. I could not have faced that without going off the deep end, as they say.

"From that afternoon on, I began a slow climb back to faith. A day, a week, more time passed, and I came to believe. Skepticism reared up from time to time, a dragon that had to be fought back constantly. I don't think it is ever really slain. I think it retreats in many of us, waiting for events or circumstances or people or a combination thereof to resurrect it with special ferocity. Becoming a Christian doesn't banish the Devil from us for the rest of our days. It seems to me that the evil one is, rather, driven to a redoubling of his efforts when one over whom he once held sway breaks loose and—"

For Philosopher, there is no doubt that Lucifer is the root of evil, the instigator of corrosive doubt, doubt that builds up a thick, high wall between the sinner and God.

He stops for a little while, sips some water, closes his eyes again, while praying, and then is ready for another segment of the evening.

"I would be very happy to answer any questions you might like to put to me."

An athletic-looking young man near the front raises his hand, and Philosopher asks him to speak.

"Sir, it has always puzzled me as to how God can be in Heaven, and yet indwelling anyone through the Holy Spirit. How can He manage to be in both of these places at the same time?"

Philosopher smiles and says, "I'm very glad we are starting with the easy ones."

There is a murmur of appreciative chuckling in the audience.

"I believe we can approach the matter in this way. Take a hypnotist— I don't approve of hypnotism and so this example is one with which I am not entirely comfortable, but it may shed a little light on the answer to your question—this hypnotist hypnotizes you, my young friend, and implants within your mind what is commonly called a posthyp- notic suggestion. It might be perhaps to eat pickles at midnight or stand in the middle of Madison Avenue and shout, 'The Martians are coming, the Martians are coming.' "

Considerable laughter . . .

"But, whatever it is, that urge is now inside you. The hypnotist snaps his fingers and you are now out of the trance into which he had put you. He stays where he is, which is Fairbanks, Alaska, and you return to your home in Tampa, Florida—many thousands of miles between the two of you. At noon, three days later, you suddenly get up in the middle of chemistry class and announce to everyone, 'I know for a fact now that the world is flat. I almost fell off the edge yesterday' "

There is no laughter this time because the growing truth of what

Philosopher is putting before them begins to become clear to those present.

"There we have it, my friend. That hypnotist is still in Fairbanks, and yet you have just acted upon what his spirit dictated to your spirit. In a very real sense, he resides inside you, and you have just obeyed him."

The teenager continues standing, saying nothing further, pondering the words that have lodged themselves in his mind. He then simply nods twice, and sits down, but he has been reached, indeed he has been reached.

"I will add that in our relationship with Almighty God, the difference is that He actually is within us, whereas only the hypnotist's suggestion has been implanted. And also, I hasten to add, for the hypnotist's subject there is really no choice in the matter—he has been taken over, in a sense. God comes in and stays, true, but He continues to allow us the free exercise of our will. But this illustration, which I heard a number of years ago, is perhaps the closest I personally have ever come to a comprehensible explanation of what the mystery of indwelling is all about."

Philosopher pauses, a jolt of pain hitting his abdomen. He feels abruptly weaker.

But he continues, managing the suggestion of a smile.

"Surely there are other questions?"

Another young man, short, bespectacled, raises his hand and Philosopher asks him to stand.

"You seem to be saying, sir, in more than one of your books, that Satan and his helpers are spreading their influence every-where. But I thought only God was omnipresent. Would you clear up my confusion?"

Philosopher responds without hesitation:

"Very simple, actually. Have any of your friends been experimenting with drugs?"

"But sir—"

"You do not have to name them—just tell me if any have done this."

"I suppose they have."

"Where did they get their drugs?"

"Sir, I couldn't answer that here!"

"It is not my intention to have either you or your friends end up in jail or murdered by some member of the underworld, not at all. What I meant was, simply, what sort of person?"

"A pusher . . . "

"Your friends obtain their supply from a drug pusher, is that correct?"

"Yes . . . "

"And then what happens?"

"I don't understand."

"What happens after the drug pusher leaves?"

"They take the drugs, naturally."

"I must correct you, young man. Taking drugs is never natural. In any event, I assume they do this sort of activity either through a vein or their nostrils or through their mouth. Am I right?"

"Yes, sir, you are."

"Do they generally buy enough of a supply to last a while?"

"Yes."

"As much as they can afford?"

"I guess you could say that."

"How many of your friends are addicts?"

"Sir, I don't mean to be disrespectful, but I fail to see what this has to do with Satan."

"You will, you truly will, and that I promise. How many of your friends are addicts?"

"More than I care to admit."

"It is alarming, is it not, when these friends of yours do become addicts?"

"Yes, sir, it is. They're throwing their lives away. I—I try to help them, but it seems almost hopeless."

"And why is that?"

"They can't break the habit."

"It has a grip on them?"

"Oh, yes, absolutely."

"And yet before they met their pusher, it was not like that?"

"Not at all."

"He does not hang around all the time, does he?"

"No, he—"

The young man pauses, a smile of awareness spreading across his features.

"Sir, you mean that once he gives them the habit, they carry it on themselves. If they don't get the drugs from him, they'll find a supply elsewhere."

"That is precisely what I mean, son. And so it is with Satan. He caused our sin nature from the very beginning. He can hook those without Christ—and even many so-called carnal Christians—in the same way a pusher hooks a soon-to-be addict. Once the obsession, the addiction if you will, with sex or drugs or money or things is commenced, all he has to make sure of is that there is a supply around to entice, to maintain the addiction. He does not need his demons for that. He himself is certainly not necessary in this regard. People aid his awful designs—the Mafia with its drug and pornography and prostitution businesses, for example. As you can see, so much of what we have around us is inspired by Satan, but he hardly needs to be on call twenty-four hours a day. Advertisers spend billions of dollars to promote so many sinful desires in order to sell their products that I lost count a long time ago. Satan created this kind of atmosphere, the moral, spiritual atmosphere which we breathe today. A brilliant chap, this Satan, this Devil, this Lucifer, his handiwork saves him a great deal of legwork."

The young man thanks Philosopher and sits down. Next, a girl in the middle of the large semicircular auditorium raises her hand. Philosopher indicates that she can stand.

"Sir, you believe, as you have stated in your books, that most of the media are under demonic influence. Have you had occasion to change your mind about that outlook at all?"

Philosopher does not hesitate in replying:

"I have not. And there are many reasons. But one of the most compelling is what the Bible terms 'knowing them by their fruits.' What are the fruits of the media? Promotion of promiscuity is often the stuff of comedy, winking with approval at that which has generated broken marriages, broken homes, diseases that breed insanity, disablement, and death. And we have the modern spectacle that involves the lifting up of perversion as—"

Shouting occurs toward the back of the auditorium. A young man is standing, angrily shouting at Philosopher:

"Son, I cannot hear very well what you are saying. Would you kindly step up to the front or at least a bit closer, would you do that, please?"

The young man climbs over to the aisle and walks up to the stage.

"I happen to practice a lifestyle that you condemn, and I am offended that you referred to my lifestyle as perversion."

"Oh, did I?"

"Yes, you did."

"But all I managed to say was a single word—perversion. You seem to have filled in the rest of that on your own."

Someone snickers, then is quiet.

The boy is momentarily flustered.

"But is it not so? Your books apparently make no secret of how you feel."

"You are correct. But I am far from being the originator of that truth. God is. And His Word is quite outspoken on that subject."

"Sir, I feel that you are wrong."

"But, son, that is the trouble. You do not know that I am wrong. Nor do you know, as you undoubtedly believe, that the Bible reflects only the mood of the times in which it was written. You know nothing of the sort as fact. You only feel that it must be so because you admitted-ly have feelings toward other men, and these feel quite normal and decent to you. Therefore, you conclude, there is nothing wrong with them. You use feel-ings as your guide, do you not?"

"Yes, that is correct . . . ."

"How many times have you been to a dentist over the years?"

"I don't understand the relevancy, sir, of that question."

"Please, would you be willing to humor an old man and provide an answer to my silly little question?"

The teenager nods, then replies, "Half a dozen probably, "

"For cleanings, fillings, that sort of thing."

"Yes, sir: Once I had to have a root canal done."

"Oh, my, yes! I have had more than one of those. Simply awful busi-ness!"

The boy adds, in agreement, "I remember one time, it was so bad, the pain, I—I thought I was going to die."

Philosopher stands, with effort, and walks over to the edge of the stage.

"You mean, son, do you not, that the pain was so awful, so intense, that you felt as though you were actually going to die? And not as a fig-ure of speech, either?"

"Yes, I—" he starts to say.

"But, lo and behold, you are here now, before God and Man, alive. How accurate were your feelings then?"

The teenager can say nothing. He stands for a second or two, look-ing embarrassed and humbled, and turns to walk back to his seat.

"Feelings are wonderful much of the time," Philosopher says. "Feelings can be God's gift. Anyone who has ever loved—and all of us have—knows what a joy it is to love. But not all kinds of love are prop-er: Can we love money and still please Him? Can we love another's spouse and still honor Him? Can we love to see naked images in a mag-azine or a film and have God honor that? Genghis Khan loved power, the real Count Dracula loved to impale little children on stakes. A mass murderer named Gacy loved to lure teenagers to his home and seduce them, and dismember them, and bury them all over his property. More than thirty boys died because he loved to hear them cry in pain.

"Love can be grand, ennobling, persuading men and women toward the finest acts, the most inspiring deeds, the greatest courage, the most honorable intent. But not all that is called love is like that. Can you see this truth? And God has said that those who love wrongly and continue to do so will be punished."

The young man, who has not reached his seat, turns around angrily.

"Sir, surely you are not referring to AIDS?"

Philosopher looks squarely at the questioner.

"Surely, young man, you are not referring to God?"

Philosopher bends down and takes off his shoe, holds it out to the teenager.

"Do you see that?" he asks.

"Yes, it is a shoe."

"It does not fit very well. There is a place at the heel which is rubbing against my flesh. I noticed just this morning that there is a blister."

The young man is silent, a frown on his forehead.

"But I was hasty, wanting to get here on time. While I knew the one shoe presented a problem, I slipped the pair on without really thinking, my haste overriding my memory and, also, my common sense."

"Yes, sir . . ." the boy says a bit impatiently.

"My heel was never meant to have anything rubbing against it in that way, but I have a choice. I can switch to a different pair of shoes, and alleviate the problem, or I can stay with these day after day, week after week, month after month, and at some point I will have worn through to the bone if I haven't caused infection, including gangrene, in the meantime, followed by a spread of that up my leg and eventually throughout my body if I do nothing, even something as desperate, as extreme as amputating my leg. If I keep that pair of shoes, and let the infection spread, and my whole body is riddled with it and, my young friend, I die, is that a judgment from God or the most appalling, wasteful stupidity on my part? Please do not lay at the doorstep of my Lord and Savior what your own blindness forces you to ignore."

It is obvious that Philosopher is very, very weak. He walks slowly back to his chair, and almost collapses into it. His family whispers to him that he must stop.

"I must go in a little while," he says with great tenderness to the audience, looking out over the thousands listening to him. "I am very grateful that you have come here this night. May we make the next question the final one, please?"

Another student, a girl, raises her hand, and Philosopher asks her to come forward.

"Sir, as you indicated earlier, you once could not bring yourself to believe in God. I cannot now, either. Help me, please."

Philosopher speaks, but his voice is barely above a whisper. He motions her to come up to him. She climbs the steps and approaches him.

"I am dying, my young friend. Let me tell you that there is a God, and even as I speak, He is welcoming me into Heaven."

He looks at her, his eyes wide, a smile lighting up his face. He reaches out his hand, and she takes it.

"Your father says to tell you that he loves you, and is happy now."

Then Philosopher's head tilts to the left, the hand drops, and he is dead.

The girl starts to sob as she turns around to face the audience.

"My father," she tells them, "died a week ago. The last thing he said —he—he said to me was that he prayed I—I—I would—would accept the gift of faith and—and—peace that he wanted to leave behind."

She leaves the stage as Philosopher's doctor rushes to the still, frail form in that chair. But he is no longer there, that suit of clothes has been shed. His spirit has left his body. Instantly he sees me.

"You have been here from the first minutes?" he asks with awe.

"Yes, Philosopher, I have."

"Are you to take me to my Lord?"

I cannot answer.

He turns, looks upward.

"Jesus," he says. "Oh, dearest, dearest Friend."

And he is gone.

Fifteen

OUTSIDE.

The night air is clear. A great many stars are apparent. Memories flood in on me. I ache to return to my home, for Heaven is my home, my birthplace. I have gone through the centuries on Earth, soared the globe, witnessed a whole encyclopedia of people, events.

It is time to—

"Darien!"

I hear the voice as I am walking away from that college auditorium.

I stop immediately, a thin trickle of dread working its way into me, expanding until I nearly continue on, not daring to turn, not wanting to face—

"Darien! Please listen, my friend."

I turn very slowly.

"Hello, Darien. It has been a long time."

DuRong!

I say nothing at first, unable to speak. DuRong, the angel who was closest to Lucifer in Heaven, stands in front of me—and—and—

"You have been looking for my friend, have you not?" he says, smiling.

"Yes, I have, DuRong. Why are you and the others not inside?"

Hundreds of other fallen angels are gathering in back of DuRong. I see them in the darkness, hovering, almost buzzing like a swarm of bees. Most are pathetic in appearance, distorted and twisted and—

"No one was willing to welcome us in," he says, laughing harshly.

He comes toward me.

"Oh, Darien, there is so much to discuss."

"Yes, there is."

"Glad you agree!"

We walk away from the others. He sees me as I cast an apprehensive look at them.

"You have little to fear from them, Darien," he indicates. "You are one of us, are you not?"

A familiar chill grips me.

DuRong looks little different, still quite majestic—the others have changed with shocking totality but not him, so much like Lucifer. His voice is as nearly as rich, as powerful, like all the greatest opera singers and all the finest public speakers ever born, and yet greater even than that.

I begin to feel a hint of old awe, since DuRong is indeed close to the magnificence of Lucifer himself. While it would be stupid to ignore so much of what I had seen that agreed with all the ghastly stories about Satan, yet other details did not. Why had Lucifer's followers become so loathsome—and DuRong, for one, had remained as grand, as awe-inspiring as ever? Beside him, Michael and the others, including myself, were pallid imitations, reflections in a mirror that had faded disastrously.

"You cannot know how glad I am to see you," DuRong remarks with apparent sincerity. "The others are hardly an inspiration in the remotest sense of the word, but you, Darien, yes, you are very, very different. But, then, I doubt that you realize how very much alike, in every way, the three of us are."

DuRong is casting a spell, I know, but then, like Lucifer he is expert at this, and I am not immune to being drawn to it.

"Let me show you the other side of Earth," he suggests. "I imagine, from the reports Lucifer and I have received, that you have been exposed to the worst that could be seen, the areas where perhaps those serving him may have misunderstood his intentions."

I agree to go with him.

"That is wonderful. You make me very happy, Darien, very happy indeed."

The first stop is an opera house. A ballet is in progress.

"That is very beautiful," I admit, pointing to the man and woman on stage.

"Both are atheists, you know," DuRong says. "They rejected God a long time ago. That has not stopped them from giving the world discernible perfection in their art. How magnificently they dance! Why not join me for the rest of the performance, Darien?"

The beauty of their moves across the stage is undeniable. Both are in their prime, slim, coordinated, well-trained. Members of the audience gasp at what they achieve in their art, knowing how very difficult it is, appreciating the self-denial indicated by years of exceptionally hard work.

"It comes only after enormous dedication, my friend," DuRong indicates. "They both get up very early in the morning, and stay at it until late at night. Everything is planned with the utmost care—from their exercising to their ballet practice to their meals, yes, everything. And it has been like that since they were quite young. "

After the performance, DuRong and I leave.

"There is beauty without God, you know," DuRong says proudly. "In mankind reservoirs of such creativity, such glorious potential, remain only to be tapped."

After the ballet, we go elsewhere—an opera singer at the Met in New York City, a stage actress giving the performance of her life on Broadway, a gallery in which stunning art is displayed.

"Most of that owes no allegiance to God," DuRong observes. "In fact, a greater number than you can know did their very finest work after they shed debilitating guilt, the inhibitions foisted upon them by what He demanded in their lives before He would accept them as having any worth at all."

"But, DuRong, that just is not the answer. Is it so wrong to expect them to be moral, to follow the Ten Commandments, to accept His Son into their lives?"

"But the implication is that unless they do all of that, they are worthless, like worms plowing through garbage every single moment of their lives."

"No, it is not that at all. They have worth, they have genius, creativity, all that is fine and good. But until they take that final step—"

"There is more to see, Darien," he interrupts.

He shows me a home for retarded children. A treatment center for cancer victims. A hospital specializing in reconstructive surgery for burn victims.

"Very beautiful, is it not?" he says proudly. "Could there be anything more loving, more sensitive, more noble than what you have seen? And, Darien, none of it can be attributed to God. All of it comes from Man's own instincts.

"In fact, the home for retarded children is financed by a life-long atheist. One of the skin specialists at the bum center had studied at one point to be a priest but came to perceive the inherent inconsistencies apparent in Christianity, Catholic and Protestant."

I keep my silence.

There are other places we visit, DuRong showing them off to me with ill-concealed relish.

We pass by a disheveled man in his late thirties. His clothes are torn, his face and hands very dirty, his hair stringy.

"What about him?" DuRong asks. "Where is God's mercy with that individual? Is that how He treats His blessed children?"

I can stand no more.

Lord, give me the words, take upon Yourself my usual ineptitude, make me a channel for Your wisdom . . .

"He ruined his life, that chap," DuRong has continued. "He is rejected, sick, alone. I fail to see God, so-called loving as He is, doing a damn thing for him."

"It is ironic that you are the one using that word, DuRong. "

"Which word?"

"Damn."

"Surely you have heard much worse while you have been here? Why does it upset you so?"

"Oh, I have. All of those words probably. The difference is that you and the others are responsible for his damnation in the first place. You put temptation before him, you created the gun that he has placed to his own head admittedly, but without the gun there in the first place, he would have nothing to use.

"I speak of a gun only symbolically. It is much broader than that, much more perverse. There is no gun, of course, it is simply another word for the alcohol that has eaten away his inside, that has destroyed his mind. God never had nothing to do with that."

DuRong laughs hoarsely.

"Show me what He has done to stop what is happening."

"God has offered forgiveness through Christ."

"And that is supposed to solve everything, Darien? I thought you were more realistic than that. If forgiveness means that an Adolf Hitler is going to be in Heaven, I am very glad we left."

"I doubt that Hitler asked for forgiveness. But then, now that you mention it, who created Adolf Hitler in the first place?"

"God? Does He not create everyone and all things?"

"True. But what God brought to life was a child He desired to be His own. What made him the Hitler he became was the world you and your fellow demons threw up around him. You turned his life upside down. You corrupted his mind. You twisted a genius into a madman.

"And Hitler was a genius. Few can deny that fact. That his genius became evil, perverted, diabolical is not the fault of God but of yours, of the others —D'Seaver's, D'Filer's . . . of —"

"You still are not convinced, are you, Darien? You hesitate even in saying Lucifer's name."

"I hesitate because if it is true that he is as malevolent as has been claimed through the centuries, then the Lucifer who once was, the Lucifer whom I once—"

"Loved? Is that what you were about to say, Darien? Why would you have loved someone so deserving of such contempt?"

"Not at the beginning. Then he was —"

"Magnificent? Yes, he was magnificent. He—"

DuRong shivers a bit. I sense the slightest change in his demeanor.

"You just said that if a Hitler could get into Heaven, you are glad you no longer remain there. But what if a DuRong, yes, what if a Lucifer could be washed clean, could be forgiven and return to Heaven as angels reborn, what if God were willing to—"

"And we would have to submit to Him? Follow His orders? Do what He desires?"

"But God has never changed, DuRong. He has always been willing to forgive. As for submission, what is it now that you are doing? You have submitted to Lucifer's will since the dawn of time. What kind of master has he been?"

DuRong is acting with growing strangeness, instability.

"You show me ballet, opera, charities. You point to the beauty of art, the decency that does rest in any motivation to help others.

"And you indicate that none of those we saw owe any obedience to the Almighty. They have run their lives without Him. And yet you admit that God created each one. DuRong, that which is noble, inspiring, artistic within them was implanted by God in the first place.

"Talent cannot be taught, it is not a serum injected, a drug ingested, something in the air that is breathed in and takes root. It was instilled even before birth, as a seed destined to grow. Anything good we have seen has come about not because of their atheism but in spite of it."

DuRong says nothing. I notice a surge of moaning among the others. They all have been disturbed.

"Just examine the way you all are reacting now. You know truth. You know it better than a missionary who has spent an entire lifetime of sacrifice in spreading the Great Commission. Take a library of all the books of faith ever written and include even the Bible, and yet your knowledge would transcend five hundred times all that!

"Which is why you work so hard to corrupt the very universe itself, why many of you also are out there!"

I make a sweeping gesture at the heavens.

"You would like to destroy all of that, and begin anew, fashion the whole of creation in the image of your master. Obedience to the will of another is not the problem. Obedience to the One who gave you life is—and so you worship a substitute, preferring the demonic to the divine, someone who promises you what that very knowledge of yours knows to be false.

"You have read the prophecies and know them word for word. If you were to be honest, you would be confronted with the spectre of your own impending doom, and so you cling to the most awful, the most evil, the most decadent lies ever spawned!"

I sense something else at that point. I hear a distant roar, rapidly getting louder, closer. DuRong and the others are cowering, so frightened that if you could say, with any accuracy, their blood was freezing in their veins, then that would hint at how they are now behaving.

"Enough!"

A single word. Just six letters. Spoken in an instant. But spoken with the most traumatic ferocity of any word in history, divine, demonic or human.

"ENOUGH!"

Again. Stronger.

"ENOUGH!"

And in a split second, if time were real, an accurate description, in a split second, there is no ground beneath me, nor sky above, nor fallen angels quavering frenziedly, themselves a blur, nor—

Only . . . around me, vivid, suffocating . . . the reality, the terrifying, monstrous reality . . . of Hell.

Sixteen

At first there is just nothingness.

A sound like that of a howling wind sweeps across my consciousness, sweeps through me, causing a chill more profound than any before now, I can still see nothing. And I experience an instant of deep, suffocating mournfulness, but even that word does little to describe my state.

I feel what it is like to be in a place without God, cutting aside all the childish rationalism and nihilism of Man, the immature playthings of deluded spirits . . . experiencing the inner core of atheism as objective, fundamental reality like a vulture swooping overhead, ready to devour.

"Oh, God . . ." I say aloud.

The entire "place" in which I am shudders as though down to its very core.

And then a voice—

"Please, do not speak that name in this place!"

The voice familiar, rich, magnetic, eclipsing even DuRong's, a chill edge to it that penetrates to—

Lucifer.

"Where are you?" I ask, trembling.

"Here, there, everywhere," is the reply.

"I do not understand," I admit.

"You are in my breast. I carry you around as a woman pregnant. I spit you out of my womb at my pleasure."

Laughter.

"You have been hunting me over history, and yet you found me almost from the beginning. You have seen me again and again and not known it. How stupid an angel you are!"

I recall the decadence. The pain. The pungent odor of burning Jews assails me.

"Let me now show you something else . . ."

A scene is played out before me or, rather, a montage of scenes, one right after the other. I am in the midst of a gala party. It is in a ballroom. There are crystal chandeliers, and diamonds, and lavish gowns and—

The alcohol flows freely. So does the cocaine.

I see two thousand pairs of shoes and dozens of Rolls Royces . . .

"I have them all," the voice says proudy. "Because they do that while they permit this."

A man, dying from hunger, sits on his haunches pleading with passersby for a morsel of food.

Other scenes, spinning, people at the altar of fame, power, sex.

There had been no real warning about the volcano. No one is prepared. Hundreds die. A little boy runs after a dog whose fur is aflame, screaming for someone to help him until the lava drowns out his thin, agonized voice.

The bodies of many are visible afterwards, some partially covered by the once—red, now—gray molten rock cooling down. Every few feet an arm or a hand is visible among the layer of death, the fingers twisted in pain, frozen that way like Arctic weeds.

A man weaves his way through the hands and arms and other half-buried portions of bodies. He takes off rings, watches, bracelets, puts them in a sack. Some of the bodies are lying on top of the hardening lava. He rummages through their clothes, finding wallets, money belts . . . . .

"I never caused that natural disaster, but I took advantage of it, Darien. It proved to be an opportunity that I could hardly let pass by, do you not agree?"

The elderly woman is temporarily alone to tend to the family store. Her husband has gone home to get her some more medicine.

Two gunmen blow her head off and get away with $35.15 . . .

"My workers stayed behind," says the voice. "They wanted to see the husband's expression. It was worth waiting for."

The man is consumed by chills so intense that they seem to infiltrate every inch of his body, every muscle trembling, shaking. His skin is covered with lesions. He weighs barely a hundred pounds.

"Oh, God, why are You doing this to me?" he shouts but never getting an answer—a hundred times a day it seems but only dead, awful silence . . . .

"That is an achievement, Darien. To get them to blame God . . ."

"Please help me. He's got a knife. Won't someone—?"

"A dozen witnesses, Darien, And no one helped."

In the midst of the town square, a man is blindfolded. Standing before him are five other men, each holding a rifle. The man is clutching a Bible. It falls from his hands, covered with blood.

"Marvelous, Darien . . . "

Image after image, a kaleidoscope . . .

"My world, Darien. Yes, my handiwork. You are coming to stay with me, are you not? To share . . . "

I am shuddering. So all of it is true, any remaining doubt buried under the weight of the evidence surrounding me. God's reasons—all true—Lucifer/Satan's exile—justified beyond argument. God knew the end from the beginning, and all else. He could see—!

Suddenly there is silence.

I feel extraordinary heat.

. . . screaming.

No more blackness. No more—

I knew, from the Casting Out, and beyond, that Hell existed, knew that it was nowhere near Heaven, knew that the evil ones of history were there. But seeing it, being in Hell, watching—

Someone on a table. A horde of fallen angels around him. They have knives. They are cutting into him. The pieces are put into an oven. And then taken out, burnt black, fingers and toes in ashes. And still alive, the body dismembered but moving, a charred tongue protruding from lips blistered and swollen, eyes—

"Oh, please, please, kill me, please kill me now . . ."

The voice is German. The man is Hitler . . .

And then I am confronted by a creature so loathsome that it could not be called human or demonic. It is bent over, almost hunchbacked. The face is rotting, wounds raw, open, with pus dribbling out, gangrenous filth spewing forth like geysers of water from a whale.

The thing is holding a baby's body in its hand, a hand twisted with arthritic ravaging.

It is laughing, this creature, shaking the tiny body like some obscene trophy.

"I have won," it cackles.

I am no longer silent. I cannot be.

"You have not!" I shout. "That is only an old suit, thrown away, useless. That baby's spirit is where it belongs—not here!"

The creature spins around and faces me as it tosses the body to one side.

"Fool!" it says, cackling. "You—"

I realize, with electrifying sudden clarity, who this creature is.

I stumble back as the cackling vanishes, and a familiar rich baritone replaces it.

"Welcome to my world," Lucifer says.

He throws his arms about, indicating the vast reaches of Hell.

"The place of my habitation once was very different, as you know."

Incredibly I detect the slightest trace of regret.

"Give it up, Lucifer," I plead. "God may be willing to forgive you. The Cross that is now the symbol of your defeat could become the instrument of your rebirth."

"You speak with great conviction," Lucifer says wistfully, holding up his hands. "But these have centuries of blood on them. These have destroyed the bodies of Jehovah's saints. These have plunged daggers into the hearts of the unborn."

He points to his head.

"My thoughts have invaded the church, the office, the home. My programs are on prime time, on cable, in syndication. My concepts are on stage. In motion picture theatres. Books. Magazines. There is nowhere anyone can turn without being confronted with me!"

Gradually that door of regret is closing, as Lucifer relishes his power, his influence, his . . . dominion.

"Return to subservience?" he begins to shout. "Return to sitting at His throne? Worshipping Him? You are a fool, Darien!"

He spins around and around.

"You probably see how lovely I am now. You probably think how grand it would be if the golden streets of Heaven were once again graced with my beauteous presence."

As he moves, portions of him erupt like giant boils pierced, sending out gushers of poison, green and yellow and smelling of decay and disease.

"This is but one me," he says. "Let me show you another."

He seems to take off that one self and put on a new one, like exchanging a suit of clothes.

"I am a judge. I undermine the legal system by voting to allow child porn. I permit the release of those who have slaughtered others because some technicality of the law has been violated. And when the public finally votes me out, I hide behind my femininity and play at being a coy little devil, if you will pardon the expression."

And—

"Look at me now, Darien."

The change this time is most startling of all, and at the same time, the most obscene.

"This is the guise with which I am most comfortable, Darien."

He is now a tall, handsome, well-built young man, naked.

"This is more the real me, Darien. Why do you think so many followed me out of Heaven? From envy? From respect? You play well the part of a fool, Darien, but I do not think even you are quite that naive."

He walks toward me, flaunting himself.

"Come to me, Darien. Blend your spirit with mine. Have the kind of experience that—"

I run. I know he is behind me, following me. I take flight through the corridors of Hell. I stumble, fall, flames leaping up at me. The spirits of condemned human beings reach out from cells in the walls surrounding me.

"Release me, please!" they cry.

"He has rats eating me. Please—"

"I am being put on a spit and roasted."

"Spiders—no—no—all over me—piercing me with their—"

I am lost. Everywhere I turn, there is horror. I am in an open room, at the end of one of the corridors. Some poor tormented souls cry out in agony. They are feasting on dismembered bodies, oblivious for the moment. And then they realize what they have been doing, and scream in utter despair and terror until they are pulled apart and devoured by others who then comprehend what has happened and hold up their blood-stained hands and—

No, no, no! I scream wordlessly. I—

Somehow they have heard, and they turn toward me. They cry in unison, You are an angel. Please relieve us of this torment. Please take us from this place of damnation.

I try to tell them that I can do nothing. They advance toward me, picking their teeth with the bones of the dead.

I remain no longer but reenter the corridor. On all sides there is screaming, a montage of ghastliness, the odors of—

Finally I can go no further. I have reached a deadend. All around me are flames, rocks glowing red, then turning molten. I trip on a severed head that suddenly looks up at me and laughs insanely—just before it catches fire, the laughter replaced by the screaming of the damned.

I am trapped. It seems I can only wait.

I sense something nearby . . . .

Observer!

He is hiding in the shadows.

"For me, there is but an eternity of this," he says in a tremulous whisper. "I have chosen my hell and now I must lie in it. But, Darien, you mustn't do that."

I look about me helplessly.

"Not about, Darien. Not this way or that. Above!"

Ahead I see Lucifer. Gathered around him are a thousand of his demons. As I look, they become one, their forms blending, and at the same time the real Satanic self returns but bigger, even more revolting, red sores erupting onto me, his breath the stuff of cesspools. He raises a hand, commanding Observer, who goes, whimpering, standing before Lucifer, becoming a part of the ungodly union.

And then Lucifer, former comrade of Heaven, now maestro of Hell, turns to me, smirking, his tongue darting in and out of a mouth filled with the tiny bodies of aborted babies being crunched between his teeth.

"Perhaps, Darien, you carry with you the quaint notion that I can be appealed to through an overture to my conscience. Perhaps you think you can reach my heart."

He cackles ferociously.

"Hearts are my fodder, Darien. I enjoy their taste. I wallow in the blood that pumps through them. I add ingredients of my own—some cocaine, a pinch of heroin, a drop of bourbon—that is my blood, Darien, and I share it with Mankind!"

He steps a bit closer. I can back away no further.

"Take a look at Observer's book. Examine its pages. He tells all. It is destined to be a best-seller. Millions will read it, my millions, when I finally ascend to the throne, and destroy God Almighty!"

He throws the book at me. It lands at my feet.

"You think of conscience. Goodness. Mercy. Silly stuff, Darien. For the weak. My strength is pain, my energy from the bloodshed of wars, my ecstasy from the dying of hope and the birth of despair. Your men of God rant and rave about my punishment sometime someday somewhere. For me, there is no wait. I mete out my punishment now. I grow stronger from the cries of starving millions. Plagues are my rejuvenation. I dine on what your redeemed ones call anarchy, barbarism, hedonism. I relish the acts of the homosexual and call them my baptism."

He is very close now,

"Kiss us, Darien," he says. "Kiss us and join us forever . . . ."

I have only one act left, the remaining weapon in an arsenal long neglected by skepticism and doubt over the validity of Lucifer's fate. I fall to the molten—red floor of Hell, stirring up the ashes of Eden, and my voice, created by God Himself, cuts through the screams of damnation.

"I claim the name of Jesus Christ, and accept the protection offered through His shed blood."

Instantly Lucifer pulls back.

"You think that is enough!" he shrieks. "You think words can stop me?"

"Not words alone, Lucifer," I say, gathering strength. "It is what they portend. You are doomed. You wallow in the excrement of your foul deeds and call that triumph."

He hesitates. His whole being seems to shake to its very core.

"You turn the womb into a graveyard spitting out its dead, and call this a battle won in your war against the Almighty. Your weapons are the bodies of babies with bloated stomachs—your elixir the blood of concentration camp victims mixed with the fluids of perverse acts in dark places of passion. You shout of victory, and yet all you have left is the torment of Hell! Your trophies have become the twisted bones of a demented grotesquerie—your former majesty an eternal mirror held up to the rotting filth that you now call your very being."

My anger is spent. I have only pity left. And I tell my former friend that that is so.

"You are without hope, by your own choice. But as for myself and my destiny, I choose, now, my Creator and yours. Take me back, Lord!"

I feel myself being lifted upward. Through the volcanic-like geysers below, there is for an instant, barely visible, the bent-over shape of a wretched creature falling to his knees and weeping . . . .

Seventeen

I AM NO LONGER IN HELL.

But I have not returned to Heaven, either. I remain in some limbo state, still on Earth, still going from place to place, century to century, like someone caught on a perpetual merry-go-round, unable to bring it to a halt, unable to get off, condemned just to stay there, spinning, spinning, spinning. During one turn, the Dark Ages flash before me, filled with overt demonic activity, during another, I see the Civil War in the United States, whole battlefields of the dead and the dying, blood staining dark blue as well as light grey uniforms, often brother having to slay brother, during yet another spin, I witness the birth of the first thalidomide babies, twisted creatures crying pitifully, pain over their entire mal-formed bodies, while profits were being made on the drug that caused their misery, faster the merry-go-round goes, dizzying, until I tumble off yet again . . .

I cannot age, but I do feel somehow old as I sit here, on a mountain-top overlooking the plain where the last great battle of Mankind has taken place. The bodies number into the thousands, and blood collects everywhere—giant, deep pools like a titanic wave over the ground, submerging it. It is possible to drown in blood down there . . . .

I momentarily turn away, the odor so strong that it ascends the mountain. I try to close my ears because the cries of the dying are loud enough to form a crescendo that also reaches me—but there is no escaping the panorama below, either in its sights or its sounds.

I decide to leave the mountain and go down to the plain where the old prophecies always had been pointing, with devastating clarity.

Some of the dying have had the flesh literally seared from their bones, and they have only seconds left, those that survived at all. They see me, of course—the living do not—but the dying, suspended, in a sense, between two kinds of life, indeed see, reach out, beg.

"Please help me, sir," I am asked again and again.

"The pain . . ,"

"I know I've been blinded, now, yet I see you anyway. I see—"

Ahead, standing as though on an island uplifted in the midst of a blood red sea, are several hundred figures. I approach them. One by one they ascend. The final soldier turns to me, smiles, says, "We did the right thing."

I nod.

. . . we did the right thing.

Yes, they did—all of them—that one group of hundreds out of countless thousands.

They refused the Antichrist. And he had them slaughtered as a result, threatening to do just that to any others who might decide to rebel.

And now—

Not one of them bore the scars of how they died—no bayonet wounds, no bullet holes. In their resurrection they had been healed, given the bodies that would be theirs throughout eternity.

But the others share not at all the same end. Every few seconds, more are dying. Bodies piled upon bodies, visible where the blood is not quite deep enough to hide them. I look about, and see hands raised against the sky, like stalks of marsh grass in a bloody inlet. For an instant only. Then cut down.

They also see me. They surround me as I go past, trying not to look at them, their eyes haunted where they yet have eyes. Some do not, seared away, only the empty sockets remain. But they see me just the same. And all turn away, knowing that they will spend eternity like that—in agony, flames searing but never fully consuming them.

The scene oppresses. I cannot stand it any longer. I leave, not sure of where to go. I have time at my disposal. I can flash forward a thousand years, two thousand, however many. I can retreat in time countless centuries.

But I have nowhere to go. An irony that presses me down inflicts on me a weariness that is so pervasive it is as though all of history has become a weight threatening to—

It does seem as though an eternity somehow has come and gone since I left Heaven. I have seen more than all the human beings since the first two were created by God. Perhaps only the Trinity has seen more.

Can angels become weary? We never sleep, true, but we have consciousness and the very essence of what we are indeed can be subjected to strain, can indeed wear down, can approximate how humans feel. After all, we are not robots without feeling nor batteries that can never run down.

I feel myself spinning again . . . .

Eighteen

"I was blind, but now I see!" says the man walking the twisting, winding street. "And my brother was lame, but now he walks."

Not a significant proclamation perhaps, not as momentous in itself as, say, the Holocaust. Nor at all meaningful against the realization that twenty million babies or more have died at the hands of Whim, Convenience or any of the other demons bedeviling those who decide that killing a baby is not murder.

And yet—

I continue walking. I see a centurion with his son.

"You were dead and yet now we walk together," the man says to the child.

I find others, one, two, a dozen, a hundred, a thousand. Healed during just three brief years.

And then . . . Lazarus.

Christ's good and dear friend . . .

Lazarus alive, walking with his family. Speaking of the warmth of the sun on his skin.

People touched by supreme goodness, snatched from ultimate evil, each a victory, one after the other like them throughout history, in Heaven instead of Hell, walking the golden streets, listening to the sounds of angels . . . singing.

I sit down on the side of a hill, next to some sheep in that ancient land. Two shepherds are nearby. I overhear them talking about their simple lives, the quiet, isolated place in which they tend their sheep.

I reflect on my journey, recalling everything from the very beginning. I have seen victory and defeat. I myself was almost seduced at the hands of Lucifer.

I indeed am tired. Normally, of course, there is no such thing as being tired for any of the angelic host. We never sleep. We have ceaseless energy for any and all tasks. But this time it is different for me. Along with it is a sense of shame and regret, that I had not simply believed God but, rather, like Thomas had to see and feel the equivalent of the nail-pierced hands and lanced side and mangled feet.

I look about, seeing the sheep, the sky well-nigh cloudless. I remember something God had told me once, about there being warfare all around, just out of sight. Later, in a world of five billion inhabitants, how many would ever be aware of this contest for their very spirits?

Surely, the vast majority scoff at the notion. Angels? How silly! Demons? Nonsense! A creature named Lucifer or Satan or the Devil? How trite and childish! A skepticism presided over by a special council of fallen angels, their job that of fostering the doubt, the sarcasm, all the careless, tongue-in-cheek media depictions of Satan that only enhanced the phony, carnival-like image with which he deliberately surrounded himself.

Of those who believed, how many would follow after Lucifer, not knowing the truth perhaps but instead attracted to him by the veneer of excitement and thrills and seeming fulfillment, beckoned like moths around a consuming flame, its dazzling colors and brightness drawing them in?

A startling insight grips me as though I had a physical body: most of his deluded human followers, seduced by him, would mortgage eternity and be in bondage without ever knowing that this was so, slavishingly responding to his role as corrupt master puppeteer, pulling the strings and causing them to dance to his commands, mixing in huge globs of guilt and regret and much else so that any message of forgiveness is mitigated, unable to get through, unable to become God's knife to cut those strings of Satanic enslavement. Call it humanism, call it chemical dependency, whatever the term, it was but another branch on a tree planted by a Machiavellian gardener.

Breathtaking clarity rushes into my very being at that point. The spirit of the age indeed has taken over Earth, and there are now only pockets of the redeemed, a few areas of spiritual oasis—the rest is a desert of damnation.

The net of delusion tossed about by Lucifer and his followers had caught even me by the hem, so to speak, and I had had a glimpse of what total allegiance could have meant, allegiance to one who deserved only contempt.

Something quite astounding happens to me now. I am near Calvary A storm is ripping the sky apart. I walk up the side of Golgotha, past the time-carved rock that looks indeed so much like a human skull, past the multitudes gathered at the top. Mary, the mother of Jesus, is there, His brothers, a contingent of Roman soldiers, onlookers including Nicodemus. I stand at the Cross, looking at the pain on His face. I am under the crimson flow now, His blood washing over me, all my doubts, all my rebellion flushed away like yesterday's garbage. I look at myself and I am suddenly very white, very pure.

I wander, later, from that place, my mind filled with arresting images. I was at Calvary. I stood beneath the feet of God Incarnate, His blood providing the missing moment in the scenario of my odyssey.

Suddenly I hear a familiar voice. My head has been bowed. I look up. Stedfast!

Not a fallen angel. Not a demonic perversion of what once was. My friend from Heaven—here on Earth!

"I have been with you from the beginning," he says. "Call me your guardian angel of sorts."

"But I thought—"

"It is all a bit different from what you did think, my friend Darien. Lucifer was actually sad that you ever left Heaven."

"I do not understand . . . ."

"You originally were to have joined him, during the Casting Out. You were as close as that. But you held back just a bit too long. It was then Lucifer decided that you would be more beneficial to him actually in Heaven, and he did not try harder to convince you to be by his side, for eventually he thought you would sow the seeds of a second rebellion, acting as his agent provocateur in heavenly places. He underestimated your devo-tion to God, though. You were torn between God and Lucifer, unlike the others who had no compunctions at all about their choice of Satan over God."

"So when God let me go on my journey. He knew what the outcome would be."

"Of course. But He also knew that you would have to discover certain things for yourself."

"And you followed me in case I really did need help?"

"Two angels are better than one, Darien."

"But I never knew . . . I—I never saw you. Nor did any of the—others. How could that be?"

He looks at me, rather like an impatient teacher at an impudent student, fluttering his wings as a telltale sign.

"Darien, Darien, do not put such limitations on the God of miracles."

❧

We walk for a while, talking.

"Earth has turned into a nightmare place," I say at one point.

"Oh, it has—call it the rape of Eden—but even so you have encountered reminders of what could have been if Lucifer had remained loyal, and not allowed pride to entrap him and the rest of Mankind."

That first family, Millie and Charlotte, so many more, redeemed ones for whom the shackles of the sin nature were eventually replaced by the true freedom of being born again.

"You know," Stedfast says, as though reading my thoughts, "so many men and women talk of freedom. They want to have no restraints whatsoever. They want to be free to have sex whenever, wherever, and with whomever they please. And then the sexually transmitted diseases started to put a real dent in that thinking, of course: herpes, AIDS, syphilis, and so on. That kind of alleged pleasure brought punishment inexorably along with it. They blamed God, but it was simply the nature of their bodies, the biological realities of being human. Each of them dug their own special grave just as surely as though they had taken a gun to their head and pulled the trigger.

"That is not freedom. That is but a death sentence—they spend the last few months or years of their lives waiting for the execution. The flamboyant piano-playing entertainer, the black ballad singer, the leading-man actor, the rotund veteran TV star, so many other celebrities-the media reports everything. And the message is loud and clear. But, Darien, it is not being heeded, not really. Unfortunately, all of them are under total delusion.

"So there is no freedom in their freedom, not a freedom that has any validity, for even while it is being shouted from the media as the lifestyle of choice for millions, all of them are in a prison—the bars may not be metal, although sometimes that is the case—and they will go on with that cry of freedom mocking them to the grave and even beyond!"

We wander to Joseph's tomb, go inside, stand by the hard rock shelf on which rests Christ's body. He is passing from death to life even as we watch. Finally He sits up, then stands, smiles at me, and says just five words, "Now you know the truth . . . ."

"Yes, Lord, I know the truth," I manage to reply, barely able to say even that, aware of the moment to which I am witness.

A short while later, someone approaches from outside.

A woman.

Our eyes meet.

I find myself saying, "He is not here, the one you seek. He has risen, as He promised."

It is as though the light of Heaven is on Mary's face, her expression sublime.

I watch her go. My whole being weeps with the joy of redemption profound, redemption purchased in blood for all of humanity and which included mercy for a foolishly errant angel.

A voice, rich, kind, familiar . . .

"Darien, are you truly ready now?"

"Yes, Lord, truly . . ."

Nineteen

I AM BACK IN HEAVEN, *as suddenly as I had left. But whereas I left without fanfare, as though sneaking out, hoping no one except God Himself would see me, I return as the hosts of Heaven stand before me, trumpets sounding.*

My fellow angels are spread out in front of me, the assemblage going on further than I really can see. The fluttering of their wings seems so loud that only the trumpets can compete.

Heaven is never dark, no clouds blocking the sun. But in that moment I perceive more brightness than I can remember, an illumination so clear and clean that everything is asparkle.

Moses comes to me, smiling.

Abraham stands before me.

Jeremiah. Peter. John. Constantine. Florence Nightingale. D. L. Moody, countless thousands of believers over the centuries welcoming me back.

And then the Holy Trinity.

What Man finds so difficult to comprehend is before me in reality, the only reality that counts.

I fall to my knees in humility and shame.

"Arise, Darien," God says. "This is a time of rejoicing. All of Heaven, angel and human, welcomes you for eternity. Shame is of earth. It has no place here. There is no need any longer."

. . . no need any longer.

How those words wash over me, cleansing me . . .

∿

I am standing next to a woman who seems always to be smiling.

"It's so wonderful," she says, "so wonderful to see that they have no more pain or want or fear."

She asks if I would sit down with her, and I gladly answer in the affirmative.

"There were indeed times when I wanted to give up, the strain was so awful," she admits.

"In what activities were you engaged?" I ask.

"I took upon myself missions of mercy. There were so many of the poor who were dying in the streets. I went to them and bathed them and gave them food. So many children! Their poor little arms were bone-thin. Their eyes were as mirrors of the suffering they underwent.

"I remember, out of the multitude, one child in particular. His name was Johann. His parents gave him that name because they had a single luxury—a little battery-operated record player and an old scratchy recording of one of Johann Sebastian Bach's compositions. When they could no longer give their son even a crust of bread, they left him by a highly traveled road, hoping some stranger would take pity on him. When I saw Johann, the battery had run down, but the player was still there, the record on it, covered by dirt.

"I held him in my arms and took him to our mission. There was no doubt in my mind that he was dying. The ravages of malnutrition had claimed him too severely for too long. He couldn't even hold food in his stomach. Once he vomited it up over me and my helper. And he was very embarrassed, but I told him not to worry.

"We found a battery for the player and kept the record going again and again. As soon as he heard it, his crying seemed to subside into a low, sad whimper. Finally he closed his eyes, but just before that, he looked at me, seemed to become very much stronger and put his frail arms around me. He whispered just one word in my ear."

"What word was that?"

"Heaven . . ."

She pauses, then: "I noticed something I hadn't before. His right hand had been knotted up, gnarled actually. As the life flowed from him, that hand abruptly relaxed and opened, and I saw, lying against the palm, a tiny, tiny cross. The pain was gone from his face, leaving only the most beautiful smile I have ever seen.

"And, you know, I left my earthly home a few years later, yes, I did. I closed my eyes to the poverty around me and opened them to majesty. Johann was waiting for me beside a wonderful lake with a sheen like polished crystal. He was tall, handsome, strong. And he introduced me to his mother and his father.

"If only those who doubt could see what it is that we have here, if only—"

She looks ahead, smiles.

"Johann's calling. Will you excuse me, please, Angel Darien?"

"Yes, of course. Oh, what is your name, dear lady?"

"Theresa," she says.

I see her join a tall, handsome young man not far away. He is not alone. A thousand others have joined him, gathering around this woman named Theresa . . . .

~∾~

God requests that I meet with Him. I am there in an instant.

"There is something I must ask you to see," He tells me. "I know it will not be easy, Darien. Are you willing to join me?"

"Yes, Lord, of course I am."

We stand before what I could call a door except that it is not of wood and metal hinges. It is without actual substance but a door nonetheless.

"I want to show you the future, except for us it is now the present," God says not harshly.

"Yes . . ."

I witness a broad overview of the Battle of Armageddon. I see, again, the lone regiment refusing to continue. They put down their rifles. Ordered to pick up the weapons, they steadfastly refuse. As a result they are shot immediately.

"Even in the midst of such an event, there is redemption," I say aloud. "My own journey now seems more needless, more blind than ever. I gave up nothing but my doubts. Look at their sacrifice."

"But that was the whole point, Darien. Those very doubts were the seed of your rebellion. In Lucifer's case, his pride compounded the problem—and the two brought about his unredeemable doom.

"Those men gave up allegiance to the Antichrist. You gave up what could have become your eternal commitment to Satan. You fought against what could have been, and won, Darien. I am very proud of you."

And the Devil that deceived them was cast into the lake of fire and brimstone, where the beast and the false prophet are, and they all shall be tormented . . . forever and ever.

A trumpet sounds.

The heavenly hosts sing with great glory.

I am allowed to see the final moment of judgment on all the fallen angels—Mifult, D'Seaver, D'Filer, Observer, each and every one on the very rim of the lake of fire, and then over the edge.

Finally Lucifer himself.

He turns, and sees me. The defiance is gone. But not the results of countless centuries of deviltry His countenance is even worse; however, instead of the flaunting of his powers, the perverse pride in what he has caused, there is only terror as he hears the cries of his fellow angels like a thick fog swirling around him.

"Darien . . ." he starts to say, strangely pitiful."Even now, God knows even now, I cannot come to Him on my knees and ask Him to forgive me. The same guilt I inflicted on others is like a thick wall between us. I—"

He turns, dancing flames reflected on that cankered face, and then he is gone.

And I saw a great white throne, and He Who sat on it . . .and I saw the dead, small and great, stand before God, and the books were opened: and another book was opened, which is the book of life, and the dead were judged out of that which was written in the books, according to their works. And the sea gave up the dead which were in it, and death and hell were cast into the lake of fire. This is the second death. And whosoever was not found written in the book of life was cast into the lake of fire.

Countless multitudes follow Lucifer—those who obeyed him in life were to share his miseries in the final death. For them all, Hell proved to be just a way station before their ultimate destination . . .

∽୧୨∼

How much "later" is it?

Can such thoughts be answered in eternity?

It is unknowably later, perhaps that will suffice, I stand before God at His beckoning.

"Your walk on Earth was akin to that which many human beings take, from doubt to pain to redemption. It has been so ever since Calvary, Darien. But never before has an angel journeyed as you have and come back. Wherever you have been, Darien, the path has been marked. And it will be called Angelwalk, throughout the totality of eternity."

God motions me forward a bit.

"Earth is different now," He says, peering down from His throne, seraphim fluttering.

I sense what is happening. That moment toward which all of history had been heading!

"It is time, is it not, Lord?" I say with thrilling comprehension.

"Yes, Darien. Join us and we go together."

I stand with Father, Son, and Holy Ghost. We pass through the Gate, into the bright, golden sunlight of the new Eden.

Epilogue

IN THE TINKLING LAUGHTER of a particular moment amid the journey of that special hour if time were any longer time, there is found beside that path of legend called Angelwalk what surely must have been a treasured book of the ancient past, pages nearly gone, lying near a kindly lions paws at temporary rest. Only some meaningless old scraps remain, none displaying anything legible except the last fragile bits of a few lost words.

A Book of the Days of Observer, Once an Angel.

Then it is gone in dust, trod underfoot by lions and lambs and bright-faced redeemed led by joyous cherubim traveling Angelwalk toward a golden temple rising out of the mists atop a majestic mount called Sinai . . .

F i n i s

STEDFAST

Human beings are promised a Heaven without tears, without pain . . .
but that is not the case for angels. It is something that we have become
accustomed to waiting for, an anticipated blessing that will be ours when
we all experience the new Heaven and the new earth.

We regularly journey to the present earth, the earth so pitiably torn
by Satan's ravaging presence, and spend a brief time there—or longer, if
we are particularly brave—and then we must return to Heaven with the
bleak and tragic baggage from that sojourn weighing us down, for we
cannot tolerate what Satan has done with the planet. We feel a desper-
ate need to engage in the spiritual equivalent of taking a bath. And that
is what we do, as we stand before the Father and let His purity cleanse
us . . . until the next time.

Holy, Holy, Holy, that day when there is no more next time, when we
do not have to brace ourselves for the battles that now take place on
Planet Earth and in the heavenlies. Wonderful it shall be, and ready my
kind and I are.

—STEDFAST

Introduction

STEDFAST IS THE THIRD ANGEL WALK BOOK, the second sequel. It is different in many ways from *Angelwalk* and *Fallen Angel*, though Stedfast was a character in both of the previous books.

But then Stedfast is different, as well. Whereas Darien of *Angelwalk* was a questioning, somewhat rebellious angel while remaining essentially unfallen, and Observer of *Fallen Angel* was an altogether demonic angel, yet a quite reluctant one in the long run, Stedfast is neither questioning nor fallen. He is one of the elite corps of unfallen angels, if I may put it that way, always steady, always serving the Trinity, always perfectly obedient and faithful with not even a thought out of place.

Legends are often born from nuggets of truth during the course of earthly history. And Stedfast, according to the mythos of this series, was the origin of the legend of the Guardian Angel.

He is wiser than Darien. Ah, he is certainly that! He knows the answers to the questions for which Darien was searching in *Angelwalk*.

Steady as a rock . . .

That's Stedfast, for sure.

But this angel is also one with an enormous capacity to assimilate the feelings of every creature with which he comes in contact, their emotions his own, to a real and vivid extent.

He is a sponge, this Stedfast.

And he yearns for the day when, like redeemed humans, he will know only the joy, the peace of Heaven.

Without the tears that only the angels, only the Trinity will continue to shed until then . . .

This indeed is a striking truth. The Creator weeps in Heaven, His human creations do not. For divinity, there is sorrow, there is anguish.

But flesh-and-blood beings who have accepted Jesus Christ as Savior and Lord have been promised freedom, forever, from such as this.

We have to wait for our full participation in that same promise, unfallen angelkind and I among them.

Until the new Heaven, the new earth, that wondrous transformation toward which all of history is heading.

That is when we shed our own veil of tears, and walk together in the special sunlight of that special day, never again looking back, the past washed always in a flood of eternal joy . . . .

Stedfast's Prologue

It is going to be soon. The ethereal fabric of Heaven itself hums and buzzes and flashes with anticipation.

That Moment . . .

Oh my, what can I do? How can I face it without embarrassing myself and the rest of my kind by emotion unstoppable?

That Moment for which we all have been waiting—how indeed we have been waiting for it to arrive! Countless have been our entreaties before the Trinity as we bow in humble adoration, but also with our incessant petitions, again and again—and been told over and over, "Not as yet, dear ones. Not as yet."

So we turn away, perhaps to welcome another soul past the Gates, perhaps to leave that place of wonder and joy altogether on a mission of one sort or another, or simply to sit beside a crystal lake and think back over what has been, the sum total of our existence until—

That Moment.

Oh, blessed Jesus, it is soon. It is going to happen soon. We will no longer be leaving Heaven to stride in our obedience across continents of bloodshed and fear, of crime and disease, of sin in every form devised by the fleshy nature of humankind.

Soon it will be that we will visit instead the new earth, cleansed and reborn, just as the faithful have been, and we will walk hand in hand back to Eden.

Oh my . . .

But then, in the interlude before that odyssey begins, as I sit here beside the crystal lake, preparing myself for what I will say to the gathered multitudes, human and angelic alike, awaiting that which has been prophesied, I think back, so far back, so long ago, and I shiver, yes, I shiver as bits and pieces present themselves to me . . . .

∼◡∽

Their souls cry out, you know.

The damned always do that as they are taken to Hell. They could have been in the company of angels, but they chose other companions instead.

They cry a great deal.

That is what I hear most of all. More than the gnashing of teeth.

The sound of their weeping, their tears.

Tears do speak in a certain way, if you listen carefully—not with words, certainly not that, but in other respects.

Forgive me, please, for being vague with this. I am so because the sensation of which I speak is not altogether definable, nor easily so.

It is a feeling, I suppose . . . .

Yes, that may be the best answer, if not a satisfactory one.

My comrades and I were not created bereft of feelings, you know. We have them, my fellow angels and I. We have our own, and we also experience the feelings of every being with which we come in contact.

When they, the mortal ones, the ones of flesh and blood and bone and marrow, are evil, when they are held often inextricably in the sway of sin, the feelings born from them tend to be repugnant. In this we get a hint of what Hell is like, a hint that is, by itself, enough to make us so very glad that we chose Jehovah the Almighty instead of Lucifer the Magnificent.

And yet any allegiance won purely by fear is tenuous at best, for the one feared the most can always be replaced by another of more fearsome intent. But it was not so with us, the unfallen. We have loved our Lord and Him only. We would gladly go into Hell itself if He only asked.

Did Lucifer?

Love Him, ever?

It cannot be said that Lucifer did, truly—oh, perhaps, after his own fashion, for the first few thousand years or so, or their equivalent, before the Casting Out. But after that, which is but a small portion of eternity, his desires overtook him, desires that made him jealous of everything that God could do, everything He was, everything indeed.

. . . everything He was.

But Lucifer forgot the love part, forgot the kindness, forgot all but the power of God.

"I want what He has," I overheard the loveliest of all of us saying. "I want His throne! I want to rule!"

He approached me as I stood in a quiet place.

"Stedfast, I need you," Lucifer purred, exuding all the charm of which he was capable, for his countenance had not as yet suffered the devastating corruption of his deeds.

How glorious this angel was, a face of great magnificence, like the finest sculpture ever done by man· during the height of the Renaissance.

"I will not," I replied.

"But you will be always in subservience to Him," Lucifer continued, astonished that I could resist what a third of the other angels had committed to in His presence.

"And not to you?" I scoffed. "You ask me not to choose freedom, which you pretend to offer, but, rather, between two masters. If it is a slave that I am destined to be, then I must follow in the steps of the greater of the two."

He waited, thinking that, surely, this meant him.

"Oh, my friend, my friend," I said to Lucifer upon realizing this. "Can you not now see . . .?"

He could not. He was lost by then. He had become the captive of his own passions.

I looked at Lucifer with great pity.

ROGER ELWOOD

"Goodbye . . ." I said.

"You will miss me, Stedfast," he replied. "You know that. You will wish you had gone on with me to victory."

This magnificent being raised a glowing hand, not yet devoid of its glory, now doubled into a fist.

"There will be a point," Lucifer said, smiling, "at which you—"

He lowered that hand, his body shivering ever so slightly.

"Why am I so cold?" he said out loud, undoubtedly regretting the momentary vulnerability this lent him.

"Judgment," I told him. "You have felt a taste of it already."

"Nonsense!" he screamed.

Our Father which art in Heaven.

We both heard that chorus.

"Why are they doing that?"

"They are singing a song of triumph."

"But I recognize it not."

"It has not been written as yet. It has not been spoken as yet. It resides only in the mind of the King of kings and Lord of lords."

Lucifer clutched his temple.

"You have not yet broken the bond," I told him. "It is still there, your mind and God's connected."

"No! I will not be a mere extension of Him any longer!"

The rage of that cry echoed throughout the Heavenly Kingdom.

And lead us not into temptation but deliver us from evil. For thine is the kingdom, and the power, and the glory forever . . . .

Lucifer was granted that which he wished. The bond between him and Almighty God was broken.

We all felt it. For a moment there was a hint of darkness in Heaven, transitory but chilling, though we and the Trinity alone felt it, human souls to be insulated from such for eternity.

Lucifer started to change in appearance even then, the glory that once had been his and his alone amongst us suddenly dimming and something else taking its place, something foul and perverse.

Sin.

Sin was separation from God, a death of communion with Him.

Lucifer had sinned. Along with ten thousand upon ten thousand of my once fellow angels.

They were finally leaving.

"I will be back," he shouted, "to storm the gates!"

Lucifer turned for the last time and saw us there, saw our sorrow, saw the tears.

"Weep not for us," he roared with defiance. "Rather, weep for yourselves. Realize what lies in store as I gain control over that planet which Jehovah created with such hope, and along with it, the rest of the universe. I will take that hope and destroy it forever!"

The horde of them, now screeching, loathsome things consumed by their own vile natures, that horde fell to the world below, and beyond, to the pit of another place, a new place, a place created for the damned and by the damned . . . like themselves.

And that is their story.

෴

Feelings . . .

We are the only creations of God to experience suchfeelings of darkness in the midst of His holy Heaven, you know.

We do that because we regularly journey between Heaven and earth. Those human beings who have accepted Christ as Savior and Lord and who have been allowed into Heaven as a result are shielded from the pain of earth, the dying of earth—yes, even the tears.

My angel kin and I all await the moment when we will experience the same kind of peace. But we do not know it just now. For us, there is little solace so long as we trod the path called Angelwalk. For each of us has his own Angelwalk, which is as much a name for the very journey itself.

Angelwalk . . . .

It is a path of pain, a path of joy—it is both of these and more.

It is the story of Darien, my fellow angel, with all his uncertainties, with his quest to piece together the reality of Satan for himself.

Another story is mine. I had no doubts, you see no uncertainties. nor did Michael. Or Gabriel.

Another story indeed . . .

We take our feelings with us when we journey to earth, and we take them back with us when we report to the Trinity. We stand before the Throne, and we weep. We weep for the lost. We know what God intended for the planet, and we weep over what it has become. We beg Him not to send us back—surely, we will not have to return, surely we can instead continue to stand amidst the cleansing atmosphere of Heaven itself and be washed pure again, without going back to the dirt below.

Surely . . .

God cries, too.

Oh, He does. Jesus truly wept in human form. That did not end the moment the Son of God ascended. This capability was with Him before the Incarnation. It remains today.

We often serve to help the blessed Comforter, and we do our best, mostly when humans are in pain, when we can step into their lives and stay by their sides.

We cannot hold their hands, of course.

We cannot rub their foreheads.

We cannot put our arms around their frail bodies and sing to them.

But we do more, much more, you see.

This, then, is my story, which I recount now as I stand in front of Father, Son, and Holy Spirit, and before all those created beings, human and angelic alike, who have remained loyal, loving followers of the Most High. It would not surprise me if some scribe is quietly marking down what I say, to be put in some form on the shelf of a majestic new library somewhere.

I know I cannot delay any longer, for as soon as I finish, I shall join these the residents of the Kingdom as we all begin the long anticipated journey triumphant from the new Heaven to the new earth, all things new, forever and ever . . . .

THE ODYSSEY

One

Every seat is taken.

On stage at the front of the auditorium are only two individuals, a fragile-looking boy and his mother. Even though the loudspeaker is on full blast, the child's words sometimes are difficult to hear.

"I am very tired now," he says, and rests his head on his mother's shoulder, and dies.

She continues to stand there, though she is obviously trying to fight back tears that are beginning to drip over her lower lids and down her cheeks.

Suddenly there is the sound of voices raised in prayer. The hundreds of men and women in that auditorium stand and—

I see Heaven opening up.

I see angels descending. They stand around little Robbie as his soul begins to leave his body.

They are waiting, I know, waiting for me, waiting for me to do that which has been ordained. And I know, how blessed it is, I know what I must do. I must take that soul, pure and healthy from that diseased and now dead flesh, I must lift it from corruption and give it to incorruption.

Something quite wonderful happens. Words come from the soul of a child, words without pain, words of sublime joy.

"Peace like a river attendeth my way . . ."

Robbie starts to sing that remembered hymn, and the gathered angels join him, sharing its wonderful lyrics as none who were still trapped in their fleshly bodies could ever do, could ever do with the same meaning.

And that expression on Robbie's face! Peace envelopes him, as water surrounded the baptized Jesus in the River Jordan. All that is finite, all that was born to perish, has passed away.

In an instant, the Holy Spirit descends not as a dove—no need of symbols or surrogates any longer.

I hand Robbie to Him—a brave and beautiful child, now glistening, now cleansed I hand this precious one to this Member of the Trinity. The Holy Spirit looks at me for a moment, smiles, and I feel His radiance throughout my very being. He smiles, yes, and He says, "You will miss him while you are here, will you not?"

"Oh, I will, I will," I admit, incapable as I am of lies, deception.

"You were with him for so long, and now you will wait expectantly for the reunion, is that not so, Stedfast?"

"Yes," I agree. "He was so fine, this child. He smiled in the midst of pain. He never became angry. He stayed faithful even as the disease ravaged him more and more severely. If I were of flesh and blood, he is the son I would want, I would pray for."

The Holy Spirit, touched by my words, says, "The Father knows. He knows, and He rejoices because of you."

I have brought joy to my Creator! I have pleased Almighty God!

"It is time now," the Holy Spirit says as He turns to the child. "Robbie, are you ready?"

Robbie nods eagerly and reaches out toward me.

"Thank you, Stedfast," he tells me. "I prayed to Jesus about you every night. I thanked Him for sending such a beautiful angel to be with me. The pain didn't hurt as much because I could feel your presence, and nothing else mattered, Stedfast. God bless you, God bless you, dear, dear angel, angel of mercy, angel of joy."

I try to control myself though barely managing to do so.

Robbie casts a glance at the crowd in that auditorium. They had come to the Christian media convention to buy and sell. They had come to hear speeches. And none would ever be the same again after listening to what his mother had to say of her struggle to save the life of this her beloved son.

Voices are now raised in praise, many present with their palms upheld.

Though none can actually see what is happening, they can somehow sense the presence of divinity. This child, now free, now whole, reaches out toward them and in a beautiful way touches each one with his gentle and good spirit, some driven to tears as they fall to their knees.

Robbie hesitates but an instant as he looks at his mother that final, final moment before, someday, they walk the golden streets together. Her tears have formed a river of their own.

"I love you," he whispers. "I love you so much, dearest Mother."

Not words at all, at least as far as she or any of them can perceive.

A sensation.

Something rippling in the air, perhaps, gossamer like.

She senses it instinctively, raising her head toward the ceiling—and at the same moment there is a touch of concern, a last fleeting reluctance to let go, to acknowledge her beloved's odyssey.

"It is well with my soul, Mother," I can hear Robbie say clearly. "I see Jesus waiting, you know. He says He will take your hand, too, Mother, and very soon. Don't be afraid. My Lord, your Lord loves you as much as I do."

And then Robbie is gone.

His mother smiles as she raises the fingers of her left hand to her lips, kisses these, and holds them out to the empty air.

"He is not there, sweet lady," I say. "He is beyond the Gates now. His feet touch streets of gold. His ears listen to the songs of angels. There are so many gathering around him. He is at peace, this child of yours. He is—"

Home.

Two

Observer also was there at the time, Satan's demonic journalist, so chained to his master, yet so reluctant. Other fallen ones had urged him not to enter, for they all were leaving in a panic. There was too much faith, too much sweetness, too much love in that room, and they could not endure it.

But he stayed. And I did.

We saw the same beautiful moments. And we left that place touched by what had happened, me to the rededication of myself to the Cause of Christ, Observer back to his puppet master.

"I could do nothing to stop it," Observer told me.

"Did you want to stop it?" I asked incredulously.

"No," he admitted. "I pray that Satan will never find out."

"Would he punish you?"

"Yes. Horribly."

And I watched him go, my former comrade. I watched him go, and I remembered how it once was, before evil began . . . .

~⊙~

Those first wonderful days!

True and I were selected by the Trinity to help Them in the process of creation. Yes, it may seem strange to say that, for surely They need no help with such matters. But it was done not for the sake of Father, Son, and Holy Spirit. Rather, it was for True, for me. Even then we were being groomed, I realize now, groomed for special tasks and special destinies.

And there he and I were as Adam and Eve came to life, Adam from the soil, Eve from his side.

They saw us, and they smiled without fear.

Without fear!

Think of the wonder of that. It is the same awe many feel when a baby killer whale is born at one of those modern sea-life-type parks, born and swimming in an instant, as though it had been doing so forever.

Thus it was with the first humans, born out of nothingness, yet accepting us with no reluctance, no doubt over whether or not they were hallucinating, just simple faith, faith together with trust.

The destruction of this is a very large part of the foundation of my hatred for Satan.

The death of pure trust.

I find that as tragic as the death of faith, for once faith is present, trust should be, yes, easier! Yet without faith, trustlessness is understandable. It cannot be transformed into what is nobler, grander. It hangs like a dark cloud, submerging all who choose to allow it to dominate every second of life.

Those who have faith and do not couple it with trust are bastard creatures, born indeed, alive and walking and doing—but with victory robbed from their lives, exaltation drained from the days accorded them.

Adam and Eve had it.

Adam and Eve lived it.

And we, True and I, saw it in their eyes, in their words, in the very walk of those two.

That was why they did not fear the serpent.

Later, other angels, including Darien, joined us. Later, the Garden was alive with them. And because of this, because of our radiance, there was no night. Oh, technically there was night, but we banished it by our presence. We set the Garden aglow with color, sparkling with some of the light of Heaven itself—for that was what we were made of, you know, the glow of the Creator transfused throughout His

Kingdom, from which we were created by His loving Hand, as though, playfully, He would grab some of it, hold it, and then let it go as another angel beamed to life, countless thousands of us, thousands times thousands, God remarkably like an innocent child in a long ago time on earth, a child grabbing at sparkling soap bubbles he has created—and there the comparison ends, for when a child opens his hand, he finds nothing, but when God did, He found us.

Three

Like a river glorious . . .

There was indeed a river named Glorious in Eden, the water like molten crystal, sparkling under an overhead sun whose pure rays were not filtered through layers of pollution spewed up into the atmosphere.

There was no industry in those days.

There was no death.

There was no sin.

Like a world glorious.

That was how it used to be, you know. Adam and Eve began in Eden, but this was intended as only the start. God was prepared to take them on a wondrous journey around the world, their Guide through the wonders of a planet that was, in so many ways, a mirror image of Heaven itself, an extension of its glories. Eden was the nucleus, with everything else spreading out from it. Eden offered to this first couple a taste of what the world was like. God planned to show them the rest.

I saw what the two humans had not as yet.

I saw a world of waterfalls of liquid gold.

I saw a world of colonies of unfallen angels clustered together, chattering about what they saw around them, comparing it to their previous heavenly home, and excited about the future, for they were to be caretakers of this new place, sprung as it was from the mind of God, as they themselves had been.

There were no battles for us in Eden nor anywhere else on earth at that time, it seemed. Satan had been vanquished. We all assumed, so foolishly, our former comrade would never again reappear.

I saw a world where no living thing died in the mouth of another.

I saw a world in which a lion sat contentedly simply looking at a color-drenched butterfly going from flower to flower in a field of orchids.

I saw a world that—was so much like Heaven itself!

I said that before, I know, but it is so blessed a fact that I cannot but repeat it.

That had been the purpose, of course. God wanted His newest creations—Adam and Eve—to exist in a world of the finest elements that He could provide.

And Planet Earth was that, the very finest.

The Father intended this to be forever. If there were no death, then mankind would never die. If there were no death, then mankind never needed to eat meat. Eating involved decay of one sort or another, animal or vegetable. But with eternal life, there would have been no hunger, no thirst, cattle and geese and lobsters spared.

Funny, isn't it, how I always took pity, somehow, on the lobsters, crammed into their glass tanks as they were, then taken out and shown to the one into whose stomach bits and pieces of them would soon drop, before which the eater would examine the eatee and say, "Yes, that's a good specimen," and into the broiler it would go.

None of that in the original Eden.

I saw lobsters, yes. I saw a whole inlet of them, they were moving about rather briskly for their kind, not shackled by the need to hunt prey, and so they had no cares at all, and could live as they were meant to live, without stress, without fear.

Perhaps talking about lobsters seems inappropriate, but it is not that at all. They are hardly of a shape and a look that engenders any degree of affection. Yet in the world of that Edenic period, they were as well cared for as any creature on the planet. It was not by appearance that they were accorded what they enjoyed but the very fact that they were, period, that they existed, that the least in God's Kingdom had all the respect of the greatest—except for man.

I saw this world in all its wonders. And I craved the day, still hence, when I could join the Father, and assist Him as we walked with Adam and Eve, sharing it with them, their guides through the most miraculous journey either of them would ever have.

For since death had not as yet entered the world, so it was that they were aware of the angels around about them. So it was that I, Stedfast, joined with them to be one of their guardians—the other a dear comrade named True.

And so it was that they were aware of us. Sin would change that. Sin would establish a barrier between us, between all humans and all angels. Future humans would talk about us, would write poems and songs about us, would speculate about us in books—but with no memory of what it once was like.

We were torn from Adam and Eve, and they from us.

That day came as a chill breeze through a graveyard, unexpected, making us shiver at the consequences.

A bright world, a world of seamless purity torn from eternal light into abysmal darkness.

Darien had left to do the Creator's bidding elsewhere,

but I remained, along with True. We tried to dissuade Adam and Eve, to whisper into their ears, to stop them in some way or another.

We could not physically do anything. Even then we were spirits only, a breeze against the cheek, an insubstantial sensation, but not more than that.

We lost.

We lost that first battle, and, thus, began the war.

That has stayed with me through the centuries since, the thousands of years of separation from God that have dominated history's walk.

We lost that first battle . . . .

All of mankind has suffered because we weren't strong enough, our words like puffs of cotton, easily waved aside, when they should have been heavy weights pressing down Adam and Eve in constraint.

Those first moments after Adam and Eve were cast from Eden are not chronicled in Scripture. Nor have I found them so anywhere in all the literature of man.

But I know them. I knew them then. I know them now. They are fresh in my thoughts, and will not be exorcised until the new Heaven, the new earth.

To have that awful time wiped from memory will be one of the Father's greatest blessings.

To no longer witness in recollection—oh, please, let it be soon, dear Father—death rushing in, animals not accustomed to pain suddenly consumed with it, many dying in their tracks, creatures large and small, creatures of the air and the sea and the land, all gasping or groaning or shaking their lives away.

And we, my friend True and I, could do nothing.

Oh, how worthless I felt at such times of remembering how we failed, trying to reconstruct in my mind what it had been like in Eden back then, those moments of communion, flesh aware of spirit, spirit understood by flesh—communion, yes, but also connection, angels and humans as almost a single entity, an interweaving of one with the other.

Joined.

Oh, yes, We were, Stedfast with Adam and True with Eve.

Stedfast and True—we were the angels with the most precious assignment of all, to be with the first human beings. We were their companions, their friends. How cherished those moments were, blessed and—

Missed.

Having tasted all that was fulfilling to us and pleasing to the Father, we could not have been less prepared for the expulsion of Adam and Eve.

To be joined together in holy matrimony.

What it was like for a man and a woman in the most ecstatic moments of their passion was very close to what True and I felt. We were "married," in a sense, to Adam and Eve. Indeed, we had the greatest possible intimacy.

Marriage, then, is yet another hint of Eden, not a relationship to be mocked by an endless repetition of marriage-divorce, marriage-divorce, marriage-divorce, a marriage license no better in such instances than the key to a cheap motel room for a night of illicit passion.

How do I describe such a moment, that moment when Adam and Eve were ripped from True and myself?

True did not want to release Eve. He cried out to her,

"Recant! Recant! God forgives. Please, please—!"

She did not. Nor did Adam.

They saw only their nakedness and they were ashamed.

There was something worse. While they lost Eden, they did not lose their memories of it. They would be tormented by this until the day they died, remembering the beauty, the peace, the joy of Eden, and doing this in the midst of the new world in which they found themselves, a world filled with death.

From neverending life to always-present death.

In Eden, Adam and Eve could stand before a beautiful flower, and admire it again and again, week after week, month after month, for years at a time, knowing that nothing would ever affect that flower, its colors unceasingly vibrant, its shape always delicate, its scent forever, no disease to kill it, no hungry insects to drain away its life, no change of seasons to make it turn brittle, then fall to the ground. It was a flower made by God simply as a way of pleasing them.

It was all for them, these first two humans, a world into which the Father had placed them for their enjoyment, for their exaltation—but also for their stewardship, a stewardship that was to have been of great sensitivity and care, for this was one way they both had of returning to Him the supreme love that gave them life in the first place—that flower and many others even more masterfully-made, that lake and its pure water, the air which they took into their lungs a gift directly from God, their only obligation so simple, an obligation to appreciate His grace and goodness and generosity, to show this appreciation merely by obeying His one outright command—not a cruel one, not a command that would limit their world to any measurable degree—and yet they turned their backs on the Father, resenting the one part of the garden that was off limits to them, where stood that one tree out of countless numbers actually more attractive than it, its fruit eclipsed in appearance by any number of others hanging from trees to either side of it— but it was the only small requirement that God had, the one simple test to which He put them. And thus went their loyalty, loyalty as filthy rags in the midst of paradise.

They were gone.

True and I stood there, side by side, watching the man and the woman as they ran into a world that showed the first encroaching signs of their foul transgression, a tiny bird having dropped from the course of its flight and landed in front of the two of them.

They paused for a moment in their sudden exodus, Eve bending down, picking up the gray and white creature, not quite dead, its head turning, looking at her, then at Adam, and saying by this, What have you done? What have you done to me, to the rest of creation?

And then it was gone, its body cold in an instant.

Adam and Eve dug the first grave . . . .

"Goodbye, True," I told my friend.

"Goodbye, Stedfast," he replied, his brilliance dimming in his sorrow.

He turned, briefly, and looked back, and I with him, the Garden the same as at its moment of creation, as colorful and alive as ever, within its boundaries the cold, awful grip of death still vanquished . . . for the moment but not for all time.

"No one can enter," he told me. "No one can enter until the new Heaven, the new earth."

"You are to guard it until the end of time," I said.

"I shall face hordes of demons, Stedfast," he said, stating something that would have seemed incomprehensible just a short while earlier, but now had become, in human terms, a fact of life.

He was only momentarily tremulous at that thought.

"Lucifer himself shall stand before me."

"But you will remain . . . steadfast."

"Yes, oh, yes, steadfast and true," he said, smiling, reaching out to me, our spirits blending briefly, "our valor our gift back to the Father who made us all."

And then my fellow unfallen and I parted, doing so for unknowable centuries ahead of us . . . my good, good friend remaining there, alone, somehow succeeding in preventing entry, until One and only One would tell him that the time had come to stand aside, stand aside indeed, and rejoin his comrades . . . and I, Stedfast, wanting to stay, to be with him, to help in whatever fashion I could, but called by the Master of us all to minister instead to Humankind, not other angels so self sufficient, as they were, of course, so able to stand and fight the enemy . . . but always my thoughts, though not my presence, were with this one angel, knowing all too well the multitude of loathsome monsters which were certain to confront him throughout the jumbled history of mankind, to offer him, as enticingly as possible, their own version of the forbidden fruit of Eden, in return for his doing something quite simple, that is, merely standing aside and allowing simple entry, but always this angel would be resisting, never giving in, a gentle angel, yet with the unflinching valor of a warrior and the spirit of a poet, turning back tides of evil for all of history, remaining, as ever he would, strong and brave and . . . yes, blessed friend . . . True.

Four

I walk the centuries. I see the effects of sin more than any historian because I see them as they occur, not simply as I plow through manuscripts that turn to dust at the slightest touch.

I see it all.

Until the new Heaven and the new earth, as promised by God to human and angel alike.

But in the meantime . . .

So much of what I have witnessed has been due to the inability of one individual to communicate fully with another. It was not that way in Eden. Adam and Eve did not need physical intimacy to become as one. They were already in total union with one another, with the Father, and with all of creation.

But they sinned, and the links were broken all around. God no longer spoke to them audibly. He did so to others in the centuries to follow, but such times were miraculous interventions rather than normal occurrences.

That first creature fell from the sky.

Cain took the life of his brother.

From that awful moment to the infamy of the Holocaust to the mass destruction of Hiroshima and Nagasaki to the Vietnam War to poison gas on the battlefields of Iran and Iraq was not much of a leap, in the final analysis, because it all sprang from the same awful abyss of mankind's rebellion against God—that and a global allegiance to Satan, sometimes knowingly, sometimes otherwise.

Families have been splitting apart since the earliest Old Testament days because they did not communicate. Governments have been at war because they did not communicate. In the latter part of the twentieth century, there seemed to be a multitude of greater than ever means to effect communication, but less and less communication itself.

All of creation has suffered.

Communication is not simply talking. It involves understanding. There was plenty of talk before and during the American Civil War, but nothing was accomplished until too much blood was shed, until the South found itself losing far too many of its men—and then the war ended.

There was not enough understanding that slavery was an abomination in the sight of God. There was not enough understanding that those who claimed the name of Christ and supported slavery were skirting blasphemy.

Once again, blood covered talk, silencing it, because understanding was the greatest casualty.

I was active during this period. I was with the North as well as the South. I took dying Rebels and Yankees to the gates of Heaven. I took slaves and free men.

And I watched many snatched by taloned creatures of loathsome countenance and dragged beyond the mouth of Hell.

It mattered not which side the dying were on. Any soldier fighting in defense of slavery was not guaranteed damnation because of this, any soldier fighting in opposition to slavery was not guaranteed salvation as a result.

General Lee went to Heaven.

That may be surprising to some . . . Robert E. Lee in Heaven!

I have not seen some quite prominent Northern generals there, men whose pulpit was a liquor bottle, the only source from which they drank, feeling no need for spiritual refreshment.

Robert E. Lee was simply obeying his commander. What Lee did, he felt was the honorable course even though, in the end, he acknowledged that he had spent many, many nights dealing with emotions that were on the other side.

Some plantation owners are in Heaven. Slaves were, to them, well-nigh members of their family, given similar privileges. Their slaves got such food, good clothes, and medical attention that were equal to that of any white person on the plantation.

I remember one group of slaves that had fought to defend their owner's property against invading Northern soldiers, not because they had been ordered to do so, but out of a sense of personal loyalty, given freely, and reacting against strangers coming in and taking over.

"What could we do?" the survivors cried. "They were bent on destroying the only way of life we have ever known. For us, there had never been hunger. Our sicknesses were healed. We had clothes to wear, quarters in which to sleep. Only our freedom was missing. And yet there were those Negroes in the North who were not slaves to any man but to a poverty more demeaning than anything we had ever known in the midst of our so-called slavery. What were we being freed from?"

Most died.

Every white man, every black man on that plantation, except some women and children.

Those men empowered to liberate the slaves were responsible for killing them instead.

Among them, I remember Jonah.

This Jonah was not swallowed up by a giant fish but by war.

He was a slave who died in the arms of the woman who had been the wife of his "master."

"I tried so hard," he told her. "I tried to do what I could to . . . to . . . Oh! I see Heaven! They're calling me to come . . . ."

"Tell me, Jonah," she pleaded, "is my husband there?"

He had been shot just seconds before Jonah was, seeing this, the black man had started firing back at the men responsible.

Jonah was slipping away, but he managed, barely, to tell her, "He is. I see him! He's smiling . . . beside him are my mamma and my papa. They've been waiting for me all these years, all these—"

Jonah let out one last gasp of pain, and then he became limp, lifeless in the woman's arms.

Soldiers were gathered around her.

She stood, yelling at them, "Is this anything to be proud of? Is this what you call liberating an oppressed Negro?"

~⊛~

I encountered many scenes like that during the course of the Civil War. I saw many that spoke of the hypocrisy of using a biblical justification for slavery. I saw black people beaten to death, black women used as sexual slaves to their white masters. I saw hangings of blacks caught for the simplest of crimes. I saw the foul, stinking domination of one man over another, the weaker subjected to the worst indignities, the baser inclinations of human nature.

But not Jonah.

Jonah's story was different.

Jonah's soul left his body as I stood before him.

"My master is waiting," he said anxiously. "I can see him just beyond."

"He is no longer your master."

"He isn't?"

Jonah seemed puzzled for an instant, then began to grin from ear to ear.

"Jesus! Jesus is my Master!"

"The moment you accepted Him as your Savior, your Lord," I told him.

"Praise God Almighty!" Jonah laughed joyously.

The plantation owner approached us as we entered Heaven.

"Dear Jonah," he said. "Dear, good friend."

And it will be that way for these two throughout eternity.

Since the beginning, societies have been groaning in near-continual pain. There has been little relief. War after war after war . . . they have caused a kind of preview of hell, with millions bombed or shot or bayoneted or gassed to death, millions more maimed in their bodies or their minds—or both, perhaps.

But there have been other kinds of wars: The drug war, the war against corruption in government, the war against allowing millions of babies to be murdered legally and in a socially "acceptable" manner.

Sometimes, though, wars are not on a grand scale, or even between countries. There is another kind that goes on within the human mind, heart, and soul . . . .

Five

Only the lonely . . .

I remember hearing a song with that title during my travels in the midst of the twentieth century. I remember the lonely I have tried to console in the final moments before they slipped off the confines of that body of flesh in which they had been trapped.

Trapped?

Oh, yes, it .was like that for many of these individuals, their bones and muscles and veins a prison as confining as any with bars and concrete. Some looked at themselves in innumerable mirrors wishing they were handsome or pretty, thinking that if this were the case, they would have friends, they would have fun, they would have a vibrant life. Instead they were confined to the wings while the stage belonged to the charming, the attractive, the "worthwhile" human beings who had so much going for them.

Self-worth . . .

They measured the sum total of their existence by what they could accomplish in their careers. Each award brought a fresh surge of vigor, as though they had at last earned the right to be respectable, to be accepted, even to function in the same universe as those they had secretly envied for so long. Each new recognition gave them some hope of getting a single moment of time from others because, look, they were saying, we are worthy.

I remember one such sufferer in particular. And sufferer is the correct designation. William suffered, his very soul knotted up continually, dragging him downward to an awaiting abyss of sorts, dark and lonely and filled with the reverberating cries of his often self-inflicted personal anguish.

William was a Christian, indeed he was, but perhaps the most trag-ic sort of all. Indwelt by the Holy Spirit, with an angel at his side from the moment of his birth until his death, he also had been picked by God as someone with a special mission, a very special mission indeed.

He had a gift.

Music.

William wrote songs—ballads, hymns. He started out in the secular world, and did quite well. But then came a point at which he decided to dedicate his talent to Christ and Christ only.

Even greater success emerged for William.

His songs were hit-parade regulars, sung in churches across the nation. He had every material thing that he could want.

Yet what William wanted was to die.

"I yearn for death, Lord," he would pray. "I eagerly anticipate the joy of walking with the angels along the golden streets of glory."

Heaven played a part in so many of the songs. People were comfort-ed by William's words, by his melodies. But for him, those words were cries from a heart long ago wounded, and the melodies merged into one long mournful cry of despair.

William had no one.

He was known by millions of fellow Christians. His personal appear-ances were in demand at Bible colleges and conventions from coast to coast. He—

No one.

And no matter how he analyzed it, that was the conclusion he invari-ably had to confront.

For William, there was no question of acceptance by others for the work he did.

"They listen to my songs, and they hum the melodies," he said dur-ing the last hour of his life. "Young people who devoured heavy metal now tune into my stuff. I can pick up the phone right now and talk to heads of record companies, world-famous evangelists and family counselors, even renowned Christian actors, actresses, and politicians."

He stifled a sob.

"Yet I am alone here in this condo. Oh, yes, 'beautiful Hawaii' is beautiful enough. This is where I always dreamed of living. I can stand on the back balcony and see some of the most beautiful sunsets anywhere in this jewel of God's universe, this world so beautiful—yet so ravaged, like my life itself."

He threw his head back, his eyes glistening with tears.

"Where are the people? Where is a wife to kiss me, a child to touch my hand, a word of love?"

"I love you," I told him. "Jesus loves you."

He broke out laughing.

"Jesus loves me, this I know . . ." he mused.

Anger flashed across his face.

"Where have you been all the years of my life?"

"By your side."

He looked at me.

"I never saw you before."

"But you felt my presence, William."

He was about to shout his denial, about to scream the pain that had isolated him so long from sharing his feelings with others, for surely if they knew the depth of it, that pain of his, surely they would fling platitudes at him and, in the end, turn away.

But he did nothing of the sort, instead falling silent in thought.

When my parents died, I thought I could not go on, no way was there that I could do this. When you have an inner world of three, yourself and two others and that is that—and that is all there ever has been—and two are subtracted, two are ripped from the tapestry of what passes for your life, if life is not a misnomer in your pitiable case, leaving a gaping hole where the only love of your life had been, when you stand by two open coffins, and kiss the cold foreheads of the only two persons with whom you have ever known intimacy, and then you

return to a motel room, and realize that there can never again be anyone to call, to really, really call, when—

"The reviews mean nothing after that," he told me.

"There is something else, isn't there, William?"

He bowed his head.

"You know?"

"I do."

"How much I hated them at the same time I couldn't live without
them, at the same time I loved them with mind, body, and soul? Is that
what you mean?"

"Yes. Tell me, William. Tell me it all."

"It is so shameful."

"Be honest."

"Before I die? Isn't it a moot point now?"

"William?"

"Yes?"

"Feel cleansed, feel whole for a few fleeting moments in this life.
Wouldn't you like that, William?"

"Yes, I would, I truly would."

"The guilt. You would like to be free of the guilt, even for a single
moment."

William knew I was right. He felt so very guilty about his parents.
He hated them, he loved them, he hated them, he loved them, over and
over, in endless cycles, until they were no longer around, until he
could no longer shout his feelings at them.

"We never talked," he said. "We fought."

"Why, William?"

"Because—"

The words were loathe to come, his tongue reluctant to speak them,
his brain rebelling at the thought of—

What they had done to him!

"Done, William? What had they done?"

"Kept me."

"Kept you?"

"To themselves. Chained. Imprisoned."

"Surrounded by love . . . is that so bad, William?"

"The imprisonment of their love . . . that's what it was. The thing cherished became the thing that stifled."

He strode over to a television set in the room, a large one with an immense screen, and turned it on. He flicked through several channels.

He looked with encompassing longing at the fleeting seconds of people together, talking, kissing, laughing, connecting in wonderful ways with one another.

"Communication," he said.

"With others?"

"Yes. Isn't that the natural scheme of things?"

"Agreed . . ."

"A man shall leave his parents at some point and cleave unto his wife. A new family is begun. When the original parents die, it is traumatic, it is all kinds of pain, but then they are buried, and the man returns to his own family. His wife and he grow old together, and their children get married, and begin their—"

He started crying.

"I wish I could touch you now, William," I told him. "I wish I could rest a hand on your shoulder, and give you what you have always lacked."

"A hand, a single hand," he sobbed. "Not out of duty, not even out of a sense of ministry!"

Not now, William, not in the flesh. But you shall truly have it . . . beyond what you could have imagined.

"Are you still here?"

"I am."

"Soon?"

"Quite soon, William."

"My parents? They'll be waiting."

"Truly so."

He stood, looking around the room, at the walls covered with commendations, with photographs of him posing with the famous of the world, the church, shelves lined with awards and statues.

"My life . . ." he whispered ruefully.

"The letters," I said, knowing what his answer would be. "Take out the letters, William. Read through a few of them."

"I have no letters. I threw them all out. I gave to the ones who wrote those letters what I could not obtain for myself. Reading what they were thanking me for only reminded me of what I was missing."

"A reason to go on living, in some cases?"

"In some, yes."

"What about the others?"

"Renewed faith. My words were instruments that the Lord used to—"

"It wasn't a charade, William, if that is what you are thinking."

"What other word is there? 'Hypocrisy' perhaps. If not a charade, then surely hypocrisy. Tell me, how could I have taught them anything? How can a blind man lead others who are blind to the light?"

"That was your mission, William. You wrote of pain. You sang of love and rejection and redemption. You took each song as a cup from the living spring of yourself and you gave it to the thirsty."

"While remaining famished myself!"

"No longer, William."

He had bowed his head, as so often before, half in prayer, half in the burden of what he felt in those sad, wrenched emotions of his, emotions that he fought with continually, trying so hard to force himself into some semblance of joy.

Now he looked up.

"Light?" he said, puzzled, feeling it at first rather than seeing it.

"Yes, William, not a nebulous light, disguised darkness from the pit of hell, not a light as that simple minded actress would describe, but the light of Heaven, William, the light of Heaven coming from Almighty God Himself."

"This is God?"

"As much as your laughter, your tears are you, yes."

"I—"

He felt it first, then he saw it as he dropped to his knees, looking around fearfully at the emptiness of that condo.

"I die alone," he said, "as always I thought it would be."

"No " I said "no you do not William, For now—"

He thought he saw me then, appearing before his eyes from nothingness.

"You are so beautiful," he said.

"But, William, you are not looking at me."

"Then what exactly do I see?"

"Yourself, William. You are looking at your own spirit now, without the burden of flesh."

"How can something so radiant be—"

He turned and looked down as the ascent began, saw the old body, now limp, alone as always.

"Me?"

I was by his side, and he saw me at last.

"Take my hand, William," I asked of him.

He reached out.

"We are so much alike," he said.

"God created us both, but it is you, as His finest, who are His greatest source of joy."

"Me? God's joy?"

"Oh, yes, dear, dear William."

A tune.

"I hear—"

A tune sung.

"Oh my I hear—"

By angels.

"One of mine! They're singing—"

At first he heard the angel chorus with that familiar melody, but now they were joined by a vast multitude, each voice raised high.

"Their arms, their arms are outstretched," William said incredulously.

"They've been waiting, you know," I told him. "Ten thousand souls singing the melodies of your heart."

I took him forward and they surrounded us, mother and father and all.

"What were you saying about loneliness, William?" I asked.

He had forgotten.

~❧~

Such a beautiful conclusion, is it not? A man taken from despair and loneliness into the greatest companionship he could ever have known.

There is another man of whom I am not fond at all, unlike William, whom I have grown to love. I doubt that this other will ever love anyone except himself, and the warped ideals he holds dear . . . .

S i x

Mercy—killing also has been given a familiar "spin" by the media.

Television docudramas with "sensitive" depictions. Well—planted news stories. Very emotional case histories.

A typical campaign by the hidden forces of darkness.

To me, though, they are not hidden at all. I see them as I enter hospitals, hovering as they are before the dying, eager to grab the souls of those who are going to be lost for eternity.

Mercy-killing . . .

That travesty is going on a few rooms down the corridor.

Her name is Norita.

She is in a coma. She has been in a coma for weeks.

Doctors have conferred. They now advise her husband to stop the life-support system.

"There is no hope," he is told. "Your wife is being sustained artificially. Her body itself is incapable of taking over. She will never pull out of the coma. We feel quite certain about that."

Shawn, the husband, does not decide immediately. He ponders the responsibility.

If I wait, how can I ever be certain when my beloved will regain consciousness from the darkness?

If I don't wait, how will I ever know—?

He could not finish the thought. He was lost in memories of what their relationship once had been like.

Norita . . .

He would never hold her again, he would never touch her lips with his own, he would never watch her smile as a sunset was reflected off her white, pure skin, he would never hear her voice whispering into his ear, "I love you, Shawn, I love you so much."

He owes her something. He owes her as little pain as possible. The doctors say that they couldn't be sure about the so-called "pain factor." Is she in oblivion? Is there nothing but nothing?

Or is his beloved actually being tormented by agony while seeming to be free of it?

If there is the slightest chance—he starts to tell himself.

He knows he has to eliminate that possibility by eliminating the woman who means so very much to him.

How can I say that? How can I conjure up even the remotest chance?

So quickly their lives had changed. Less than a year after their beautiful island honeymoon. The other driver was not even hurt. Alcohol. The courts let him off with a stiff sentence and a large fine, but that was all. Norita never even knew what hit her.

I prayed and prayed. I begged God to touch your body and heal it. I wrote letters to men on TV and my envelopes were included in piles over which they prayed. Nothing worked. And now the doctors say she'll never wake up . . . .

To see Norita so pale, to see the tubes in her nose and down her throat, to see the chest moving up, falling back, then up, then back, kept going only by ingenious devices that had nothing to do with life but generated a grotesque caricature of it, like those people who had their pets stuffed and then placed on mantels or tables or elsewhere, often holding them in their laps and patting them as though nothing had happened, the only difference being that the stuffed remnant in each case didn't have an air hose stuck through its mouth so that the sides could be pushed out, then drop back, then out, furthering the illusion.

It cannot go on, he decides. It has to stop. He has to ignore a thin little wisp of a voice that seemed to be saying, Wait. Please wait. Don't anticipate the actions of a Holy God. Surely you must wait.

He buries those words under the immediacy of the moment.

Hours later, Shawn stands again by Norita's side. He has told the doctor that he wants to be there, by her side, when the machines are unplugged.

But he cannot stay. The tubes are being taken away. He feels a great, drowning surge of sorrow. He has to leave before he changes his mind, before he tells them, No, no, it's wrong. Put everything back. Please, I don't want to—

Shawn turns, pauses for a moment in the doorway to her room.

"Shawn . . . I don't want to . . . die . . ."

He assumes he has imagined those whispered words, that they had crept to the surface of his mind from a corner of wishful thinking, idle fantasies.

He turns, in any event, and sees Norita's eyes closing, those attending her frantically trying to reconnect the life-support system.

A single tear slides down her left cheek, and then she is gone,

They have to sedate him to stop the screams.

⟨∘⟩

Can there be any question why my kind hungers after the new Heaven and the new earth? Though we be as insubstantial as mist, we think, and we feel, and we listen to the screams of a man who has realized what he has done to his beloved, we listen, oh, that we do, my comrades and I, and we shiver from the impact.

We almost give up. We beg Almighty God to keep us in His Kingdom, to give us the peace, the joy with which He has graced redeemed human beings for thousands of years.

That must not be, we know.

For if He were to grant us what we craved, He would deny countless numbers of men, women, and children that which we can give them from time to time. For if we were to be allowed only Heaven, then God Himself, to be consistent—and He is never less than that— would have to abandon the world for all time, and in that case, He, like us, then would be insulated from the pain, for it is that insulation which we oft crave and cannot be granted for the sake of humankind.

Seven

Sometimes unfallen angels can take human form.

Satan was jealous even of this, knowing that neither he nor his demons had a similar power, so he started the practice of possession, taking over an existing man, woman, or child.

I myself have been in human form, but not all angels are allowed to do this—only those on special missions.

I remember a midwestern family with a devoted relationship to a little poodle named Gigi. Eight year old Chad especially loved Gigi. He had some emotional disorders and would often withdraw, seeming to lose touch with the world around him. But he was different when he was with Gigi. A special rapport existed between them from the beginning. The two were, in a real sense, in communion constantly.

Then the dog contracted cirrhosis of the liver, which led to a liver shunt condition causing waste products to be diverted into the bloodstream.

A painful two year battle for Gigi's survival began.

The last night of Gigi's life, Chad was holding her in his arms, rocking her back and forth. They had all been taking turns with her throughout the night . . . first, the father, then the mother, then Chad's two sisters.

For the past two years, Chad had been slipping back more and more frequently into his internalized world. As Gigi's life faded, so it seemed to be with Chad.

But that night, Chad was drawn back into reality. He asked if he could be the next one to hold his friend.

"She'll know it's me," he told his parents. "She'll be calmer. Oh, please, she needs me now."

When his mother or his father had been holding Gigi, she would go through periods of intense, sudden jerking motions as though spasms of pain were tearing through her. Then she would seem to relax a bit, but later, another awful moment of abrupt movement—yet there were no sounds except a vague little whimpering.

Chad had overheard them talking about putting Gigi to sleep.

"No!" he begged. "You can't do that. I . . . . I prayed that God would take her home to Him. Let Him do that. I want her to follow Him into Heaven when she's in my arms."

They looked at one another, and said nothing further. They were skeptical of the idea that animals had an afterlife. And they didn't want to fill their son with false ideas. Yet his expression then, tears in his eyes, conveyed such desperation that they felt they could not destroy that hope of his, and they decided to let Chad hold his beloved Gigi for the next shift between them.

It was a warm summer night, and Chad took her outside.

They had played a lot together in that same yard. Briefly Gigi opened her eyes, and looked at him. There was no pain in them, just simple trust, for it was enough that he held her, thus enabling her to ignore the torment being experienced by her tiny, frail body.

I took on a form then, for only a few minutes, my appearance that of an old, old man, and I entered the yard, and stood there looking at the boy, gently holding his dog.

Chad's eyes widened.

"Are you—?" he started to ask.

"God?"

Chad nodded.

"No," I smiled. "Just someone who cares about you very much."

"Me?"

"Yes, Chad, and your pal there, Gigi."

"Have you come to take her from me?"

"I have, son, I have."

"But I don't want her to go yet. I love her so very much."

"You had some wonderful times together, didn't you?"

Chad smiled broadly then.

"You know?"

"Yes, Chad, I was there."

"When she warned me about the snake?"

"I was there."

And he talked about other times, times when Gigi helped, if only by being with him, resting her head on his lap, and trying to reassure him by her presence that he was loved, truly, truly loved.

"And now I won't have her anymore," he said.

"She'll be safely in God's hands."

"You mean—?"

I looked at him through my human form.

"You're smiling?" Chad said.

"I am, yes, I am."

"But why?"

"It's time."

"No!"

He held Gigi close to him but as he did so, she groaned.

"Pain," I said. "She's tired of the pain."

He heard little sounds escape from her emaciated body.

"Goodbye . . ." he whispered.

For an instant, Gigi's eyes were open again just as he had spoken.

"She's looking at me," Chad cried. "She—"

"Not at you, Chad. She's looking beyond you."

Just then, Gigi let out a gasp. Her body grew limp. Chad bowed his head, unable to hold back the sobs.

"Is she—?" he asked.

He looked up when I did not answer.

"Sir?" he said. "Sir, where are you?"

As Chad stood, a puzzled frown on his forehead, with the lifeless apricot colored form in his arms, and went back inside, we waited and watched for a moment, Gigi and I, spirit both of us, and then her Master called her home.

ঙ৯

Being involved in such moments does truly keep me going. Being with human beings governed by love is so beautiful. Being with animals for which love is all that matters makes me yearn even more for the old days of Eden when it was always so.

Cruelty is another story. I cannot abide it. Animals seem incapable of indulging in cruelty.

But not humankind, truly not them . . .

Eight

Dietrich Burhans.

His death was a shock to the community of Wheaton, Illinois, where he had lived and worked for several decades as a financial analyst.

He died at home, with his large family gathered around his bed.

He spoke just two words before his ravaged body twitched a couple of times and then was still.

"The Jews! The Jews!"

At the time no one knew what he meant. And in the wave of sorrow that followed his death, Dietrich Burhans' final "statement" was overlooked.

Even though an atheist, he had maintained good relationships among the evangelical community that dominated Wheaton, the "Protestant Vatican," many thinking they would be the Lord's instrument in bringing him to a redemptive faith, others as much concerned with his favorable impact upon their financial health as anything else.

He never did change. He died an atheist. Yet Wheaton was at a stand still until the day of his funeral. His impact upon the community was felt among too many families for him to be ignored.

The minister delivered an impassioned eulogy as he spoke of Burhans' humanitarianism, expressed through outreaches he funded to reach a variety of worthy recipients around the world: starving children, AIDS researchers, many more.

His three daughters and two sons each gave their own brief remarks, speaking of a devoted and generous father. They all would find that their financial concerns would be nonexistent for the rest of their own lives. His widow, who met Burhans not long after he came to the United States from his native Germany, caused tears to flow more freely than any of the other speakers when she told the assemblage how very much her husband meant to her.

I thought of everything I knew about this man, based upon many years of being near him, of seeing what he was like, of wishing he would come to Christ, and knowing how many, many times he had rejected the Savior.

You fool! I would shout with words he never heard. You have a good life. You think that that is enough. You are certain you will never have to pay an eternal price for your stubborn rejection.

I liked Dietrich Burhans, despite his atheism.

I liked this man with such a kind heart that it seemed to compel him to do whatever he could that was benevolent. He died wealthy, with a mansion as a home and seven family cars, but far less so than would have been the case if he had proved significantly more selfish with his money.

I had met far too many Christians who hoarded their money, who forgot that it was only being loaned to them, and that they had no right to hold onto it with a kind of zeal that would have better served the cause of Christ if it had been directed toward the Great Commission as opposed to their individual bank accounts.

Not Dietrich.

I had gotten to know him well enough as a young man, and traveled with him as he made his way to the United States. I did not stay with him permanently, for I had others to minister to but he seemed especially in need of help, a man fleeing his own country's horrors and trying to construct a new world for himself. But, he appeared, after a fashion, to be remarkably self-sufficient, and yet so stubborn in matters spiritual. I remember one time in particular, when he came very close to death after a car accident.

He sensed my presence without knowing what or where I was.

I could see him consciously pushing that awareness away, denying its existence.

"But how can you do this again and again?" I asked, hoping that something would get through to the man.

"There is nothing that I hear now. It is a voice in my mind, some silly fragment from the past."

"It is not, Dietrich, it is not that at all. You know that I am standing right next to you."

As he lay in that hospital bed, he brought his hands to his ears, trying to shut out my voice.

"You pretend that I am nothing because your belief system has no place for me, for my kind. If you admitted that I existed, then you would have to stop denying so much of what you really believe."

He spoke softly then, almost a whisper.

"There are so many things I do not want to face."

Dietrich's eyes widened. I could see tears slipping from them onto the pillow beneath his head.

His mouth opened and closed, and he seemed to be saying something but what it was could not be heard.

Abruptly another angel appeared in the hospital room.

Observer.

I was on Dietrich's right side, and Observer was on his left.

"You cannot have this man," I said.

"My master has already prepared a place for him," my former comrade-in-Heaven replied.

"It matters not. God can overturn Satan's machinations in an instant."

"Not with this one."

I knew he was wrong, of course. God could snatch Dietrich from the arch deceiver at any time—but Dietrich needed to change from his atheism to acceptance of the Savior, whose very existence he had been denying.

He would not. But I did not know that to be the case when I was contending with Observer. Only God had the ability to tell the future.

So I continued what would prove to be fruitless while Observer tried to come back in rebuttal.

Finally, defeated on the theological level, he simply looked at me, quite sadly in fact, and said, "You do not know everything, Stedfast."

He was gone then, the faint sound of dancing flames accompanying him.

~ⓢ~

The eulogy had ended. The minister was about to step from the podium.

"No!" an elderly man, thin, pale, screamed from where he had been sitting in a pew at the back of the church.

He stood, holding up his right wrist.

I could see numbers tattooed on it.

This old one was in the aisle now, walking toward the open coffin in the front of the church.

"How can you do this?" he asked as he passed row after row of astonished gazes. "How can you pay homage to that—?"

He finally reached the mahogany coffin, and before anyone could restrain him, he managed, despite his frail appearance, to kick out from under it the stand on which it had been resting.

The coffin crashed over onto the floor, and the body of Dietrich Burhans toppled out, which sent screams of shock through the gathered mourners.

"Remember Maidanek?" the old man shouted at the lifeless body. "Remember the 1.5 million who died there? Remember the coarse sound of your laughter as you watched them drop, often at your very feet?"

He spat on the body, and then strode with uncommon vigor from the sanctuary.

I liked this man with such a kind heart that it seemed to compel him to do whatever he could that was benevolent.

I leave the mourners a short while later, having found reaffirmed another truth among many through the centuries of my existence.

Angels do not know everything . . . .

Nine

Karl Leemhuis was a Dutch billionaire who had become fed up with what was happening in his native country, epitomized by the influx of drug peddlers and sex merchants turning such a beautiful urban area as Amsterdam into a place of filth, filth of one sort or another, with drug deals in the square in the center of that city, with prostitutes in picture windows along the polluted canals, and, in general, a sense of absolute moral and spiritual decadence that had caused many travelers to change their plans and spend far less time there than originally anticipated.

So Karl moved to the United States, and built an isolated estate in the mountains of Colorado. He hired locals to make up his household staff and bought everything he needed—food, clothes, furniture—entirely from the local merchants. By himself, even with such immense wealth at his disposal, he couldn't have been responsible for turning around the depressed economy. But the very fact that he had given the location such a vote of confidence drew in other individuals, along with the companies over which they had charge. He became a hero to the people of that town.

Five years later, his doctors delivered the news he had secretly suspected for some time.

"I have five billion dollars," he told a very special friend, "but I cannot buy a cure for this cancer. I can fund a dozen hospitals but I have no power to turn back—"

Interrupting himself, he stood and walked over to the large window in his office on the second floor of his vast house, twenty thousand square feet of glass and timber and concrete set in the midst of fifty acres of alpine meadows and fir trees. For a few moments he gazed silently at the beauty of his mountain estate.

"From the beginning, I liked this spot because of the elevation," he said. "I can see for miles in every direction."

He chuckled as he added, "I didn't think, when I moved here, that I would be able to see the end of my life so soon, and just as clearly."

Then he confided in his friend what he intended to do. He did this because it seemed natural to tell her, for he trusted this woman more than he trusted himself. She listened to his plans, every word of what he was saying, loving him even more for the mixture of compassion and wisdom that he was showing.

When Karl had finished, she sat without speaking for several minutes, then started weeping.

"They will hate you," she said honestly.

"Oh, at first, yes, I agree," he replied. "But the alternative is that if I don't act while I still can, they will end up hating each other. Can you imagine the squabbling, dear, dear Colette?"

That she could, indeed she could.

Karl had five children. None of them was pleased that he moved to the United States. It seemed that he was deserting them as well as his country. But, finally, they each followed him to America, however reluctantly. When he told them, five years later, that he had fallen in love, they found that somehow as difficult to accept as the move from one country to another.

"I tried to make them understand that when their mother died, my life changed," he went on. "But they never did. They're children of wealth, Colette. They have always had full bellies and dressed in the most expensive clothes. I've never denied them anything, I'm afraid."

Years of regret danced across his face on leaden feet of despair.

"They couldn't even exist on their own," Karl said with a husky voice. "Whether they would admit it to themselves or not, they had to go where Papa was, where the money would be banked. Each one is drawing a salary from my corporation but none is working, not really, none, that is, except—"

"Rebekkah?" Colette finished for him. "It is Rebekkah, isn't it?"

Karl nodded.

"You are perceptive, as always, dear," he told her. "The rest. . . ah, they're all betting that you and I are sleeping together, you know."

She blushed at that remark.

"I know how you feel," he said. "But—"

"You're a Christian, and you cannot have sex with me unless we're married," she mimicked amusedly. Then her expression changed to one of concern. "But surely, now that you're—"

"Dying? You think that would make a difference?"

She was blushing a deeper red this time.

"You think God would understand?" he said. "You think He would give us this final pleasure before I go? I agree. He would want the two of us to be happy."

She shot to her feet.

"Oh, Karl!" she said joyously. "I know God wants nothing else for us."

She started to embrace him, but he held her at arm's length very briefly.

"That is why," he told her slowly, passionately, "I am now asking you to be my wife, Colette. Would you consent to marry a dying old man?"

⚘

Colette and Karl were married a few days later. The wedding was not an elaborate one, there had been little time for preparation. Karl was wise—if they had waited any longer, the children surely would have mounted frantic opposition to it. But now they had no maneuvering room whatsoever, they could only sit back in cold, bitter acquiescence.

After their father and new stepmother went on their honeymoon, they fumed among themselves, calling Colette a tramp, this bright, beautiful, middle aged woman who married someone twenty years older than she, someone who was obviously in bad health. It could scarcely have been for reasons of sexual fulfillment, they surmised.

"She's after only one thing," commented Erika Leemhuis. "And once she gets hold of our money, we'll have to come crawling to her for every penny. She doesn't have hands, she's got claws, and once they dig in, they'll stay there, sure enough. You can bet she won't be pried loose from anything that has our family name on it!"

"Father must have a few remaining fantasies, whether he can ever realize them or not," remarked Hans. "He might well just want to prove to himself that he still can attract a beautiful woman—"

"What's he going to do with her?" interrupted Anna, another of the Leemhuis offspring.

They all broke out laughing.

All except Rebekkah, though her brother Peter had since joined in with the others. She felt uncomfortable with this ridicule even if she had initially resisted the idea of a father she knew was dying suddenly getting married.

"But what if they're happy, really happy?" she said finally as they all sat in the large dining room of that massive house.

The others turned to her, almost in unison.

"Of course she's happy," Erika pointed out." What would you expect? After all, she'll soon be included among the beneficiaries of our father's fortune. A hundred million dollar pot is sure to make anybody happy! I tell you this: Colette won't let go of our father. Once she's got hold of him, she won't let go."

Grumbling, they pushed back from the table and left the room. Rebekkah remained seated for a few moments, lightly caressing the polished wood of the huge table where she had joined her father for many, many meals.

Then she stood and walked into the hallway. Everybody was heading outside.

Hans turned around, asked, "Are, you coming, Rebekkah? We're heading into town for the music festival."

She smiled, thanked him, declined the offer, then walked upstairs to her bedroom, and sat down in a large leather chair, holding an envelope her father had given her a couple of days earlier. He had wanted her to read it sometime in the future, maybe years hence, because specific instructions were written on the front: "To be opened only after I have died."

"Please forgive me, dearest father," she said out loud, as she could no longer restrain herself.

She gasped as she read the contents:

I am writing this to you because you are the only one of my children with whom I can feel any rapport at all, dear Rebekkah.

The others have taken my worst tendencies and magnified these while discarding all of the good ones, anything that could be called right and proper, yes, I must say, that which is Christ honoring.

They want only that which is material—more money, more cars, more diamonds and clothes and real estate holdings and trips abroad, and they want this from the labors of another, and not their own. "What is the point of having a rich father if we have to work for a living?" they ask.

They do not know that they can get along perfectly well on a great deal less. They do not know that money spent to help others brings with it the most profound blessings of all.

But they will find out, my dear Rebekkah, and they will find out quite soon. I have provided enough money in my will so that they will not starve, of course, but nothing beyond that. They will have to earn anything else with their own labors. They will have to continue my business dealings in a profitable manner for them to be able to continue anywhere near their accustomed standard of living. Yet, dear daughter, once they do, they will learn, in the process, not to throw away money as they have been doing. They will learn that the finest sports car means little if there is no peace deep down in their souls. I know, Rebekkah, that they do not have that peace now because their joy, as transitory as it is, is based upon their possessions, and their insecurity arises from the nagging fear that they might somehow have to give up that which has been the very foundation of their existence.

As for you, fair child, I am secretly leaving you more than I have your siblings. Because I know your heart, and I know what you will do with it. All the rest of my fortune will be put in a foundation, a foundation to fund the spread of the gospel of Jesus Christ throughout the world. I want you to head that foundation, because I want it to be run by someone for whom the salvation of otherwise lost souls will be a magnificent compulsion.

As for Colette, she is to receive no more than the others. This is, by the way, at her request, for she knows well enough what they think of her.

Goodbye, dearest child.

Your father

P. S. I want to encourage you to study more about angels. I have sensed one by my side.

～✑～

Rebekkah pressed the pages to her chest and wept.

As soon as the tears stopped, she knew what she would do. She would go to where her father and his new wife were honeymooning, she would go there, indeed she would, and beg them both to forgive her for acting just like the others, and then she would return, keeping the secret as though it was something holy.

I went with Rebekkah, though, naturally, she was not at all aware of this. I went with her to that cabin beside a clear and beautiful lake where her father and her new stepmother had spent hours sitting happily on the shore, watching the fish swim in water so clear that their multicolored bodies could be seen without squinting, listening to birds calling, and—

The air.

Yes, just inhaling it into their lungs, its sweet purity radiating throughout their frail, tired bodies.

I know. I was there with them earlier, before I went back to their house, before I sat with Rebekkah as she read her father's letter.

Before—

That moment came as they were walking inside.

"Colette?" he said. "Did you see that?"

She smiled.

"Yes, my dearest," she told him. "He's quite astonishing, isn't he?"

"So beautiful dear, so—"

He stumbled then, fell into her arms, his body nearly lifeless, as his soul reached out to me.

Colette managed to sit down on the front porch of that little cabin, and wrap her arms around his chest, and rock him gently, singing softly in his ear.

"Thank you, dearest," he said with infinite tenderness, the last words of his life as I took him to his awaiting Father.

Colette sat there, still rocking him, even as he gasped—not from pain, she knew, no, not pain, but from what he saw, and what he heard, and the glory of it.

"Save a place for me, my beloved," she whispered as his body became limp, the life gone, but only from there.

～⊙～

They were still like that when Rebekkah arrived, Colette holding the lifeless body, her head pressed next to his, lips touching his cheek in one last kiss, her back resting against the closed front door.

None of the children knew that Colette had been dying, too. Not even Karl had known. She had had her reasons, very personal, very fine. She simply told no one, and since angels cannot read minds, I could not tell either. There was some speculation in days following that the shock of having Karl die like that, as she held him, was perhaps the final link in a chain, compounding her heart problems.

Rebekkah stood there and waited while paramedics tried to pry them apart. Colette had been firm in her hold, as though afraid to relinquish his body.

The words came hauntingly back to Rebekkah from that awful meeting with her brothers and sisters, words that made her shed tears in front of strangers.

Colette won't let go of our father. Once she's got hold of him, she won't let go . . . .

She didn't.

Ten

I have been present at innumerable funerals. I have heard the eulogies, seen the tears of mourning, appeared in human form to give a word of consolation to those for whom grief threatens its own kind of death.

True grief or remorse can reshape even the cruelest of human temperaments.

I think of Heinrich Himmler, who was one of the worst human monsters in history, he lived that way more than a decade—but it is quite possible that he did not die the same man who was one of the principal architects of the Final Solution.

No man, woman, child, or angel can mourn the passing of one such as this. Every Jew can breath a sigh of relief, except those—perhaps the majority—who would have preferred that he had been captured, put on trial at Nuremburg, and then hanged.

That was not to be the case. Most of the top Nazis—Hitler, Himmler, Goering, Goebbels—committed suicide. All but Himmler did so to avoid the ultimate defeat: being executed by their enemies.

Yet that is why the world believes Himmler took cyanide.

But I know otherwise. I was with this man when he died. He poisoned himself out of guilt, guilt that crushed him from the first and only time he visited one of the concentration camps that were his brainchild.

"I sentenced millions to death," he said, his voice getting weaker and weaker. "I saw the bodies of thousands littering more than one battlefield. But it was not until Auschwitz that the reality of an intellectual principle—"

He was nearly gone, and began to ramble.

"Those pathetic bodies, skeletons covered by flesh . . . they should have been dead, skeletons do not live . . . but these did . . . they were moving, they were breathing, their mouths opened, closed, opened, closed . . . and they looked at me, some with anger, some with resignation, others with pity . . . they were pitying me . . . I approached one, and he reached out a hand . . . my guard raised his rifle butt . . . I waved him back . . . that bony hand, the veins pronounced, the skin touched with jaundiced yellow, touched my chest."

I remembered. The man had whispered, "I go from this hell to the Lord's Heaven, I escape it, but not you, Herr Himmler, not your kind. There will be no escape from the Hell that awaits you!"

He knew fear then, along with the pity that he felt for this abandoned human being.

Abandoned . . .

He shivered, for an instant, hoping that no one saw this. The same guard roughly brushed the prisoner aside, and Himmler came very close to reprimanding him for doing so.

That night, he had the first of many foul and terrifying dreams. He saw the man who had spoken to him die. He saw the frail, ravaged body thrown into a ditch. He saw lime poured over that body and a hundred others.

And he woke up screaming.

"I had not been to one of the camps before that day . . . I used a pen to seal the doom of six million men, women, and children—but this was a simple act, you know, ink flowing from my pen onto the appropriate sheet of paper. Even the dead on the battlefields of that war could not have prepared me for Auschwitz. There is a vast gulf between a soldier valiantly giving up his life and an old, tired Jew, barely alive, but alive just the same, being shoved into an oven!"

It is interesting, though few men have made the connection, that Heinrich Himmler henceforth was known to have favored the dismantling of the death camps.

"If we win this war, we want to win the world along with it," he had said. "If we lose this war, we do not want the world to view us as barbarians."

He was blind to the fact that the world knew everything by then, that Himmler and the other creatures with him would never, under any circumstance, be viewed with other than the rawest loathing.

And so he pushed ahead with the possibility of razing the camps. But the change in Heinrich Himmler did not stop with that. He befriended countless numbers of Jews, sending them secretly into Switzerland, or redirecting them to camps where there were no ovens or gas chambers—though this hardly protected them from the cruelty of the guards themselves.

It was the children, I think, children who looked like their own little dolls but with the stuffing sucked out of them, so pale, so afraid, so ill.

The children were being shoveled into the ovens, two or three bodies per enclosure—more if tiny babies were involved, a practice to which Himmler put an immediate stop at Auschwitz and other camps.

The cries of boys and girls dying in the awful heat!!!

He bolted up straight from where he lay, his eyes bloodshot, the poison throughout his system.

"Oh God!" he cried. "You could never forgive me!"

Yes, I tell him. Yes, you can be forgiven. You were once a devout Catholic. Take your words beyond words and let them reflect the yearnings of your very soul.

"Oh, please," he begged, tears streaming. "Please help me."

Then take the hand of the Savior who is reaching out for you now . . . .

Himmler started to do so, reaching up physically as well as spiritually, to grasp the hand of this Messiah, this Jewish Messiah.

He fell back on his deathbed, the years of anti-Semitism making him withdraw at the last instant, a sob escaping him, encrusted Nazi dogma pulling him down to a furnace unlike any in Auschwitz.

True grief or remorse can reshape even the cruelest of human temperaments . . . .

I cannot say that "reshape" is the most accurate designation for a Heinrich Himmler. But I also cannot deny that even he was capable of something approaching kindness, if only as an effort to drown those cries of anguish at night.

In the end, this was not enough for Heinrich Himmler. The thought of reaching out to a Man who was incarnated two thousand years before as an itinerant Jew, a hated Jew, was impossible for him to accept, and he threw away salvation because of this.

Coming close is not enough . . . .

Eleven

There is something else about grief. It confuses matters. It screams out the word "tragedy" and applies this to the deceased when it is better used to describe the survivors.

In a Christian context, grief is not for the dead husband or wife or mother or father or daughter or son. Grief is the realization that those left behind are now going to have to get used to living life without someone very important still around, someone who has meant a great deal to them.

That really is the essence of grief. As such, grief is a bit dishonest, a kind of charade, if the dead person is a Christian and as soon as death has claimed him or her, their soul is ushered by my kind into eternity. Grief wails and moans about the tragedy of someone so young dying, while so much of their life remained unlived.

Why is it a tragedy for them if they live again, instead, by the Father's side, in the company of angels, and walk streets of gold?

If they have died, that is, in their mortal bodies, if they have died through a long illness, an illness that caused continual pain, that took life from them with slow agony, and then, brain dead, heart no longer beating, lungs stopped, they are transformed into a body very much like an angel's, and now have entered Heaven where such will never afflict them again—where is the tragedy?

If death comes through a murder, if life is torn from them by another human being for anger or money or whatever the insane reason might be, or even accidental death as in an automobile accident—then the tragedy is still not for the one who is dead, if dead can ever be the right word for somebody who has accepted Jesus Christ as Savior and Lord. The tragedy is for humanity itself, for what this shows as to the depths of the perversity or "mere" carelessness of human nature. And, yes, as accurately as before, perhaps more so for those left behind, for the wife and mother whose husband has been taken from her and who now must raise a family quite, quite alone, for the husband whose beloved marital partner has been raped and murdered, and who is thrust into the dual role of father and mother to their three children— yes, again, this is where the essence of the tragedy is found. But not, no, not for the victim who is beyond fear of what the night holds on the terror stricken streets of cities and towns, around the world.

Here, however, is the true tragedy, the tragedy that transcends all others . . . .

If the victim is not a Christian, if they have rejected Christ as Savior and Lord, and death whisks them away instead to damnation, their opportunity for salvation gone forever—this is the tragedy!

Picture a young, intelligent, attractive woman with a future in her profession, always busy, always planning the next "campaign" for a promotion. For this individual, for this woman, accepting Christ as Savior and Lord is a decision akin to that of an oft delayed mammogram, something she knows she must do someday—yet not now, for she is far too busy, but later, for sure, later. And then, later, the good intentions blow up in her face in a dark alley, her clothes shredded, her body violated, her soul leaving its dead, cold mass, surrounded by demons as she is dragged, screaming, into the abyss of flames.

But then she is hardly alone. Others, men and women both, who tend to put off, put off, put off everything ranging from raising a family to tests for cancer to a personal relationship with the Savior face the possibility—and the longer it goes on, face the probability—that they will never do what must be done if they are to survive pain in this life and in the life just beyond.

This is where grief, for this woman, for that man, for them and a thousand, a million, a hundred million others, for those left on this planet who find such souls torn forever from their presence, this is where talk of true tragedy is right on the mark. For the only way there can be a reunion with loved ones is if they, too, are damned. Yet, in one of the ghastly ironies that have followed the sin of Adam and Eve, it is a truth, a pathetic but unchangeable truth, that in the punishment of Hell, love dies, has no place—love goes up in smoke, you might say.

Twelve

Grief is capable of doing something else for which it is seldom given credit. It takes hold of memories and transforms them.

Dying can take a very long time. I know this all too well. I have been with thousands of dying men, women, and children over the centuries. I have personally guided many, many of these into Heaven as they take off that which is corruptible and put on that which is incorruptible, immortal.

Some of the people with whom I have grown close during the final days or weeks of their lives have seen their senses sharpened as they come closer and closer to the end. I remember one old woman named Dottie.

"I never knew the air could be so clear," she said that final day as she sat on the front porch of the home she had occupied for half a century.

"It is the same as before," I told her. "It hasn't changed."

"But I have, haven't I?" she said, understanding.

"It happens, Dottie."

"I would think that coming so close to death would cloud my mind, put me in some kind of befuddled fog."

"It is that way often. But that occurs mostly with those in great pain."

"The Lord gives them His own kind of sedative."

"You could say that, Dottie."

She sighed, and smiled.

"I see you sometimes," she told me. "I see you all shimmering and iridescent, lit up with a hundred colors."

"And then—?" I probed.

"Other times I don't see you at all."

"The life force ebbs and flows. One minute you are a bit closer to death, another a bit further away."

"Like a river?"

"Somewhat, dear Dottie."

"You call me dear. Surely all of us blend together at some point in your memory, indistinguishable from one another. You couldn't possibly remember everyone you have been with."

This time I was indeed visible. She could see a smile on my glowing face.

"I do," I replied. "We are children of God, Dottie. We are extensions of Him. We remember just as He remembers."

"If there are a hundred million people over the years, a hundred million identities that you have comforted, you can recall all of them?"

"All hundred million."

She stopped rocking.

"What an amazing thought," she said softly.

She turned and looked at me, studying me carefully.

"How many like you are there?" she asked.

"How many grains of sand are on a beach, Dottie?"

She gasped then.

"So vast a multitude!" she exclaimed. "And you know each one of them, too?"

"I do."

"What about the third that rebelled and were cast out, along with Satan?"

"Them as well."

"What a mind you must have!"

"The same humankind was meant to possess."

"And sin in Eden shut off all that as well?"

"It did, Dottie, it did."

She rubbed her forehead.

"I hate forgetting," she said, "and I do forget so much."

"There is a purpose even to that."

She sat up straight, waiting for me to explain, eager to have this newest of revelations explained to her.

"What you remember is often filled with pain, Dottie. What you remember is carnal more often than not. When you shed your fleshly body, when your soul is freed for the journey ahead, you shed many of the memories as well, the sad ones, the sinful ones, gone in an instant."

"I won't remember people?"

"The best people, Dottie, the kind ones, the ones who have added much joy to your life."

"The ones who are in heaven ahead of me or will follow after me."

"Those people, Dottie, yes."

Her mind went back to her husband.

"It was quite awful with Harold," she said. "He became very ill, you know: He would wake up in the middle of the night, screaming, and thrashing about."

She was shivering.

"I feel so cold now," Dottie remarked. "Is it going to be warm in Heaven?"

"It will be," I told her, "truly the sweetest, the most total warmth you have ever known."

She started talking about Harold again.

"Just after he died, I looked back at our life together, and all that pain, all that suffering of those last few weeks were, can it be, almost forgotten as I concentrated on the good times, the moments when he had his appetite, and he could control himself in various ways, and. . . and—"

She brought her hand to her mouth.

"Harold was so very embarrassed," she said. "He had been so strong, able to do everything on his own, you know and, yet, now I had to change his diapers, I had to force spoons of food into his mouth, I had to sit by the hour, and hold his hand, and talk to him, or sing to him, hoping, oh, how I hoped that I could calm him down, that I could quiet that low, awful moaning that seemed to go on and on and on."

After wiping her eyes with a lace-edged handkerchief, she added, "But that's not how I usually think of Harold, you know. I see him water-skiing in his youth. I see him rocking our baby daughter to sleep or playing tennis with our son and so much else. The dying part of it almost never intrudes."

"Death will do that, Dottie. It will transform your memories."

"Just as Heaven transforms so many things, is that it?"

"A little like that, Dottie, just a little."

"How much longer?" she asked.

"Soon," I replied as gently as I could.

"Soon?" she repeated. "It's coming—?"

She fell back on her chair.

"I'm frightened all of a sudden," she said as she closed her eyes for a moment or two. "Please, help me."

"Dottie?"

"Yes?"

"Open your eyes, dear lady."

"Will it be soon?" she repeated.

"Oh, Dottie, it already is!"

She did as I had asked, and saw, then, ten thousand like me standing before her. Their colors glistened under a radiance quite unlike anything cast by any sun in galaxy after galaxy.

"Harold?" she asked, her own face aglow.

The angels stepped aside.

Ahead she saw a white throne, and a Figure sitting on it, and kneeling in worship and adoration before that Figure was someone familiar yet transformed, who now stood and turned in her direction.

"Bless you, Stedfast," she said, "bless you, dear angel, for being by my side Down There."

"And here as well, sweet friend. We will never leave you."

"You call me friend," she said, a bit puzzled.

"I have known you for many decades," I told her, recalling in a kaleidoscopic surge moments that we had shared without her ever knowing this was so.

She could scarcely comprehend that.

"So long," she mumbled.

"Only the beginning," I smiled, "only the tiniest beginning."

Her new hand touched my ancient hand, for just an instant, but enough so that I knew how she felt, and she stepped forward, briefly hesitant, then more confident as she experienced, in that transcendent moment, what eternity was all about.

∼ତ∽

This is a good time, I decide, for me to visit True at Eden, which I do periodically, passing on from one assignment to another. It has been centuries since I was with him, and he must surely need some encouragement after so long . . . .

Thirteen

I am at the entrance to Eden, guarded as always by my comrade. True has remained there for thousands of years, alone much of the time except when ones of my kind have been able to pay our friend a visit, to talk with him, to tell him what has been going on in the world.

"There have been so many tragedies," I say, my mind swirling with the history that has elapsed since the last time.

"I can understand that," True replies. "I remember the awful darkness that fell upon this place just after Adam and Eve left in shame."

His radiance dims momentarily, a sign of intense sadness.

"Oh, what they gave up, Stedfast, what they gave up," he says, his sorrow almost palpable.

"And what they brought upon the world!" I remind him, though "remind" is scarcely the right word, for he could never have forgotten.

"How can the Father forgive them?" he asks. "How can even mercy itself be so merciful with such as those two? I have been told by others about Calvary, of course, I know all about it—but, Stedfast, the sacrifice the Father underwent!"

True's presence shines with extraordinary brightness at the mention of Jesus.

"I love Him so very much," he says.

"As do I. That is why we serve Him with such loyalty," I reply. "Actually, I have talked with Him quite recently."

"You have? It has been so long for me."

"He admires you a great deal, True," I remark. "You have certain qualities far beyond what most of us possess."

"They liked Lucifer as well, Stedfast."

That was accurate, of course, which was why Lucifer had been the

highest expression of the Trinity's desire to have beings such as us pop-
ulate the Holy Kingdom.

"But there is a reason, True, a reason why you are so adored," I tell
him. "Can you imagine what that is?"

"I do not know the answer. Please, please tell me."

"They knew, Father, Son, and Holy Spirit. They knew."

"Knew what? No riddles now, Stedfast."

"Knew that you were the only angel who could endure staying here
until the end of time."

True looks at me, believing my words because no unfallen angel is
capable of lying. He is astonished by what I have just told him.

"Out of so many, I was the only one?" he asks.

"That is my understanding."

The weariness that had attended him a moment ago seems somewhat dissipated now. I sense that he is looking at himself through a
kind of mental mirror, and, in memory, at the multitude of angels to
whom he had belonged before being called to duty at the entrance to
Eden, trying to cope with the singular mission which he, above all others, had been assigned.

He turns toward the interior of the Garden.

"Smell the scents, Stedfast," he says, a curious note in his speech.
"Are they not as strong as ever?"

I do what he has asked, and I lend my agreement to his words.

"The same," I tell him, "the same as before."

I shiver, gossamer strands of light coming from me.

"It has been thousands of years since I walked its path," I say, musing.

"Do you want to enter?" True asks.

I nod, embarrassed that I seem so obvious.

"Go, then, my kindred spirit," he urges me.

And that I do, not quite sure why the impulse gains my attention,
nor why I succumb to it.

I step into Eden after millenniums away from it, this my first visit, which I am ashamed to admit to myself because of the sense of deserting my friend that it suggests.

It is not the same. It is far, far different from that which I left. It was once a place of lush life, the very sounds of life, the color of it, the scents.

No longer.

Dead.

Everything has died, at least that is what seems so upon first glance. The trees have become dead husks of what they once were.

"How can that be?" I ask out loud, puzzled, knowing what I detected before entry.

I hear True in back of me.

"Your memories of Eden are so powerful and you anticipated something so strongly that—" he says.

"—that I made it so, in images that no longer have any basis in reality," I finish the sentence for him. "There are no scents except of decay."

True cannot leave the entrance to Eden but his mind connects with mine, born as we were from the same Father's mind, retaining a measure of His consciousness in our very selves, as does Satan—which makes the tragedy of what he became all the more pathetic, since he is still "connected" to the Trinity, and yet still rejects everything that They are.

No glory left in Eden.

All is dust. The remnants of gray and brown and black where there once had been pink and blue and orange—a vast array of other colors signaling vibrant life.

So sad, Stedfast, so very sad.

I know that True has been there throughout the process of deterioration.

It was not all at once, was it, dear friend?

A pause.

No, Stedfast, it came gradually, through the centuries, as sin abounded more and more in the world. The greater the sin, the quicker the collapse of Eden.

Until the Flood.

That cleansed the world, for a time.

What happened then, True? Can you tell me?

Another pause.

I feel from True a wave of exaltation that is quickly overcome by despair.

Eden bloomed again. Dying animals revived . . .

I am startled. True senses this.

Quite so, Stedfast. Not all died the instant Adam and Eve left. Eden was a haven for those that remained, animal and plant and bird and fish alike. They thrived . . . for a while.

But Eden became corrupted by the world around it!

The Flood stemmed the process for a time, but a cleansed world saw men and women with their sin natures intact going back into it and beginning the infestation allover again, blind to the lessons of history .

Those that were left . . . oh, Stedfast . . . they died with agonizing slowness . . . enduring pain that puzzled them, unaccustomed as they had been to it . . . I saw them go before my eyes . . . I heard them as they came to me, and begged for mercy, begged for—

The funereal atmosphere in Eden seemed to grow stronger as images flooded my mind.

A bird . . . and another, and another, falling dead just like the one I had encountered directly after Adam and Eve lost Eden.

Lizards . . . they took a much longer time than did the birds, which tended to go all at once. The lizards became white-toned, vibrant green shades no longer apparent, their little eyes bloodshot, their sides collapsing, their tongues protruding.

The fish . . . yes, the fish! The clear streams of Eden became polluted because they were still connected to the outside world. The fish died more recently than other creatures since the problem of contamination accelerated only with the advent of the Industrial and, later, the Nuclear Age.

Suddenly I hear movement!

How could that be? Life no longer exists here.

Wrong, Stedfast, terribly wrong! Some small fragments of life have remained. But those clouds, those ghastly clouds—!

"From the oil fires set during the last war?" I ask out loud, forgetting myself.

"Yes, my comrade, yes, that is the cause," True replies out loud. "This monster succeeded in his attempt to devastate, to ravage at least part of the earth."

I turn and see him there, next to me.

"You have left the entrance!" I exclaim.

"I still guard Eden, Stedfast, even if I am a few feet from that usual spot." His expression is gentle, concerned.

"Our Creator is loving, merciful, understanding," True adds. "He knows that you will truly need me by your side when the last living creatures of Eden come into view."

And come they did . . . a rodent, a single large bird, a gorilla-like specimen, others, but not many, considering the vast numbers that once populated the Garden.

All are ill.

"Of the air," True says, "the poison comes invisibly. Of the water, burning their throats even as they need it so desperately. Of the soil, sending up twisted fruit that must be eaten even though it destroys them."

He walks forward, and they gather around him.

"At least they have not lost that!" he says. "At least that is something."

He refers to the sensitivity between such creatures and the angels.

"Even when the last dog contracted rabies," True tells me, "he went about snapping at others, grabbing a poor squirrel, attacking his own body—but he stopped as I came upon him. He sat before me, whimpering, the pain throughout his little form so great that the madness seemed almost a blessing since, at the last, he did not know what he was doing, could not have known when he bit at his own flesh in an uncomprehending outburst."

He looks at them, and I sense the sadness in his spirit. True must fight emotions, for all angels have emotions . . . as Almighty God, as the only begotten Son, as the Comforter . . . as they also have emotions . . . these emotions every bit as traumatic to angels as any experienced by humankind.

Most profoundly, my dear friend feels pity for those in our presence who will not be alive another earthly season. All have existed since Eden was first created. All are thousands of years old, since this was to have been a place of eternal life, as much as in heaven. None have sins, animals being incapable of that, but all have been affected—even in this place!

"Think of the years!" True exclaims. "This must be one reason why I guard Eden, and do naught else."

"I would agree," I say in confirmation. "If sinful man were to discover this spot, were to realize what these creatures represent, it would be a carnival overnight."

"I have heard the stories from others," True replies.

"A carnival," I add sadly. "The Protestants have water from the Jordan and the Catholics have water blessed by the pope, all sold at a premium. There have always been people who profited from simple faith sold for much money."

"It is amazing what a thousand years will do to an angel," True remarks. "When you were last here, you were not quite so cynical."

"Your task is to guard Eden," I remind my friend. "My own is to guard human beings. Here you have the remains of sinless perfection. Out there, just a few miles from where we stand at this very moment, a mad man, the latest of many in this region, is slaughtering anyone who opposes him, and the opposers' families along with him.

"I can stand anywhere in the world and feel the nearness of Satan's armada, True. I can feel them waiting, always waiting for an opportunity to grab another soul away from me, waiting for me to be less than diligent even for an instant, and then, without hesitating, they move in."

Screeching . . .

"If I had blood, True," I continue, "it would freeze within me the moment I hear that screeching."

"Yes, yes," True nods, knowingly. "I have detected it, too. They would like to get into Eden, dismember every portion of it, hold up the pieces in front of us, and announce that they will be victorious in the end, as they were in the beginning."

"If you were not here, that would happen."

"I feel so weak sometimes, Stedfast."

"I will stay with you this day, my friend."

"Bless you, Stedfast."

I smile.

"Stedfast and True," I say, "as it was meant to be."

I stayed with my fellow angel for a while. In eternal terms, it was not long. In finite ones, it spanned decades perhaps. We watched the last of the animals die, the last links with the original creation of Eden. They died horribly, the sins of the world at last literally crushing life from them through diseases, through poisons, through the ravages brought on by man.

Each came to True, or to me, and flopped down before us, sighing audibly before it died.

I remember the rabbit, no longer fat and white but thin and splotched with dirt and a hint of caked blood. It seemed to be smiling, if animals can smile, as it looked up at me, and said, in words clear and strong, humanlike indeed, "The pain has vanished. I feel no pain." It closed its eyes, tilted its head, and then was gone, truly gone from that once paradise.

Fourteen

I am often in the company of people consumed by regret. They regret past deeds. They regret the present. They stand and face the future with little but anxiety. Everything is a source of worry, of fear, of endless speculation.

But some of the regrets are understandable.

I am now with a middle-aged couple who have come to visit the husband's quite elderly parents.

"What a bore!" he says. "I wish we didn't have to do this."

"It's only once a month," she replies, "sometimes not even that."

They are sitting in their family car, outside the same home in which he had grown up many years before.

"I wonder why they never left," he says. "I guess they just felt so comfortable."

"The tyranny of the familiar," she muses.

"No, no, it's not that. Some people find comfort in a life that is predictable, the same rooms, the same pictures on the walls, the same furniture. It's almost a tragedy when something wears out and just has to be replaced."

She leans back against the front seat.

"Wears out . . ." she whispers.

"It's such a strain on them to pick out something new. You'd think they'd lost a dear friend instead of an old rug."

She closes her eyes.

"Are you feeling badly?" he asks.

She shakes her head.

"It's not that," she tells him. "I'm just remembering . . ."

"Remembering what?"

"My own parents."

"I'm really sorry they died before we met each other. Both of heart attacks the same day, wasn't that it?"

"My father died that way. Not my mother."

"How did she die?"

"Slowly. Some blood disease."

"Leukemia?"

"Probably."

"You never knew before then that she was sick?"

"Mother kept it from me. Father apparently felt I should know, but she was the one to say what happened."

She says no more, for a moment, thinking of that single funeral years earlier, the dark, cold trip as she came home from college, realizing that if she had known, she would never have left. She would have been willing to give up her education, or at least delay it, just to be with her mother, just to whisper the kindest, the most loving words to her.

"Just to hold her hand before . . . before—" the wife tries to say.

The husband reaches out and touches her shoulder.

"You were spared—" he starts to tell her.

"Spared?" she responds a bit angrily, pulling away. "I wouldn't have described it as being spared."

"I didn't mean—" he says, genuinely sorry.

The wife smiles.

"I know," she tells him. "I know. I still have a few lingering fragments of guilt left, despite—"

"Despite what?" the husband asks.

"Despite what they told me."

"They?"

"Yes, their doctor. He's a family friend, still alive, still practicing."

"What did he say?"

"That—"

She brings a hand to her mouth, trying desperately to force back the tears.

In all these years, she had never really discussed her parents with her husband. She preferred to keep her emotions in a neat little box somewhere deep within her.

"You don't have to—" the husband remarks.

"I know that," she says, her voice trembling. "If not now, then later. It comes back periodically, you know, it sneaks up on me and announces its arrival, along with the memories, all those memories."

Until what that doctor told her is recalled, for it had, over the years, helped. And now, in another moment of reliving that brief interlude . . .

"They weren't themselves," this dear, caring man had said, gently, his eyes misting over.

Then, the doctor cleared his throat as the two of them sat on the front porch of her parents' house.

"Your mother had lost so much weight. That dear lady was just a network of bones, with a little skin stretched over it.

She was nearly blind. She—"

"In just six months?"

"Oh, yes."

"But they never said anything. When I was home the last time, I saw that she seemed a bit pale, I asked if she was feeling all right. She just looked up at me and said, 'I'm feeling as good as I can expect.'"

"And she was being truthful."

"But there was a hidden meaning to those words, wasn't there?"

"Yes, there was. She knew even as she said them. She didn't believe in lying, so she said nothing that was not true. She felt as good as she could expect."

"But how could she feel good at all, knowing what was wrong with her?"

"She talked a lot about the Lord's gentle touch. When there was any pain, even very severe pain—"

I, Stedfast, was there, you know, by her side, as she came closer to death, her guardian angel, her ministering spirit, and she sensed my presence, smiled contentedly even as her friends visited and saw the edges of pain reflected in her bloodshot eyes and whispered among themselves about her courage . . . .

"But I could have been a comfort. I should have been a comfort."

The doctor looked at her with compassion.

"Then, perhaps, but you could not have endured the ugliest part."

"You mean Mother losing weight, is that what you're saying? Am I so weak that I could not—"

He put his fingers to her lips.

"She was nasty, and loud. She threw things. She became what she was not. She could not hold any food in her stomach. She—"

"Please, no!" she said in a loud voice. "I don't want to hear—"

"—any of the details? That's right. You don't. You needn't. But how could you have experienced any of it if you cannot bear to hear any of it?"

She was silent. They sat quietly, both of them, a slight breeze dancing across their faces and weaving gently through their hair.

"I missed seeing a mother I would have not recognized, a mother who became someone altogether different," she finally offered.

The doctor sighed as he said, "That is what you missed, my dear. She had lost control of everything, her mind, her emotions, every function of her body."

"She had been so strong . . ."

"At the end, just a couple of minutes before she died, she had regained some measure of that strength, of spirit if not body, and she took your father's hand, and she smiled."

My hand, also, the hand of an angel . . . just for a moment, holding onto a man she had loved for most of her life, not wanting to leave him, and, as well, being lifted from her body by someone else, than to meet, a gossamer moment later, yet Someone else.

"He said he could feel her leave," the doctor went on. "Your father said he could see his beloved turn for an instant and look back at him, and some creature of inexpressibly bright and shiny countenance by her side."

"In his imagination, of course?" she asked. "He couldn't really have seen anything, isn't that right?"

He saw us, he saw this sweet reborn child of the King because he had already begun dying himself . . . .

"I can't say," the doctor replied. "But delusion or glimpse into the other side, whatever it was, your father was comforted. He left that room, and sat down in his favorite old chair in the living room and, a short while later, when I went out to check on him, he too had gone."

The doctor handed her a sheet of paper that she unfolded and read aloud from.

☙

Do not be sad, Sweetheart. Your love was here. Thoughts of you were here. We talked by phone. We wrote letters. Your spirit was here, brought on the wings of an angel who knew how much the writing of your hand and the sound of your voice filled your mother and me with the greatest joy we could ever experience. Rest easy, my child. The same angel now attends you. He does so with our love as a gift eternal, to whisper into your ear when you think of us as you stand someday before your own family and give yourself to them.

☙

She reread those words, then glanced at the doctor. She found it so very difficult to speak but managed somehow, somehow.

"How did he realize this?" she asked.

I know, child. I know. I have the answer. I am the answer, sweet child.

A voice intrudes that reverie.

Her husband.

"You weren't here for awhile, were you?" he asks.

She nods. "Back in those days, that day."

"Did it help?"

"Yes, yes it did. Let's go inside."

"Boring day ahead of us, honey."

She reaches out and grabs his shoulders, but gently so.

"Don't ever say that," she admonishes him.

"But they're old, they're failing, they can hardly hear, I have to keep repeating things. That's a hassle."

She smiles with love, with understanding risen from the memories.

"But they're here," she says. "You can hug them. You can eat your mother's cooking. You can sit back and reminisce with your father. And you can say goodbye, knowing that it's not the last time."

She leans forward to kiss him.

"That's everything, my love. It is everything, you know."

They embrace, and then get out of the car and walk up the path to the front door. The husband knocks, and his mother answers, after a few seconds, and for an instant she doesn't quite recognize either of them.

"Mother?" he says with sudden warmth, with love. "It's us. We're here to visit, remember?"

She comes back to awareness just as quickly as it had left her, and she reaches out to hug her son, her daughter-in-law.

The wife looks at her husband, wondering if he is as irritated and uncomfortable as usual.

His tears are his answer.

Fifteen

The old man named Thomas had been a lighthouse keeper most of his adult life. He and his wife had built their entire existence around the requirements of that job. Not far away was the cottage they had shared.

But no children.

They had wanted boys and girls to hold, to laugh with, children for whom they could wipe away tears and to whom they could be a source of strength.

It was never Your will, Lord, Thomas thought as dusk dropped around him, and he stood just outside the whitewashed lighthouse. But my beloved and I got along because we had each other. And we had the presence of the Holy Spirit within us.

And me, good Thomas, and me.

I said that not defensively but lovingly. I enjoyed being with Amy and Thomas. They had separated themselves from the world, and while that mayor may not have been the full intent of the Father for all Christians, it indeed worked for this couple. They had no television. There was one radio in the cottage and one other in the lighthouse. They got all their news from these, for they subscribed to no newspapers or magazines. When they had each other, they had no need of anything or anyone else.

Succumbing to a severe case of pneumonia, Amy had passed away several years earlier. Thomas had buried her himself after having a coffin delivered from a town which was ten miles or so away, the same community where he got his food and other essentials. Several people offered to help out, but he politely refused.

So he laid out his Amy in her favorite dress, and gingerly applied makeup on her face, and combed her hair as she would have liked it to be. During the last few months of her life, she was too weak to do anything for herself, and he had had considerable practice taking care of dressing her, making her up, holding a mirror in front of her and asking, "Amy, is this the way you want to look?"

She would nod, and smile weakly, and say in a hoarse voice, "Thank you, Thomas. I wish—"

He would put two fingers gently on her pale, thin lips and say, "We are here to help one another. You mean so much to me, beloved. How could I ever do less?"

She would start crying, and he would dab away the tears from her cheeks. And then he would get into the bed beside her, and she would lean against him, and he could feel her slow, uncertain breathing.

Thomas' beloved died like that, just a little after sunrise one October morning, leaning against him, that breathing suddenly ended, her body limp. He didn't move at first, afraid that he might be wrong, afraid that her heart might still be beating, and he hated to disturb her rest.

Even after he could no longer deny it, he remained like that for nearly an hour longer. Finally, he moved slowly, and her body fell over on the bed, and he stood, and bowed his head, and sobbed until he nearly passed out from the effort, every muscle in his body tortured by the strain.

Then he started to pull a blanket up to her neck, stopped a moment, looking into that sweet, familiar face.

"It's as though you are still looking at me, dearest one," he whispered. "There is almost a smile on your face."

It is indeed a smile, dear Thomas. Your Amy was leaving that body just then, and she had been looking into the face of the Savior in whom you both had believed for more than half a century . . . .

Thomas turned and left their bedroom. He used an ancient telephone to call into town.

A day later, he was taking care of her for the last time. He slipped into the coffin a bottle of her favorite cologne, Chantilly, which she had been using ever since he first met her, its gentle scent much like Amy herself.

The grave had been dug with a slope at one end so that one man could carefully slide it down to the bottom.

One shovelful at a time, he piled dirt on top. Thomas was very tired by the time he had finished, and he went back into the cottage and fell down on their bed. Closing his eyes, he prayed that the next time he opened them he would see Amy standing at the gates of Heaven, waiting for him.

But when he awoke, that had not happened. He was still in that bed, and when he got up and walked to the front door and looked outside, he saw the lighthouse still there, standing as it had for more than a century.

Nothing had changed, except that now Thomas was alone. Or so he thought.

Thomas went on, day after day, for weeks, for months, for years.

One morning, though, Thomas was sitting on the beach, just beyond the reach of the surf: A beautiful sunrise had begun.

It is like that every day in His kingdom, I said.

"Is it like this in Your kingdom, Father?" Thomas said out loud, unexpectedly, with much hope reflected in his voice.

Had he heard me, somehow?

"Oh, Lord, when Amy passed unto You, did she see a golden red hue suffuse all of creation? Was it so fine to her eyes that she smiled at the sight of it, and then was quickly gone?"

Thomas jerked abruptly, feeling a pain in his chest, but that moment passed. He had grown accustomed to the brief spasms, and he always felt fine after them—a little more tired, perhaps, but fine nevertheless.

"Another day of sunrises, Lord, and sunsets?" he asked of the air and the sea and the gentle breezes.

Thomas stood breathing in the age-old scents, and then he walked the distance to Amy's grave.

"What was it like for you today?" he asked, realizing that this foolishness had been going on for years, and always it was the same, only the pounding surf to provide an answer of sorts, whatever that answer was.

Pain again. More severe this time.

He fell to his knees with the severity of it, but then, in a moment or two, it passed, as before, though he had had to shut his eyes for a bit.

He opened them to the sound of children.

"Where are—?" he started to say.

Still on his knees, he looked up.

Six of them were running toward him, joy on their faces.

"Where did you come from?" he asked weakly.

None of them answered. But two did walk over to Thomas, and helped the old man to his feet.

"Thank you, dear ones," he said.

He responded with unmasked joy to that tiny, tiny bit of kindness, perhaps more so since it was evidenced by bright faced children. That particular region was not overflowing with youngsters, so he had precious little opportunity for fellowship with any of them. Occasionally they could be seen in town, but only two or three at any time—often just one, hanging on the hand of a parent. But never had he experienced so many together, so many intent on him, instead of just passing by on the street. It was a place instead primarily of the elderly, a quiet town and its environs, where people wanted to be isolated, away from neon signs and heavy traffic and, certainly, dirty air.

Thomas asked if the children wanted to join him in the cottage so that he could give them something to eat.

"Are you hungry?"

They shook their heads.

"May I show you the lighthouse, my new young friends? All children seemed to be fascinated by lighthouses."

They nodded.

Thomas walked with surprising energy to the tall, narrow, whitewashed building, and unlocked the door, and went inside, climbing the steps as though he were once again a young man.

He showed his new friends the huge searchlight.

"At night," he spoke proudly, "if I've maintained it properly, this light can be seen for miles out to sea."

By the time he was finished telling them whatever he thought they could grasp, he was tired but happy.

"All these years, Amy and I wanted children. From the beginning we wanted precious little ones, and talked about them, dreamed about them, prayed for them to be given to us, to be able to talk with them as I have been doing with you," Thomas told them. "It's a miracle that you've come all the way here to see me."

A miracle? Good, good Thomas, you really have no idea how much of a miracle all this is . . . .

We looked at him sweetly, my fellow angelic impostors and I, knowing how much he wanted to be with children, thankful that we could give him that momentary little pleasure, though, for him, it was not so inconsequential.

As he smiled at the half dozen of us, Thomas asked, in his ignorance, "Are you all from town?"

We said nothing.

Not the town to which you refer, Thomas. We come from a city, an extraordinary city. You'll be there soon, old man, very soon....

Thomas became weak just then, and had to sit down at the same old desk he had been using for over half a century.

"Forgive me, my young friends, but I feel my age suddenly," he acknowledged. "It means so much to me, though, that you all are here with me. What a blessing you are! Do you know that?"

He started to hang his head, finding little strength to do anything else.

Thomas . . .

He turned to say something to the children.

The others were gone, on to other missions, and with my gratitude that they had taken the time to help out, but not me, for I had to remain a short while longer, though I continued to be without visibility to his sight.

They were gone.

He scratched his head.

"Am I losing my mind?" he said.

No, Thomas, you are not.

He cocked his head.

"Is someone there?" he asked.

He looked momentarily at the familiar surroundings, the search light, the curving steps leading down to the base of the lighthouse, and detected, as so often over time, the odor of carved wood, salt air coming through an open window. He breathed in deeply.

Pain gripped his chest again.

He got to his feet, and walked falteringly down the stairs, and then stepped outside.

No children. Just the bare landscape, every rock familiar to him.

He could no longer stand.

Thomas did not feel the impact as his body hit the hard ground.

Everything—the cloudless sky, the old lighthouse, the tiny cottage a short distance away—was spinning in his vision.

"Oh, Lord, is this that moment?" he whispered.

I assumed the form of a small child again and reached out and touched Thomas on the cheek.

He looked into my face.

"You're not really a child, are you?" Thomas asked with wisdom, his expression knowing.

"No, I am not."

"Will there be any children where I am going?"

"We all are children, Thomas," I spoke with warmth, tenderly, to this dying old man. "We all come to our Heavenly Father in the utter simplicity of our faith and pledge to serve Him throughout eternity. Is that not the way, my friend, that things were meant to be?"

Thomas smiled then, the last smile of his life, as he said somewhat tremulously, "Can I see you as you are?"

I gave him that privilege.

"Where is Amy?" Thomas asked, the last words of his life.

Thomas, my beloved, you have come at last!

I stepped aside as the scent of Chantilly and the laughter of children filled the air.

Sixteen

I think a lot about animals. I have seen them transform humans into wonderful beings—and I have seen them horribly abused at the hands of the very ones they long to love them. They do not deserve that of which they often find themselves the object, whether in laboratories or city streets or wherever it is that cruelty is inflicted upon them, cruelty elevated to the so-called service of mankind or, simply, the blind and stupid cruelty from children who delight in hearing their victims scream.

These are the obvious manifestations of cruelty, that to which many human beings would raise their voices in protest, cruelty deemed by the media as newsworthy from time to time, especially if some radical group with placards happens to be involved.

And then there are others, occurring daily in every community across the nation, this nation, and others as well.

Simple cruelties, perhaps, but no less hurtful, no less cruel.

Love. Love and concern are the catalysts to everything good and pure for most animals, especially the everyday kind.

Having a dog or a cat "around," without allowing it to participate, keeping it "outside," to which I might add, in more ways than one, forcing the animal to live without being totally loved, which is the ultimate cruelty, it seems to me.

Having without giving.

Animals are meant to love, and to be loved in return. Consider the elderly comforted by their presence, bereft of human companionship but surrounded by the love of a special friend, the purest love—that is the truth of it, you know, love so pure, so dedicated, so unquestioning and total that it stands second only to the love of God Himself, a hint of the love that mandated Calvary, love with total abandon and sacrifice, love filtered through the gaze of gentle brown eyes or the touch of a pink tongue, giving the slightest hint of the love that suffuses the distant corners of Heaven itself, love without spot or wrinkle or, even, motivation except to love.

Sitting there, looking up, eyes wide, body swaying ever so slightly from side to side, almost unnoticeably perhaps, eyes closing a bit, then opening, then—

Human beings love animals, and animals respond with themselves, until the end of their days. On the other hand, God loves human beings, and human beings so often respond with nothing but their rebellion, their rebuke, their sin flung back into the face of the Almighty.

In such instances, which is the lesser creation?

～⚭～

Not the collie. Not this one. All it wanted was to be accepted. All it wanted was to be part of their family. They took him in, true, but only into their home. Their hearts remained closed.

It was the thing to do. In an age of concern for the environment, an age of animal rights activism, they had a pet. They fed him well. They gave him a clean place to rest. When he wanted attention, when he wanted them, they couldn't be bothered, and turned their backs.

I communicate with animals, you know. I perceive their thoughts. I cannot do this with human beings because the minds of mankind have been off limits for a very long time, a netherworld into which Satan often intrudes—no, that is wrong, in which he often ventures as an invited guest—and yet God, Jehovah, the Almighty, the King of Kings, must wait until Satan is evicted because the two cannot reside together in the corridors of the subconscious.

The collie . . .

So grand, so devoted, so ignored.

I could perceive his confusion. I knew his question: I must not be loving them enough. Could that be it?

I wish I could tell this splendid creature that it had nothing to do with him, but I cannot. I feel impotent, then, often.

. . . not loving them enough.

Oh, never, you are their friend, their companion, their loyal one, though they are too busy among themselves to know it.

There was a blizzard that year. The youngest member of the family was caught out in it, not far from their house.

He got confused, his seven year old mind unsure of the direction in which to turn in order to go back home.

He wandered farther and farther away.

By the time the rest of the family was aware of what had happened, the blizzard was so fierce they couldn't get outside. They had to wait until the severity of it lessened.

The boy's mother was hysterical, certain that her son would be dead when they found him.

Hours later, the snow stopped altogether. The boy's parents threw on their heavy coats and hurried outside.

Over a mile away, they found their son, curled up inside the collie's embrace, in fact, so completely that they thought they had found the collie but not the boy.

They grabbed their son, and started off back toward the house. The father stopped, tears coming to his eyes, and turned back, bending over the nearly dead animal. Then he picked it up and carried it toward home.

The collie looked at him for a moment, eyes wide, heart beating faster, licking his hand several times, and asking—I know, I heard him—asking without words, but certain of a response from grateful parents—Do you love me? Do you love me now?

Seventeen

I want to pause for a moment. No, that is not quite right. The word is not want. The word is must. These poignant moments, tears and joy mixed together, these moments being spoken for those who will soon journey from the new Heaven to the new earth, these are preferable to the ones of battle. Spiritual warfare is that, very, very much that—fallen meeting unfallen in the heavenlies and, often, on earth itself. Oh, it happens, it happens often, former comrades contesting against one another for victory. Satan's plan is a multi-layered one, battles in human hearts and souls, battles between nations, battles among the stars, the astronomers seeing what they do not realize they are seeing, an explosion, a flash of light distant through the lens of multi-million-dollar instruments—not a world, like they say . . . something else, collision between evil and divine.

When my Creator has needed me, I have joined Gabriel and the others, out there, standing up to the forces of darkness—but, also, back on earth where the battle is not so spectacular, not between worlds, not amongst the stars, but in awful places, dark alleys, smoke-filled bars, theatres with flickering, obscene images, battles just the same, requiring warriors just the same . . . .

Warrior angels.

Gabriel is one. Michael another.

And sometimes Stedfast. Yes, sometimes me.

What is wonderful, truly so, is that the warriors are often able to minister as well. They go from their battles against forces of darkness, during these occasions, leaving the tumult behind, and perhaps quietly enter the room of a dying child, taking that little one into the Father's presence.

I remember once when Gabriel had just finished defending a group of Christians in Haiti. All the terrors of Satanic voodoo had been called against them, and he was summoned to vanquish the demonic entities. When that was accomplished, he learned that his next mission was helping some Kurdish refugees in Iraq after the government there had violated yet another international guarantee of protection.

"They're starving, Stedfast," he told me just before leaving on that next journey. "They are sick, dying, their bodies dropping by the roadside. Satan is getting at them through their Islamic fundamentalism. They have no hedge of protection. Yet, while what they believe is heretical, I must at least try!"

Gabriel was in great anguish.

"Oh, Stedfast, how I yearn for that day . . ." he said wearily.

"Yes, I know," I replied, "that day when all this will be over. The war will have been won, and our battles far, far behind us."

He was gone, then, off to the Middle East as a ministering angel— after that, surely the role of a warrior was again waiting for him.

I stood watching him leave, proud of my friend, and I realized what I did not often admit.

He yearned to minister.

I yearned to fight.

In those words should be taken no hint of rebellion against the will of Almighty God. I think, in such moments, that it amounts to something else. I minister because demons have caused pain. I minister because of the sin and the corruption that their master—and he and they are one, just as God and the rest of us are one—has propagated since Eden, because of Eden. I see tears. I see faces contorted with the effects of disease. I see people dragged off to Hell by his debased puppets.

And I want to strike a blow against my former comrade in Heaven. I want to stand before the collective demonkind and shout, "Enough! I am a gentle angel, I dry tears and sing away the pain, and give light to those in darkness—but now I am in battle mode. Now I am as fierce as any warrior in the rest of God's army. And I declare that you shall not gain victory this time!"

. . . our battles far, far behind us.

Sometimes those words are uttered in anticipated relief as my kind grows weary. Sometimes those words are uttered for an altogether different reason, as we emerge from the cesspool of evil deeds into which we must plunge on our various odysseys and are consumed by a passion, a passion not simply to minister to the victims but to strike back at the foul beings responsible.

I change when I go into battle.

I change a great deal.

I am no longer gentle. My kindness is a casualty. I am not seeking to ease suffering. I am committed, in a sense, to inflicting it upon those who brought the necessity of all this into a once-perfect universe, a suffering awaiting them that is of far greater consequence than anything they had been responsible for showering upon mankind.

Is that possible?

The world itself has been called Hell of a kind. And those who view it as such cannot be thought to be irrational, for they are correct. Can there be any other description that does justice to what is visible before one's very eyes—if those eyes have not been blinded by the master of deception?

I see, and I become angry, and, often, that is that. Then I move on to the task at hand, doing what I can to ease the pain of a hundred million demonized lives. That number is a modest one, considering the billions alive on this planet.

But I am not alone. There are other unfallen ones such as myself. Sometimes we meet on our journey. We communicate and commiserate and anticipate the new Heaven, the new earth.

∽⦿∾

"No more tears!" Samaritan told me once, thinking of what was to be. "No more absorbing their suffering into our very beings so that we can become better able to do what has been our mission for so very long."

The eyes confused . . .the flies landing on parts of the tiny body, the parts where there was more flesh than bones . . .the stomach puffing up with gases, poisons, disease. . . the last cry, "Yamma, yamma!"

"Yes, good comrade," I replied to this special angel, my thoughts becoming verbal. "And what you say is especially sad when it involves the hunger of a dying, malnourished, quite innocent baby."

"Ah, you are thinking of Ethiopia."

"No, I am thinking of the Sudan. I have not been there, but I have heard the reports about what happened."

"Of course! The Muslim leaders decreeing genocide for people in the southern part of the country."

"Simply because those people are not Islamic fundamentalists."

"A sad and terrible situation it is," Samaritan acknowledges. "I have been there with some of the babies, Stedfast."

"I did not know," I told him, with deepest empathy.   "You must have faced such devastating sorrow."

"It weighs so heavily on me, Stedfast. Would you be at all willing to listen, my friend?"

"Of course, I would," I said, sensing his need to talk at that moment. "Please . . .go ahead."

"They are so confused. Their mothers cannot provide for them. Their fathers as well are impotent in this regard. So they lay back on the warm sand, and insects gorge on their blood, and the days stretch on and on until-"

Oh, how they change when they see me! There is a smile on each face, faint at first because they are still trapped in a ravaged body of flesh. But gradually the flesh is shed, the smile is broader, deeper, more wonderful. There is peace within it, lighting up their countenance. I extend my hand, and each one of the children takes it in his own, and one by one I lift them to Heaven, I lift them into their Father's presence, and He looks at me, and says the words that I treasure so much, so much. He says to me, "Well done, thou good and faithful servant."

"Oh, Stedfast," Samaritan continued. "We are hardly empty will-of-the-wisp phantoms, just flukes of nature, as some will say—the unbelievers, you know—we are so much more."

I looked at him, and knew that this moment would soon pass, and the Father's enabling strength once again would take over. But then—then, Samaritan seemed more like a human child, looking out at the world around him, seeing the evil, the darkness., and not wanting to step out into it.

"As I go from one bedside to another," my friend said, "one battlefield to the next—and not always a battlefield of rockets and tanks . . ."

"—but one of the soul?" I offered.

"Yes, of the soul, often enough, it is truly that—and I am dealing with a teenager who is about to stick yet another needle into yet another vein, and he is desperately searching for one that has not collapsed . . . and . . . and I whisper to that soul, I whisper, 'Stop, stop, you must stop,' and he hesitates, and I think I may be gaining a victory, Stedfast, I may be the Master's instrument in keeping that soul from the flames. But then the needle is plunged into the flesh yet again, the victim's eyes close, fleeting ecstasy filling his body, while bringing him yet closer to death, to Hell. They are so blind—Stedfast, they are so blind, and I have failed yet again!"

It is not difficult for us to be concerned with failure, and it is not difficult for us to think that the failure is our own.

It is not.

It is not the Father's.

Failure comes through the choices made by men and women every second of every hour of all the time of history.

People fail. Divinity does not.

Judas was the betrayer of Christ. Christ was not the one to sell him for thirty pieces of silver.

We know this, the other unfallen and I. We know it very well. And we know that when a soul goes off, screaming, to Hell, we are not to blame.

But we feel it, you know. We feel as though we have failed without ever having failed at all. A single question rears up at us: Were we not wise enough, strong enough, present enough to do something?

Yet there is one source of consolation for us. Humans have other humans, they have family, they have friends, they have clergymen, they have so many sources of comfort and encouragement.

But not us, not the angels who refused to rebel.

We have one source of consolation.

I smile whenever I think of that, whenever the demonic gloom threatens to overwhelm even me, unfallen that I am.

I smile because of what we have, because of where we obtain that which we all do need.

Where, yea . . . and from Whom.

How could we, ever, ask for more?

Seventeen

Rob me not of my joy . . . .

There are people who delight, it would seem, in taking joy from others and grinding it as dust at their feet. They live miserably themselves. They have seldom experienced a lightness of heart that lifts the spirit to levels of sublime fulfillment that are a glimmer of what is awaiting any who accept Christ as Savior and Lord, and, thereby, gain entrance into Heaven where there is joy unbounded, unencumbered by the sorrows of the flesh, by the twists and turns of moods that afflict every human being at one time or another.

For such individuals, those twists and turns are not from happiness into despair but, rather, from depression into greater depression, from a melancholic outlook on life to one that is near suicidal.

They seem to be saying, I am not happy, therefore, I won't allow those around me to be happy. I will enrage them, offend them, disturb them in any way I can, because in a perverse and awful way, I derive some modicum of pleasure from THAT!

When people of such disposition are by themselves, at least the rest of the world can distance itself from them, as it usually tries to do. But when they are in a temporarily pleasant mood, and they meet a member of the opposite sex, and there is, soon, a marriage, with some children later, it seems that joy has supplanted the dark side of their nature or perhaps, held it at bay.

Not for long.

I tried very hard to help one such individual, a man who was a prominent and talented attorney for the public defender's office. I on the outside tried to do so in concert with the Holy Spirit on the inside—and, yes, let me interject, what I have just mentioned is surprising. Can a Christian, with the Holy Spirit indwelling him, ever be so dismal a person as this one? How is that possible? Shouldn't the joy of the Lord be on the throne of his life, displacing all else?

The Holy Spirit has taken up residence in Albert, but He is not in control. This member of the Trinity is a boarder. He rents a room, He has the key to the front door, but that is that. Albert's sin nature still holds the deed, still pays the bills.

You see the validity of my analogy?

While Albert was indeed a Christian, he seldom proved a proper witness. Oh, theologically he might have held his own, he might have been able to defend the faith in corridors of intellect, perhaps. But where everyday living came into play, he was at best inept, at worst someone who repelled others from the faith.

Including his wife. His son. His daughter.

"Why do you think so ill of everyone?" his wife would often ask. "There are some good people left in this world. Not everyone is out to commit a crime of some sort, against you or another."

Albert's reaction to the latter point was understandably shaped by his days in court.

. . . not everyone is out to commit a crime of some sort.

"Are you so sure?" he would reply. "Can you be certain that there is not the psyche of a criminal in each one of us? The Bible calls it our sin nature. How can you dispute that?"

Yesterday he came to the end of a trial during which he defended a man guilty of murder. He was so good, so clever. He succeeded in getting his client acquitted. That man is now free, and may kill again, not stopping at one more victim. Albert, hired to see that justice was served, perpetuated infamy. Where is the justice in that?

"But there are good people, good deeds in Scripture in addition to those that illustrate what you suggest," his wife retorted. "Consider one of the thieves on that cross next to Christ. He repented. The Lord recognized this, and accepted him into the Kingdom."

"That thief had little choice. After all, he was at the end of his life. He might as well have."

"What about the Good Samaritan?"

"What about those who ignored the man that he eventually helped? Their number was greater."

"The apostles gave up everything for Jesus."

"Peter was certainly an apostle. Look at his threefold denial that he even knew his Master."

"But he wasn't a criminal," she pointed out.

"You're right. He was instead a coward. Is that necessarily better?" Albert replied. "A coward in battle can cause the deaths of his own comrades. So in reality, isn't such a man no more than a murderer as well?"

She became exasperated, as usual, unable to talk any longer, unable to break through to the man she loved.

Eventually she left him, along with his son, his daughter.

Months became years. Albert never remarried. But he went on to become a nationally known attorney. More often than not, he was assigned to defend serial killers, mafioso dons, discredited political figures, and many others of that caliber—though, judging by numbers, these types comprised the smallest number of his clients.

It might have been deemed inevitable that his personal outlook would become even more cynical than it was. Could it have been otherwise?

Yes . . .

Albert could have refused cases involving criminals, those where no doubt existed in his mind that such men were not interested in justice as much as in manipulating the justice system. They merely wanted Albert to see to it that they would either never be punished for their crimes or, at least, get a much lighter sentence.

Justice has a price, he would tell himself again and again. It is yet another commodity in this country, available to people with money and clever attorneys.

The spillover from Albert's courtroom behavior crept more and more into his personal life. Though a Christian, he got further and further away from anything resembling a strong, Christ-centered testimony. The ethics of many of his clients subliminally worked their way into his own makeup. He discovered that he could make more money leaving the public defender's office and hanging out his own shingle. Soon Albert found himself catering more and more to these high-paying but questionable characters.

It was only a matter of time before Albert ended up being on trial himself.

For extortion.

It involved one of his corporate clients. A less polite word would have been blackmail.

He lost that case.

And he was imprisoned for five years.

Finally, after being released, he went back to a life that could not be reconstructed the way it had been. Though barred from ever practicing law again, Albert was far from being penniless. He had no financial worries.

But he had no one.

No, that wasn't quite right. The people he associated with were like those he had been with in prison, the same type, but not behind bars, men and women pursuing their schemes in absolute disregard of ethics and morality.

I am a Christian, he told himself one afternoon. I indeed AM a Christian. So what am I doing with the swine, instead of being in the Master's house?

He had fallen to the very bottom of the abyss in his soul, and he no longer could tolerate the cold despair.

My wife, my children, he thought. Surely I can go back to them. They will greet me with love, despite all that has happened.

But he had to find them. He hadn't had any contact with them for five years.

It took him several weeks.

But he did find his wife, his son, his daughter.

He found the grave where his wife had been buried. She had committed suicide. She had become infested with his own outlook, and this was spread to their children. When both turned to drugs, she could not endure the struggle to keep the remaining part of the family together, so she split it apart forever.

. . . beyond redemption.

No individual is beyond redemption until the moment he dies, because he has until then to stop rejecting Jesus Christ as Savior and Lord, and, finally, to accept Him into his very soul. But some relationships cannot truly be redeemed. They have become buried, suffocated under a pile of harsh words and unfortunate acts. There is nothing that can be done to resurrect them, except by a miracle of the Holy Spirit.

That did not happen with Albert.

His wife was buried, and he stood before the tombstone on which had been carved her name.

I dug your grave myself, he admitted. I placed you in it just as surely as if I—

He remembered her face when she could still tolerate the sight of him. He enjoyed the feeling of her hair through his fingers.

Now . . . now only the children were left.

He knew he had to find them.

He did.

But what he found showed him the bankruptcy of the way he had been living. He found his son and his daughter in the same drug rehabilitation center.

"They are among the toughest cases we've ever encountered," one of the doctors told him.

"But why?" Albert asked plaintively, still not quite comprehending.

The two men were standing in a corridor.

"Would you come with me to my office, please?" the doctor asked.

Albert followed him. A few doors down the corridor, they stepped into the doctor's well appointed, wood-panelled office.

After both were sitting down, the doctor looked quite seriously at Albert and said, "You see, they feel there is no hope for them."

"But what were they looking for in drugs?"

"Not hope, sir."

"What could it have been?"

"Oblivion."

Albert leaned back in the chair, his hands starting to tremble.

"But they had so much," he said, "nothing but luxury from the moment they were born."

"A fine suit of clothes is worthless if the one who wears it is filled with pain." the doctor said.

"Because of me—that's it, isn't it?" Albert guessed.

The doctor nodded sadly.

"Look at what you are," he said. "You have already admitted becoming like the clients you represented, absorbing their values, their outlook. Is it so impossible to understand that this is precisely what happened with your own children?"

"I don't know what you—"

"Forgive me, but I have to be frank, however difficult this will be for you. According to your children, if you saw a sunny day, you would wonder how long it would last, rather than be grateful for its warmth, its light at that moment. If you earned a six-figure salary one year, you would worry about the next, hoping your income wouldn't drop. If you—"

"— if I read of Heaven, I would worry about Hell. If I saw a smile on their mother's face, I would be consumed with the fear that an hour later there might be pain on it."

"Exactly what I am trying to tell you, sir."

"But there are good people, good deeds in Scripture in addition to those that illustrate what you suggest.'" his wife retorted, "Consider one of the thieves on that cross next to Christ. He repented. The Lord recognized this, and accepted him into the Kingdom."

"That thief had little choice. After all, he was at the end of his life. He might as well have."

"What about the Good Samaritan?"

"What about those who ignored the man that he eventually helped? Their number was greater."

Albert glanced at the doctor.

"Rob me not of my joy," he said.

"That is surely appropriate. Who said it?"

"I did."

"You?"

"Yes, I wrote it during my college years."

"Why?"

"Because everything was going so well. And I became worried—"

"Dominated perhaps?"

"Yes, that's more accurate. I became dominated by the fear that my joy would slip away between my fingers like tiny grains of sand."

"And you guaranteed that that would be so by making it a selffulfilling prophecy."

"My wife, my children," Albert sobbed, "sacrificed at the altar of my own insecurities."

"And from those insecurities were born a life-view that placed trust in no one, that portrayed everyone as evil."

"The Bible says that is so."

"How easily you raise your Christianity before me when it is convenient, sir."

"But it is what I believe."

"No, what you believe, sir, is not true Christianity. You accept the evil of others, while ignoring the possibility of their redemption. You have accepted it for yourself while denying its validity for others."

"You cannot compare me to the swine that I have represented."

"Consider this: How many of them, the swine to which you refer, and accurately, I suspect, have wives who remain loyal to them, have children who are loving and have never taken drugs, and who eagerly await the opportunity each day to welcome their fathers home?"

"I don't see the point," Albert said.

"That you don't is the point, sir."

. . . wives who remain loyal . . . children who are loving.

He had seen the point, yes, but he pushed it aside, not quite able to deal with it, not wanting to face even more pain.

"But how can they, being evil, send forth good fruit?" Albert mused.

"No one is completely evil."

"You speak as a Christian."

"I am a Christian."

"How is it possible that a mobster who may have been responsible for the death of dozens of human beings, how is it possible for such an individual to be worthy of anything but condemnation?"

"When it comes to family, when it comes to those depending upon him for his unfettered love, such a man was more worthy, sir, than you. What is the value of the gift of prophecy or tongues or teaching or any such gift if there is no love?"

"It is empty, it is cold, it is stale, it is—"

Albert could not go on.

"You did give them yourself," the doctor went on, "but it was that part of yourself that you would now like to exorcise . . . ."

Albert continued his silence.

"Do you wish to see your children?" the doctor asked after several minutes.

My children . . .

"Do you really want to see them?" the doctor added.

I must. I must tell them how sorry I am. I must tell them that I love them, that I love with every bit of my mind, my heart, my very soul.

"Yes . . ." Albert said.

The doctor stood, and Albert followed him. The children, Martin and Julienne, now teenagers, were in a special section of the hospital.

"Constant care," the doctor said.

"Constant?"

"Oh, yes. We could keep them in straitjackets continually, but that has its limitations. So we stay with them nearly every moment."

"But why? They're both locked up, aren't they?"

"You have no idea how violent they can become."

"Violent!" Albert started. "Even my little daughter?"

"Neither of your offspring is little anymore."

It has been a very long time, Albert, I whispered in my wordless way, the Holy Spirit prodding him to listen through his emotions, through a tap on his soul, a gentle touch saying, Try to understand. Try to—

"But you can help them, right?" Albert asked confidently.

The doctor shook his head.

"Neither will ever be anything more than a ticking human bomb, set to explode at the slightest provocation. Their brain cells have been severely affected by the years of drug abuse. And I'm afraid it won't get better. Brain cells cannot regenerate as others in the body can."

Albert's shoulders drooped. His voice shook as he asked, "You're saying they're doomed?"

"I would like to be able to put it in a gentler fashion, sir, but that is exactly what this amounts to, I'm afraid."

Albert felt perspiration covering his body.

I'm a Christian, Lord, how could this have happened? He whispered to the air around him.

That was my chance! He had reached out.

Because you have Christ as Savior, but not Lord!

He could not hear me in the normal sense. But he could sense something, something nudging his conscience, the Holy Spirit and I together in this. Albert could still be put under conviction, moment by moment by moment.

And he listened, to me, to the Spirit, inside himself.

Yet it seemed too late for his children, too late for their flesh-and-blood bodies as well as their souls. Surely he had lost them, lost them forever. He was convinced of this as soon as he saw his son, and then his daughter.

They were just human shells. They could barely speak. All over the visible parts of their bodies, the flesh had sunk in pathetically where the veins had collapsed from constant puncturing, from the unholy wrenching demands of injection after injection, always a search for a fresh vein, a vein that could still do the job their addiction had forced upon them.

They had escaped AIDS, and that seemed a miracle in itself—but AIDS, as nightmarish as it was, could not have ravaged them any more than had been the case already by other means.

So thin.

Albert reached out to touch his daughter's cheek. She pulled back in that padded cell of hers and screamed at him.

"Don't!" she said. "It's so sore, Father, Father, it's so very sore. I couldn't stand anyone—"

Father! Father!

Albert rejoiced that she recognized him.

But then he heard the other words coming from her.

"—touching me. Please stop this man, whoever he is. You promised to help me whenever I needed you. Get this man out of here!"

Albert left, and went down the corridor to his son's room, which also was padded. The boy did not move when he entered.

There was no indication that he even knew he had a visitor. He just stayed on the floor in a fetal position, as though he were dead already.

"Son, son, I never knew what I was doing to you," Albert said, barely able to speak for the emotion that had been building up. "I was so concerned about the pain of life, the rotten people, the corruption—I could never give to you any joy because I did not have it myself. There was nothing but venom, nothing but hatred, nothing but suspicions, nothing but the darkness."

His son's eyes opened for just a moment, only that, and he turned to his father and asked, "But, Dad, the light—what about the light?"

And then he fell back into that inner world that had captured him so completely.

Albert thanked the doctor and left, stepping outside the hospital.

What about the light?

He sat down on a bench on the front lawn and bowed his head.

"They're headed for Hell because of me," he said out loud, weeping at the same time. "They're lost forever now."

A voice intruded.

"Sir, forgive me for this, but I think it is more correct to say that nobody's lost until God says that they are. Wouldn't you agree with that?"

Albert looked up.

No old man. No wavering phantom.

A beautiful red-haired nurse.

"I'm . . . I'm sorry," Albert said, his face nearly the color of her hair.

"That's all right," she replied. "Tears are cleansing."

"There's just so much sorrow in life."

"But that isn't all. You've got to realize that. You've got to grab hold of what is good and decent and loving and never let go."

"But my kids . . . they're here. They're dying."

"You don't know that for certain."

"But they look so pale, so weak."

"So does a neglected flower until it is watered. Your young ones are thirsty, sir, thirsty for your love. God loved you enough to give you the gift of salvation through the sacrifice of His beloved Son. You accepted this a long time ago. Why do you turn your back on the rest?"

"You mean the peace that passes understanding, that sort of thing?"

"I do. Exactly that."

"If only I could—"

"Your life had too many 'if onlys.' Give up this one. Banish it. Tell yourself, 'I can go back. I can stand with my loved ones. I can be the Lord's instrument for whatever He hungers to give to them.' "

"If only-" Albert repeated, out of habit.

"No more!" the nurse told him, undoubtedly louder than intended.

"You really believe it's not too late?"

"I know it isn't. Go, sir! Give them yourself, that loving side of you. Wipe away their tears. Tell your son about the light. Tell him, sir. Tell him about the light of the world. Leave the darkness in our Father's hands."

Albert nodded, stood, thanked the nurse, and turned toward the hospital.

. . . tell your son about the light.

"Hey, how did you—?"

He spun around.

But I was gone.

Ultimately there was victory, even in such a hard and stubborn soul. And that is something over which we all rejoice.

But another of my encounters during my odyssey shows victory of another sort, victory that is as wonderful, as touching, as grand as any I can remember . . . .

Eighteen

Craig wanted to be in the Olympics as a pole-vaulter. He had dreamed of this ever since he was a small boy.

"I pray that the Lord will make me strong enough," he said again and again to anyone who would listen. "I'm working on my legs. My arms are pretty good, but my legs need some work."

The family garage had been converted into a gym. Craig was there every day, after school and on weekends. By the time he had become a teenager, he had managed to break away on occasion, make some friends through social activities, go on a few dates—but, always, the primary focus had to be his physical conditioning. Few other activities could be allowed to intrude.

While pole-vaulting was the center of his attention, Craig proved to be a top athlete in two other areas of high school competition: wrestling and basketball. Even though he was a bit short, he nevertheless did well because he had a special characteristic that some of his many Jewish friends described rather colorfully in Yiddish.

Craig was young, good-looking, strong, popular. He had many opportunities for witnessing for Christ.

This young man was what I would have wanted to be if I had been of flesh and blood.

I was assigned to stay with Craig during those final months of his life. That sounds sudden, to say it like that, yes, I know that it does, but the Holy Spirit felt that this young man would be particularly sensitive to demonic oppression since he had been given so much in his life, and it seemed that the tragedy, from a human standpoint, that occurred had the potential to peel away some part of his faithfulness like a movie studio facade.

Satan did attack. He did not assign any of his demons. He wanted to devastate this young man directly, without any puppets, heaping discouragement on him, trying to break his will, waiting for a fist raised against Almighty God. He would fail, this leader of the fallen ones, he would fail, and yet he would not stop trying, no matter how often he was rebuked.

Craig was diagnosed as having a particularly severe bone disease. In time there would be not only pain but something else, a byproduct as much of drug treatment as the disease itself.

Craig's bones would lose their firmness. They would become almost elastic, like somewhat hardened rubber bands, and when they could no longer support his body, he would die.

One week before that happened, Craig spoke at his high school commencement ceremony. He was too weak for crutches. There was no wheelchair to carry him up to the podium.

A sack.

Oh, it was a bit more elaborate than that, but it still could be accurately described as a sack. His father and mother carried Craig in it, and then, when they reached the podium, as three thousand students and family members were seated inside the auditorium, his father held his son's head up so that it wouldn't flop to one side, like a rag doll. Craig spoke, his voice so weak that the sound system had to be turned up nearly to full volume.

"I love Jesus!" he said. "I love Him as much now as when I first accepted Him as my Savior, my Lord. He wanted all of me: my mind, my body, my soul. I don't have much of a body to give Him now—"

As tears started to stream down his cheeks, and his father's and mother's, rugged football heroes and geeks and cheerleaders and a very tough principal and every teacher in the school shed their own.

"—but I won't have this for long, you know," Craig continued. "It's gonna go. I'll discard it like the useless thing it's become. And you know what? The Lord has promised me a replacement, one better than the original, because never again will I have to face disease or pain or even a cold. All that will be in the past, over, ended, finished forever!"

There was surprising strength in his voice then. The microphone let out a high-pitched squeal.

"Don't go sobbing around about how all this could happen, me a Christian and all. I never made it to the Olympics, but I think—"

He turned his head slightly, trying to whisper something to his father. The words came through the microphone, "Dad, will you wipe my eyes for me?"

As he faced the audience again, Craig was smiling.

"—I know that I will be doing something better in His

kingdom. I will run without getting tired. I will jump as high as—"

He just couldn't stop the tears, he just couldn't, and he was terribly embarrassed that this was so, yet through the emotion, the remaining words somehow came through.

"as . . . high . . . as . . . the . . . stars!"

Craig had no strength left after that. His parents carried him off the podium, and down the center aisle. Before the three of them had gotten past the first row, the entire audience stood and applauded. One girl broke away from the rest and hurried to the piano on stage, and sat before it, and started playing, "On Christ the Solid Rock I Stand." Those in the audience who knew the words, and not many of them did, sang along with her, those who didn't hummed the melody.

Craig asked that they stop for a few seconds before leaving the auditorium altogether. He whispered something into his mother's ear.

She turned toward the gathered faculty and students, and, raising her voice through her own tears, she said, "My son wants me to tell you that he loves you all."

She brought a hand to her mouth, her own strength wavering, and in her mind she said, over and over, precious Jesus, precious Jesus, help me now, dear, dear Lord, help me!

She lowered that hand, and tilted her head back slightly as she added, "Because Christ first loved him! And . . . and Craig has tried so hard to share that love with others."

Satan was there, though no one knew it except me. He stood at the entrance to the large auditorium, his wings drooping, his head tilted sadly to one side.

"You could have inspired acts like that, if you had not done all that you have done over the centuries of time," I reminded my former comrade.

"I know, Stedfast, I know," he replied.

"Can you offer anything that comes even close to what that one frail young man has done?"

Satan the Deceiver turned and looked at me, an expression of regret and shame on his repulsive face.

"You are so beautiful," he said with surprising softness.

"As you once were. The ugliness is of your own making."

He shrugged, layers of pus and slime shaken from his awful countenance, and then he went outside, observing the teenager's parents as they carefully put him in the back seat of the family sedan.

"I wanted him, Stedfast," Satan admitted. "I wanted to tear him apart, and feast on him in Hell."

"You lost," I said. "This one rejected your doctrine of hate, and surrounded himself with love."

"Yes . . . as with so many others, Stedfast . . . so many."

And then Lucifer the once—Magnificent was gone from that place.

～◈～

That was on a Friday. By Wednesday of the next week, Craig's earthly life had ended. He died at home, in his room, the walls lined with photographs and certificates, the shelves stuffed with trophies. Every empty spot was filled with flowers.

One arrangement had come from his coach. On the card attached to it was a brief message: "Dear Craig, please forgive me for pushing you so hard."

Craig's mother, at his request, wrote a note back to the man. It read, simply: "No harder than the Lord, sir. God bless you . . . ."

People were camped outside on the front lawn, and on the walkway leading up to the front door. Only his parents were in his room with him when his spirit soared.

And I.

He was mumbling briefly, nothing that they could understand, but I heard his words fully.

"There really isn't any pain, is there?" he asked, amazed that he was at last truly free of it.

"None at all," I told this remarkable young man. "Pain is of the flesh, banished as the spirit takes over for those—"

"Jesus," he said, only a breath or two left.

Waiting for him at the gates.

"My Lord," he said. "He's holding something. It . . . it looks like—"

"Go to Him, Craig," I said with joy. "Gather your new strong legs and jump."

He did, always the athlete, jumping without a pole to guide him, vaulting beyond the confines of corruptible flesh and blood and bone, and reaching for the flaming Olympic torch that his beloved Savior held out for him.

Nineteen

Adam and Eve were close to God before sin entered their lives. Every human being since then has been closer or further away from Him in direct proportion to the extent to which they let their sin nature hold sway. Never again will there be the kind of spiritual union that once existed in Eden, at least not until the new Heaven and earth—but, glimpses, yes, there will be glimpses of what once was, very muted, even nearly nonexistent, and every now and then, much stronger.

Mother Teresa can experience a closeness that is not shared by a Donald Trump. That may be stating the obvious, but it is indeed quite true. This is not because of her works, for true spirituality cannot be built on a works-oriented foundation. Rather, her spirituality comes from the redemptive faith that has motivated her to serve Him in the only way that she knows how. When she gets down on her knees and says to her Lord, "I am giving You all that I am, all that I have, all that I will ever be in the flesh, and yet I wish, dear Jesus, there was more that I could offer to You," she receives, in that moment, a glimpse of what once was in Eden.

Contrast that spirit of sacrifice with another sort of spirit altogether, a spirit that is rampant in the Body of Christ, a spirit that makes demands of Him—prosperity, health—a spirit that postulates the heresy that it is more important to maneuver Almighty God into serving the human race than His creations feeling compelled to serve Him.

We should please God so that He will give us the desires of our heart . . . .

I have heard that, oh, I have, though I would have wished that I had not. It is part of the gathering storm, a storm that will sweep over Christendom, that will subvert whole congregations, though some members still may be saved, that will add the symbol of the dollar to that of the cross, the two intertwined in the minds of many.

When I see the flash-and-dash of so much of what passes for Christian service by the leaders of the faith, I know that the Rapture is not far off. I know that my Creator cannot tolerate the travesties much longer, that He must take true believers out of a world, especially a Christian world, that threatens to collapse of its increasingly virulent hypocrisy, pulling all but the elect down in the process.

And I think of the children, especially the retarded children.

If the adults around them only knew . . . .

So often, retardation in one form or another is given as a justification for abortion. Slaughter the babies before they enter a world in which they will be miserable, in which they will inflict so much suffering on others, in addition to their own—for isn't that the kinder act in the long run, the more merciful, a few seconds of pain, perhaps, rather than ten or twenty years of shambling disability?

If a baby cannot possibly measure up to society's standards, then how can there be happiness?

And yet the proponents of this carnage deny intellectual elitism! They scoff at comparisons with the Aryan mentality of the Third Reich. But their very words condemn them. They say it stops at the unborn and cannot possibly be a forerunner to eradication of the elderly.

They lie . . . .

Severely retarded children cannot lie, you know. They cannot lust. They cannot murder, or steal. But, most striking of all, they cannot deny their Creator.

A body of twenty years that houses the brain of a small child is that of a human being forever without the will and, really, the opportunity to sin in ways that are acquired through the years of the lives of "normal" youngsters.

It is true that Scripture indicates human beings are born to sin or perhaps born into sin. But when there is severe retardation, that tendency to sin is blocked off.

No such youngsters can ever be reached by Satan or his emissaries. Oh, he has tried again and again, but he cannot get into their minds, their souls. He fails each and every time.

And for the most beautiful, the most wondrous of reasons.

If those who want to snuff out these children knew the truth, they would never be able to deal with the guilt.

The truth?

I said it was beautiful, I said it was wondrous.

It is, every bit that, every, every bit.

For you see, each retarded child is in a state quite similar to what Adam and Eve experienced in Eden—but even more blessed. Adam and Eve went on to sin. Those severely retarded simply do not have the capacity to do so. Perhaps they will seem to have a bit of temper, but it is actually more a sense of frustration than anything else.

They will never strike another human being. They will never kill or rob or maim or rape.

They cannot!

A retarded child would never have taken of the fruit of the tree of the knowledge of good and evil because—and this is the wondrous part—he would never have considered disobeying his Creator.

There is a why to this, a sublime why.

Ones such as these have a bond with Almighty God that no one else can approach. If sin is essentially separation from Him, then they have never been separated.

I have seen retarded children sitting by themselves, laughing. I have heard adults look at them with pity and say, "Poor child! He's off in a world of his own."

Precisely!

It is a different world, that it is.

They walk with angels. There is no barrier between us. Unlike the rest of mankind, they do not have to wait until they are dying.

They are not lonely.

They may be alone. They may sit quietly by themselves and seem to be looking into space. But they are not looking into nothingness.

They see . . . you see.

They see a great deal.

We give them glimpses, my kind and I. We give them glimpses of the new Eden, which will be the entire earth. We run a kind of cosmic movie projector and on a kind of cosmic screen we show them what will be. They see thinking, reasoning, handsome adults playing with lions, lions licking lambs, lambs without need of a shepherd because there is no longer any danger.

"Who is that?" some will ask.

"You, dear child," I or another will say.

"Me?" responds a tiny voice, with beautiful eyes flashing brightly.

"You," I tell the child. "You, as you were meant to be, as you will always be in that fine day."

Sometimes they cry. Sometimes they just sit, uncomprehending. Sometimes they are scared and they ask me to hold them, and I say that I cannot, not just yet.

I love having the privilege of escorting them to heaven. Even as they die, they reach out to father, mother, brother, sister, and they smile, nothing more than that, but enough it is, a smile of love, of joy, a smile that says as much as words themselves, "Thank you for loving me. Thank you for taking care of me. God will take over now."

I remember so many occasions when I would sit with a mentally handicapped child and talk with that sweetly innocent one about what awaits him in the new Heaven, the new Earth. Mentally handicapped, yes. Spiritually handicapped, no.

"You will sing," I said to one boy as he played quietly with another child.

"Mmmm," he hummed in the only way he knew how, in the only way he could, since he had never been able to speak more than that.

"You will stand before the hosts of Heaven, and you will sing a great ballad," I continued. "You will stand with your friend here, and the two of you will delight precious Jesus Himself."

His playmate was also retarded. In addition, she had been born without fingers on either of her hands.

Her eyes told me that she wanted to know what she would be doing there, by her friend's side.

"You will be playing a guitar," I told her, "right in the midst of a whole new existence, first in Heaven and then in Eden."

She understood, for she held up those fingerless hands and studied them, then started crying.

"Mmmm," the boy put his arm around her and their heads touched, temple-to-temple.

He wanted to say a great deal, but the confines of the flesh gave him no words.

These two would be among the children caught up in the Rapture, and would not see death. I know the moment. Angels are not given glimpses of everything by our Creator, but this one He allowed, this one indeed.

Home.

They would be in their family homes, not in an institution like so many other children of their sort. The boy would be sitting on his father's lap, his mother running her fingers through his soft golden hair.

"Mmmm," the boy would hum as usual.

But his parents would sense something different this time, for he knew sooner than they, his sweet, sweet Jesus even then leaving Heaven and coming to earth and reaching out His arms.

They would look at their child, and smile.

And they both would reach out and touch him, each a different cheek, feeling the so-soft skin.

"It's time, Mother," he would say, turning to his mother, and to his father, "It's time, Father," and then to the two of them, "Blessed Jesus is here."

At that moment, they would be the ones without words.

Only a block away, the little girl would be in her bedroom, her parents in the kitchen washing dishes. Jesus the Christ would call her first and give her the fingers she never had, and a brightly shining guitar, and she would use it without human training, and she would call to her parents by a melody all her own, and dishes would fall to the floor as her beloved ones were caught up to be with her, together, taken unto glory, with a robust voice instantly joining in, the voice of a dear young friend, the two of them singing and playing to the delight of all throughout eternity.

❧

Children . . .

The defenseless ones, subject to the desires of another generation, in or out of the womb.

Children reach out so often in their lives, for love, for help in dealing with pain, loneliness, hunger. What of the anguish of a starving mother who cannot give her starving child the food for which that child has been crying all day, all night, many days, many nights? The child knows little of this. The child simply reaches out for the only human being he or she can trust, and even though there is no food in return, even though there is no water, the child sinks back into that deep pit of suffering without blaming the mother, somehow sensing that she has done the very best she can, and there is no more which she can provide. At least—though no food, no liquid, nothing but slow death—the child has love.

But in countries where sustenance is not a problem, where there is plenty of meat and potatoes and beans, where there is plenty of clear, satisfying water—children still have other needs, the need to love, the need to belong, the need to laugh.

❧

The clown had brought joy to so many bright faces over the years.

Now, he had one more show that he wanted to make.

"I've spent my life out there," he told a friend who hovered over his bed. "I just can't leave this world without one final appearance under the big top."

His name was Sammy . . . Sammy the Clown.

He had given his life to his craft. He had embraced it mind, body, and soul. There was little else for him, little else he knew.

He was in the business of laughter.

He made little children laugh. He made their parents laugh. He brought joy to the sick and to the elderly.

He was the best clown there ever was, the most famous, the most loved.

And he was dying.

"I'm going to die in the center ring," he once told an interviewer for a midwestern newspaper. "The sawdust will be under me, the canvas will be above me, the smell of horses and elephants will fill my nostrils, and in the background I'll go out of this world on the laughter of the crowd."

"They will laugh at your death?" the other man asked.

"You don't understand. They'll think it's just part of the act because I'll be very funny even then."

Tears came to his eyes.

"I will miss it all so much," he admitted. "There can never be anything like what I do."

"You don't know what will await you on the other side," the other man pointed out. "Maybe it'll be something better."

"If there's anything at all. I may end up as nothing."

. . . as nothing.

Those words stayed in his mind, repeated in lonely moments after one stint closed and the circus moved on to another location somewhere else across the nation, times when he was looking out through a rain-streaked car window at the unfamiliar places through which he passed, at the strangers who walked by.

Sammy ran away from home when he was fourteen, and never saw his parents again. His brief marriage had failed miserably. But he still had a family. One brother was a dwarf. Another brother ate fire. One sister rode elephants. A third brother trained lions and tigers. Circus people—they were his brothers, his sisters.

"It's hard to believe," one had said years before.

"What's hard to believe?" Sammy had asked.

"That someday those often raging beasts will actually be resting side by side without a whip to tame them, or a sharp voice to direct them, and a lamb will wander by and see them, and sit down with them."

"You're dreaming!" Sammy scoffed.

"No, my friend, it's been promised."

"Who's the screwball who did that?"

The animal trainer looked at him sadly as he said, "Sammy, Sammy, Almighty God has promised this."

Sammy shrugged and walked off.

Sammy's version of Heaven was the big top. Sammy's version of Hell was anytime he didn't happen to be in a ring, performing.

The animal trainer would talk again and again with him about spiritual things, about redemption and damnation and the rest.

And always Sammy's reply would be along the same lines, if not in the same words, then in the meaning behind them.

"I've known Heaven, I've known Hell already," he would say. "Your religion can't give me a thing I've not experienced here and now."

"But, Sammy, you need to be prepared."

"You can't mean that! For something that is nothing more than a mere game played on the gullible? A few magician's tricks? You forget, I've been a magician as well. I just like being a clown better."

The animal trainer would walk away, shaking his head regretfully, praying for another opportunity to witness to this man.

And so it went.

Sammy had his circus, he had his family—the animal trainer, the dwarfs, the giant, the others. Most had been with him for decades.

There was no other life, as far as he was concerned.

But Sammy started to outlive them all.

One by one, his adopted brothers and his adopted sisters died. One by one, new faces replaced them, strangers with whom he felt not at all at ease. Then there were new owners. The circus became a business, it ceased being a way of life, as it had been to Sammy for more than fifty years.

Sammy was losing his heaven. The alternative for him was hell.

I've spent my life out there, he thought to himself as he struggled to sit up in his bed. I just can't leave this world without one final appearance under the big top.

And he made it.

The audience really enjoyed Sammy that night. As he finished, a six-year-old child broke away from her mother and ran up to him, and put her arms around his left leg, and hugged him.

"I love you," she murmured.

He picked her up and kissed her on the cheek, and then, after returning the child to her mother, he told the crowd that this was his farewell performance.

"Ladies and gentlemen, I am a very tired clown," he said. "This will be my last performance."

A gasp of shock arose from the onlookers, and a chorus started shouting, "No, no, no!"

He shook his head sadly, and added, "I wish you all were right. But, you see, my blood is messed up. It's because of years of breathing this sawdust. It's like the condition a coalminer gets. Sometimes it settles in the blood, sometimes in the lungs."

His shoulders slumped as he walked out of the centerring and toward the back of the tent to the secluded dressing areas.

The crowd forgot him soon enough, turning their fervent attention to the beautiful prancing ponies and their sequin-collared canine riders.

～ღ～

That night, after everyone else in the circus was asleep, Sammy found himself tossing and turning.

He slipped on a heavy robe, opened the creaky door to his trailer, and walked outside.

My last night . . .

He didn't know how he could tell that. It wasn't a premonition. The soon-to-die often feel the life force weakening somehow.

I startled him as I stood there, having assumed the form of a man every bit as old as Sammy himself.

"I . . . I mean . . . where did you come from?" he asked, his deeply-lined face pale in the moonlight.

"It's been quite a distance, Sammy," I told him.

"How is it, sir, that you know who I am?"

"I indeed know many things about you."

"But how could that be?"

"I've been with you more than you know, Sammy."

"Where? When? Stop these games!"

"I do not play games."

"Then answer me!"

"When you were divorced, Sammy. . . I was there."

"Did you work for the attorney?"

"No, Sammy, I worked for his boss."

"Oh . . ."

"You gave up your wife for the circus."

"I had been raised under the big top. What was I to do?"

"She tried to live the life you wanted, but she couldn't. She wasn't emotionally capable of shouldering the burdens you placed upon her."

"But she wanted me to give up everything I had ever known, everything I had grown up with!"

"As you wanted her to do."

"But she pledged in her marriage vows to let nothing separate us."

"Those were vows you took as well, Sammy."

He turned toward the huge tent.

"That has been my home for fifty years," he said. "How could I just—?"

"It is but a thing of painted canvas and rope and metal poles, Sammy. Nothing more than that."

"I've had my greatest triumphs in there."

"And you will carry its legacy to your grave."

He turned away from me.

"Do not . . . torment a dying . . . old man," he said, his voice broken, weak.

"Your torment is in there, Sammy, not out here with me."

He became angry then, and swung around to face me.

Gone.

To his physical sight, I was gone, even though in spirit I remained.

"Where did you—?" he started to ask.

He was very confused at that point, worried that his ailing body was affecting his mind, as well.

Suddenly he felt the need to walk over to the big top. His gait was slow and painful, but once inside, he looked at the empty seats, the "dome" of the tent, and smiled.

"My cathedral," he whispered to himself, lost in memories.

"And you have worshiped well, Sammy," a voice abruptly interrupted his random thoughts.

Three clowns were standing, together, in the center ring.

"How did you get in here?" Sammy demanded.

"None of that is important," the tallest, most garishly—painted of the three told him. "The fact is that we are here."

The clown next to him, shorter, less flamboyant, added, "You said this has been your cathedral. You speak the truth. For it is here that you have found your gods."

Sammy chuckled.

"You make more of my simple comment than I ever intended," he said.

"That is not so," commented the third clown, shorter than the tall one but taller than the short one, and with almost no paint at all. "You have given your life to this temple. You have fallen at the pedestal of your own conceit."

"Meaningless piffle," Sammy grunted.

"You call it such because it accuses, it entraps you, old man," the third clown added darkly.

"Please don't misunderstand us," the first one interpolated. "We are delighted, more than you will perhaps ever know, that you have done what you have done, Sammy the Clown."

Sammy felt a chill then.

"Delighted?" he repeated. "Why are you delighted if what you say is true? For what you paint is a picture of a vain old man who—"

His eyes widened.

"Do you now see a measure of the truth, Sammy?" the first clown asked. "You gave up your family for the circus. But you also ignored Someone else."

"I ignored only those who would come between me and my—"

"Passion, Sammy? Isn't that what you should be saying?"

"No, no, obsession!" the second clown interrupted. "It is not bad to have a passion in life. But it is otherwise to have an obsession."

"I stand corrected," the first clown agreed. "Your obsession, Sammy, has come between you and anyone not connected with this enterprise."

A gloved hand swung around, indicating the big tent.

We are delighted, more than you will perhaps ever know, that you have done what you have done . . . .

Sammy felt another chill as he recalled those words so recently spoken. He turned to go, intending to walk as rapidly as his old legs would carry him.

"It is not so easy as that," one of the clowns called to him.

"What do you mean?" Sammy shouted back.

"You know you cannot possibly leave this place, you funny old clown. You love it all too much!"

Sammy was scared, scared of the clowns, scared of what they were saying to him, scared of what he sensed about them.

You love it all too much!

But there, in that single statement, they had hit upon the truth. They had pointed out to him a singular fact of his very insular life.

And now that my life is almost over, what does it all mean? he thought. I gave my last performance tonight. There will be no more cheering or clapping for me. What would I be giving up if I just continued on my way? I am too old, too ill to exert myself again. I can stop now of my own accord. It is not that difficult. I can spend whatever time I have left, quietly, feasting on my memories. I will no longer have to arise at five o'clock each morning to help feed the animals or to move on to another town.

I spoke to Sammy then, after he had put some distance between himself and those three clowns.

I was not a clown, as I did, but a middle-aged man, someone who had seen Sammy many, many times. That was not a lie, you know. The God of Truth would not allow us to lie. Indeed I had seen Sammy often, though he had never been aware of my presence when I was purely spirit. Only when I became a child hoisted up on his knee was he able to see me, albeit in another form.

A flash of insight, inexplicable, fled across his ancient face.

"We have met before, haven't we?" he stated.

"We have, Sammy. You wiped away my tears."

Sammy's eyes widened with sudden realization.

"You were that little boy, weren't you?" Sammy asked, somehow aware, though not sure why this was so.

I nodded.

The little boy rushed out to the center ring more than thirty years earlier. Sammy grabbed him gently and lifted the child up onto his left knee.

"And what can I do for you, child ?" he asked.

At first I did not answer but simply looked at him. Tears began streaming down the cheeks of that adopted body.

"Why are you crying?" Sammy asked as he reached out to wipe the tears away. "You are too young to be crying like this."

"For you," I replied through the voice of a seven year old.

"For me? Why is that so? I am very happy. Why are you crying for me, a clown, a stranger?"

Sammy's attention was distracted then, the next act ready to enter the ring. He took the little boy off his knee, patted him on the head, and walked off . . . .

"Can you answer me now?" Sammy asked urgently, never having forgotten that singular incident. "Can you tell me what this is all about?

"There is your answer," I said, pointing to the three clowns behind him who beckoned from the canvas tent doorway.

"They're evil, aren't they?" he asked.

"Yes, they are."

"Why do they want me to go back there? I performed tonight for the last time. What could they possibly offer?"

"They want you. And they will try anything."

"They want this old, dying, stooped over body? Why? It's a wreck. They'd be getting damaged merchandise."

"It isn't your body, Sammy."

He pretended not to understand, but he knew well enough.

"Why should I side with you? Why should I not at least hear what they have to offer?"

"Because having heard, you will accept."

"Accept what?"

"One more night, Sammy."

"One more night in the center ring?"

"That is what they will claim."

"But that's impossible. I don't have the energy any longer."

I looked at Sammy, his eyes and mine locked into a gaze that he could not break for a moment or two. My human form shed tears, just as it had so many years earlier, tears for the same clown, now so old and frail.

"Are you sure that you would not give up everything for one more night, Sammy? The crowds cheering, the music playing, the smell of the sawdust in your nostrils? Are you so sure?"

"I have already done it," he said matter-of-factly. This was my final performance."

"Only because you thought that it had to be, that there was no other course of action open to you, as you came face to face with your physical limitations."

"I can scarcely walk now. I'm far too tired to give even one more performance."

"They would speak to the contrary, Sammy."

"I don't care."

Sammy smiled defiantly.

"Will you join me in my trailer?" he asked. "There are some things I'd like to show you."

Sammy!

Shrill, insistent voices were calling to him from the big top, night-time sirens beckoning him.

Sammy the Clown turned quickly, startled to hear his name shouted in such an eerie manner.

He shivered with the cold, but he smiled at me again, though with much less certainty than a moment before.

"They sound so confident, don't they?"

"Yes, they do," I agreed.

Just listen to what we have to say. What can you lose, Sammy?

He looked at me sheepishly.

"Come on," he said. "A nice hot cup of tea can do wonders for the cold."

Sammy the Clown walked to the trailer, oblivious to the fact that I was no longer with him, for I knew, with an awful sense of pure-white clarity, that I could do nothing more for this old man, this lost soul.

He stopped momentarily at the metal doorway, turned, and said, "Hey, mister, I've got a scrapbook of my—"

There was nothing except the dust his arthritic old feet had kicked up, scattered about for an instant by a slight, passing breeze, and then gone altogether, as though it had never been, like everything else in life.

~∞~

The circus tent was full.

The media were there, regional as well as national.

World-renowned Sammy the Clown had been convinced to give one more show, even after that so-called "last" performance.

Word spread from household to household, children to adults. . . one more night with the master clown, one more night with Sammy.

Three minutes into his act, he died of a heart attack.

Three other clowns carried him off.

A trapeze artist reported later that he had never seen them before, since Sammy was the only clown that circus had ever had.

"Another odd thing," he said to the television newscaster interviewing him.

"What was that?"

"Look, I'll be the first one to admit how crazy this will sound, but, well, I heard some pretty weird noises, mister."

"Noises?" the reporter asked. "Can you be more specific?"

"Crazy stuff . . . yeah, very strange . . . coming from the four of them as they all disappeared outside."

"What kinds of sounds?"

"Weeping."

"Weeping?"

"Yes . . . weeping and . . . and gnashing of teeth. Isn't that crazy?"

End of the Odyssey

I cannot say how it is that I know but know I do that I do know.

The wind perhaps? A strange new wind from the east? Does it carry the echoes of hapless demons with it, as they realize they will soon be dealt the destiny that had been foretold for so long?

I hear cries, I think, from Hell itself. Somehow, damned souls know what is on the verge of happening, the event which they chose to ignore or dispute. They who turned their backs on the Savior—their only source of escape from what they are now experiencing, and will experience forever—their cries are far worse than any I had heard before, even as I stood at the brink of Hell and pulled Darien from it, cries not only of torment but salvation lost, salvation pushed aside and spat upon, and now they know it is as real as the very flames around them.

I sit at the top of a tall mountain, high above the clouds. The sky is without blemish. The world below is shrouded under a blanket of soft whiteness.

Another sound supersedes that first, that wail. This is different, and familiar. I have heard it often in Heaven my home, the sound of many wings—a million wings, ten million, more perhaps—beating together, wings of spirit, like threads of shaped mist, all coming from above. I stand as tall as I can, looking upward.

Most mortals below will never know, not those left behind. They will turn around and find a brother, a sister, a spouse, a friend, a co-worker gone.

They will assume any number of explanations: a gigantic worldwide terrorist conspiracy . . . mere coincidence involving a number of disappearances at the same time . . . some fundamentalist religious charade . . . on and on . . . without opening their eyes and grappling with the truth.

I see blessed Jesus now, coming through the clouds, His arms outstretched, a single word from his lips, a word that connects with the souls of millions, forming an immediate, irresistible link, pulling them upward.

I leave that mountain and scurry about the planet, eager to witness those precious moments of rapturing in every place that I can. I move quickly, before these have all passed by, before that instant, tragic and foretold for so long, when I must leave as a consequence, along with all other angels, leave those humans now standing in their puzzled unbelief, leave them behind in the grip of Satan more completely than ever before.

After a pleasant luncheon, a man walking from London's Simpson's in the Strand to Trafalgar Square is taken just as he is pulling his coat more tightly around himself. He forgets everything, this man does, the chill London air, the traffic sounds, the paper vendor calling out the latest headline, the ancient odors that set London apart from any other city in the world. Yes, he forgets because he is looking into eyes, now, that are beyond any he has ever encountered, for they offer peace unimaginable in his finite frame, a frame that slips away even as the body itself is transformed, incorruptible from corruptible, words of joy escaping from his mouth as he is helped into everlasting life.

Helped into everlasting life . . .

That is a description of what it is like in Heaven with which some theologians perhaps might well take issue. After all, as they would point out, those in Hell also have everlasting life.

Up to a point, I must say in reply, adding that being in Hell is hardly "life" as it was envisioned in the mind of a holy God, hardly life that is worth living. No, I would have to say everlasting life is only for the redeemed. The damned have something else altogether.

I come next to an abortion clinic, and go inside. There is confusion.

Babies are disappearing! Some as they are being scraped from their mother's wombs, others as they have been temporarily tossed onto a cold metal table.

Gone!

Nurses are screaming. Doctors are trying to calm them. Mothers recoil in terror.

&

I wish I could capture the moments that I now am seeing, capture these on video tape and show them to a society that might change its ways with such evidence before it.

I wish I could, but I cannot. What I see is for myself and, hopefully, for the consciences of other witnesses.

I see a baby who has been aborted whole, one who is supposedly dead, yet continues to live. I see a doctor order a nurse to "dispose" of the "thing." The nurse looks at him, and then at the living miniature human form in front of her, and she hesitates, wanting to obey her boss, the man who controls her livelihood, but not quite able to take her hands, put them around the baby boy's neck, and twist. Or shovel him into the oven on premises. (Heil Hitler, eh!)

Grumbling, the doctor pushes the nurse aside. As he is reaching for the tiny form, the baby is raptured—the baby is taken up, but not instantaneously. There is a transitory moment in time when he turns toward the doctor who would be his slayer, turns toward this man intent on atrocity, and, possessed of a growing wisdom, wisdom that stems from He Who is calling him, from that child issue forth the final tears of his brief existence, the last shreds of what he once was. Now there is only love in the tiny eyes, love mixed with pity—hence, the tears—love so supreme, so unconditional, so undeserved that the doctor breaks into uncontrollable sobs as he reaches upward toward the child, and the child down toward him. But it is too late, too late for conscience or regret. There is no more time. There is nothing for the child but the loving arms of His Savior and nothing for the doctor but the sharp talons of his own master as he runs screaming from the room to collapse in the corridor outside, not propelled by a vision of incalculable horror, but of a baby's blind, beautiful love beyond reason itself, a deep and total forgiveness he can scarce imagine, and never abide. That is why he can say only, "It cannot be, it cannot be, oh, God, it cannot be," again and again until the clutching darkness has him in judgment unassailable.

~ფ~

It is nearly completed now, this my sojourn on earth, as well as the Rapture. I see others going to the Savior in the air. The elderly, once gripped by pain, suddenly find that it has left them. Those men, women, and children dying of cancer are taken, the ravages of that killer disease eliminated all over the world. The retarded have regained all their faculties as they reach their hands high, and He calls them home. Women suffering through the trauma that has followed rape are now completely at peace as they leave the ground, and He gives them a security that will never pass away.

So many . . .

Millions are saying goodbye to sin, to disease, to fear, to despair, to loneliness.

To doubt, indeed that—in its place the reality that faith all along had been telling them was true.

True!

I have not seen True. Could my comrade still be there at the entrance to Eden? But why? Surely he must know. How could he not know?

I go to the Garden, and do find him as I had suspected, exactly where he was when I last left him.

"It is the Rapture, True," I tell him. "We all can leave now. There is no more place for us in this world."

He shakes his head sadly.

"All but me," he says. "My task is not yet ended."

"But there is no more need—" I start to reply, then stop myself, for I had been about to say, "But there is no need to stand guard."

He smiles, seeing my expression.

"You understand, do you not?" he remarks. "There is more need than ever that I, the last of angelkind here on this planet, be twice as vigilant, twice as strong, calling upon everything with which the Creator has fortified me."

"And you will need all of that, dear friend," I agree now that I understand that he must remain, what he must face.

For there is to be a wave of evil so intense that it will sweep over everyone who is left. Some will resist. Some will come to a saving knowledge of Jesus Christ. But most will not, seduced by Satan in this climactic bid for supremacy.

"I have heard them planning, Stedfast," True says.

He shivers then, as though the memories are shaking him to the very core of himself.

"I have heard what they will be doing with the living," he continues. "There will be more and more manifestations, you know, appearances by demonic entities as the veil between Hell and this planet is rent asunder. And mortals will not be able to cope. Many will be driven mad, you know. Many will take their own lives. Others will fall in slavish devotion to the new gods of this age. They will become as one with the evil one, and follow him on the path to damnation."

He pauses, then: "Devilwalk! That is what I have heard it called. That is surely what it is."

Together we shiver at that thought.

. . . the veil between Hell and this planet is rent asunder.

No angels to keep it in place, no Holy Spirit to hold back the onslaught.

"Pure evil, Stedfast," angel True says. "And I will be the only one of unfallen creation in the midst of it."

There seems to be fear in his manner at that moment, but if that is what it is, it is gone in a millisecond. And now he stands, his presence emboldened by a special determination, a divine valor.

"I can take it," he remarks. "I can take whatever offenses they fling at me, whatever foul tricks they might try."

"I will stay with you," I offer.

"You cannot. That would displease the Father, I am sure. He has given me my holy charge and I shall not dishonor Him by shifting responsibility to another."

True is being what he could never cease being. His nature did not permit disobeying the Father.

"I will come back, True," I say. "I will come back, and we shall walk side by side through a restored Eden."

For a moment, images of the original Eden consume me.

For a moment, I stand there, anxious for the future. I hear True calling to me, "I will be here, Stedfast. I will be waiting. Trust on that. Believe it!"

And I am gone elsewhere on earth.

Twenty

The last man to be raptured is named Jonathan, and he is very old. He walks at sunrise in a green English meadow with his beloved black-gray-white tabby by his side.

They have been together for sixteen years.

"It's a beautiful morning," Jonathan says. "Smell the heather, Boy-Boy?"

He thinks the cat can understand, and in some respects, he is right. This one does understand that he has spoken, and even if the sense of his words is lost on the animal, merely the sound of his master's voice is enough to set Boy-Boy apurring.

"It's been a rough four months, my dear friend," Jonathan continues. "First, there was that hernia operation. It was hard to recuperate at home. I still think they rushed me out of the hospital too quickly. And with Jessie gone, I—I—"

He hasn't stuttered for a long time. He did when his wife Jessie's heart failed, and he tried to revive her somehow, and cried out for her not to leave him. But that was a long time ago.

He reaches out and pats Boy-Boy, who digs his claws into the soft earth, a sign of momentary contentment.

"You were so faithful," he recalls, "always stretched out in bed right smack up against my right leg. Whenever I would groan with pain, you would look up at me, and it was almost as though you were asking if there was anything you could do to help."

This unusual companion had shown the loyalty and devotion of a dog. There was a great deal that Boy-Boy did to show his unconditional love. He would greet Jonathan and Jessie at the front door as they came in from a bicycling jaunt through the countryside, and fall down in front of them, and rollover on his back because he knew that that pleased them. And if they were pleased, he, too, felt happy.

When Jessie was in bed, that horrible arthritic pain constant for her, and Jonathan found it necessary to go into town to get a refill of some medicine, Boy-Boy would set himself on the pillow next to her and comfort her in ways that helped, that really helped. Once, after finding some relief from the pain in a deep sleep, she woke to find that Boy-Boy had wrapped his four legs around her and was resting his head in the palm of her hand, his warmth radiating through her, soothing her tired spirit.

"You mean so much to me," Jonathan says as he looks down at his side, and finds that Boy-Boy has crawled some yards away, and is now standing uncertainly, his legs very weak.

"No!" the old man cries as he struggles to his feet, and rushes over to the cat, sitting down beside him, and taking his friend in his arms.

"Come on, Boy-Boy, you can make it," Jonathan begs. "We've been together so long. I can't bear to be without you, too. Losing Jessie was so bad, and you helped me more than you can know. Please, Boy-Boy, hang on a while longer."

But the cat has no more strength. He had been close to death three times over the past four months, as a siege of tremors had racked his body, each making him more and more weak.

Now, as his beloved master holds him, he opens his eyes wide, and looks at the man he loves with all his being, and tries to tell him what he has just now seen, something bright and beautiful, sparkling light and music, and, yes, the woman, the woman he also loved, waiting, her arms reaching out to take him.

Boy-Boy's chest vibrates for a few moments.

"How can you be purring now?" Jonathan asks. "How can you—?"

Then the cat reaches out, and does something then that he had done often through the years, he folds his front paws around Jonathan's wrist, and pulls that hand closer to him, closer to his fur. How he enjoyed the feel of human flesh against him, and he sends forth for the last time a surge of warmth from his body.

But that is it. He has nothing more to give. His body sags as though with relief, but he is not quite gone. Some small spark of him lingers.

"I can't let you go!" Jonathan screams. "I need you just a little while longer!"

It is time for me now, time for me to appear before this old man.

"Let him go from that body," I say. "Let him put aside what is now of no use to him. It does not function anymore, you know, that earthly body is—"

"No, stranger!" Jonathan interrupts. "No, do not say it. It cannot be! I need him. I do need him."

"And your friend, your very good, friend needs you to say that it is time now. He must go, for his sake. Release him, Jonathan. I know that you love him far too much to ask him to suffer another moment for your sake."

"But I'll be alone," Jonathan retorts. "I'll have no one."

"You will have me," I reply. "I will stay with you."

"But for how long? How long will you be with me?"

I am about to speak when he interrupts me.

"You have just arrived here. I knew Boy-Boy for sixteen years, Jessie for many more than that. Why should I expect a stranger to comfort me?"

"Listen, Jonathan, listen please."

He does that, he listens as Boy-Boy lets out a sigh, the body now limp, a slight breeze stirring through the soft, beautiful fur.

"I can't bury him," Jonathan tells me desperately. "My hands, my fingers, the arthritis!"

"It's okay. Just put him down on the ground," I say.

"But there must be a grave," he protests. "My beloved Jessie is buried only a few yards from here."

"No more graves, Jonathan, no more dying."

With great tenderness, Jonathan lays the still, thin body on the cold rocky ground.

I pause, smiling, and then say, "Now look up, old man."

He does. In an instant his tears are gone.

"You are the last one," I say, "the very last one."

Even for me the emotions are too strong, and I must stop. I realize that it is all over, this phase of God's plan for the ages, and what Jonathan and I will leave behind is not a world in which we could ever want to remain for a single additional moment.

"I promised to stay with you, Jonathan," I finally tell him. "I will do that. You asked for how long? I can tell you now."

"No need," he whispers with awe. "I know."

There is the sound of a final beckoning trumpet. No longer bound by age or ailments or grief, Jonathan is swept up from the earth, and I with him, beneath us the grave of the woman he loved for fifty years. Nearby lay a black-gray-white body as useless as hers had become. But above, ah, above, someone familiar, her arms outstretched, her smile the very light of Heaven's own radiance, and, waiting, at her feet, loyal, loving, beyond flesh itself, a familiar friend, a special gift from the Creator, now returned to them both, to be enjoyed again. No more parting, no more waiting for sweet devotion to be jerked away by dark death.

How long, Jonathan? You asked me, now you know. How long will I be by your side, and so many others I have come to know and to love with a measure of the love of God Himself? Isn't the answer truly, truly wonderful? Isn't it?

That is why the Father, my blessed, blessed Creator, called me by the name that He did in that ageless instant when I came into being, for it was to be the purpose of my life, the sole and holy reason for my very existence.

That is why I am what I am, and will always be, long after the lion lies down once again with the lamb.

Stedfast . . . as ever.

True's Epilogue

I watched that first couple go, their nakedness covered, their shame exposed. They left as a storm arose and swept over the whole of the earth. The first murder in the history of the human race followed, one son killing another . . . .

It is peaceful now. The sky is clear. The air is warm, dry.

I await their return.

I have been waiting for thousands of years. Every epoch of human history has passed by.

And there have been visitors, human and demonic. They have stumbled upon this place, but none have gotten past me.

I have been capable for this my assignment. I need no food. I need no water. My sustenance comes from the Father of all.

I feel His power. I need His power. I am but one angel, and yet hordes from Hell have stood about, taunting me.

They have stayed with me for long periods of time, have talked about the old days of unblemished fellowship in Heaven before they followed Lucifer.

"For us, there is no boredom," one said. "We go where we please. We do what we want. We have no restrictions. We are free, True, and that is true."

I recalled the times when we walked the streets of gold, when we were in harmony, when the world below was untainted.

"You left," I replied. "I did not."

"To be in service to a new master."

"A pretender to the throne."

"The rightful heir—big difference."

"Deceit. Lucifer is the master of that, and nothing else."

They cannot tempt me, cannot seduce me into their perversion.

And always they went away, though always they returned, with some new taunt, some foul breath of deviltry.

Once, just once, it was Lucifer himself, not his underlings, not the duped spirits of a rejected Heaven.

Lucifer.

My once comrade.

That is truly how it was. It was Lucifer, Stedfast, Darien, and True. Close in Heaven, close to one another, close to our Creator.

To have him leave, to have him turn into what he became was like wrenching a piece of myself away and throwing it into some eternal sea. But I healed. So did the others. Even so, we retained the memories.

And the memories were what Lucifer tried to use against me.

"You are lonely," he said.

"No, I am not. I am alone. But I have visitors. And I can callout to the Father anytime I wish."

"So said Another. And yet even He was driven to cry, 'My God, my God, why hast Thou forsaken me?' Remember those words, True. Remember them during those nights when there is no one, when there is nothing but darkness, and you are alone with the memories of what we once had, what we once were."

This fallen being named Lucifer knew what to say. He knew how to say it. He had, after all, persuaded a third of all my kind to join with him in his rebellion in Heaven.

But I was called True from the beginning. And that has never changed. My name is not Inconsistent. Or Wavering. Or Weak. I am True, and so I shall be to my Father, and to myself, and are these not one and the same?

Lucifer lost his veneer of propriety.

"You are stupid, True," he screamed.

"And you are false, is that not true? You reek with deceit. You shroud yourself with treachery. I serve the Almighty Father. You are the father of nothing but the foul deeds of your compliant demonkind. You stand before the human race and offer yourself as a messiah. Yet you are the very voice of Hell. You offer nothing but damnation!"

That got him, I think, at least for the moment.

Lucifer had no immediate reply. I thought he was going to leave, but he turned at the last moment, and looked back at me, beyond me, to the hint behind me of what Eden had become.

"Once so beautiful," Lucifer said. "Once so alive . . ."

His voice trailed off, and he bowed his loathsome head as though regretting—as much as he was capable of anything of the sort—what he had wrought through the ages of time, epitomized by this dead, dusty, melancholy place.

Something happened then, one of the last remaining creatures made its way to the gate where we stood, a tall creature, rather like a young giraffe, born to be free and proud of its beauty, born to live without disease, born to last forever, without death to take it away into the dark night.

It had aged inexorably. It had become ill, contracting some sort of repugnant disease that reduced its colors to pale blotches and its gait to a pitiable shadow of what once had been.

Then it fell past the gate at the feet of its executioner, at the feet of Satan—and just as it died, it looked up into his face, and there were tears in its eyes. It groaned once, and that was all. There was nothing more. It was gone.

❦

That was ages ago, centuries past. There are no more creatures left, the husk of once—Eden shriveled and ugly, and I continue to be alone. I have seen no demons for a very long time. Perhaps they have gathered together for Armageddon.

Is that music I hear? Has someone somehow slipped past me after all my efforts and broken into that which I have tried to guard for so very long?

I turn for a moment, to look beyond the entrance into that place.

I am startled.

A flower is blooming, looking much like an orchid. I enter Eden and stand beside it. I drink deeply of the scent it offers.

How can that be?

In a nearby stream, I hear the trickling of water over rocks at the bottom.

And swimming just below the surface are silver and gold fish.

Life!

I turn, and see green leaves unfurl on a tree that had been dead for five thousand years.

On one of the branches are two birds.

Singing! They have returned to Eden, and they are singing their joy!

A bush is green. The soil is rich and brown.

That music I hear . . . again . . . so beautiful!

I turn around and around. Before me, in an instant, Eden is coming to life, its own resurrection ascendant at this very moment.

I walk almost numbly to the entrance. I look up at the sky.

I see heavenly hosts descending. I see my fellow beings forming a glorious river of light and life.

I see the Son. He stands before me. He smiles as He reaches out and touches me.

I kneel before the Father in adoration, my head bowed, my wings—

Two voices!

I look up.

Oh, Lord, how many times has there been temptation? How many times have I been asked by demons to turn aside? But I did not. I stayed, Holy One. I stayed for Thee.

"Hello, dear, dear True," the woman says.

"It has been a long time," the man adds.

They are changed these two, cleansed, as radiant as the angels accompanying them.

"Will you give us entrance, True?" the couple inquires of me.

I say nothing, I can say nothing. Words are useless when souls are united.

I step aside for the first time since sin entered creation.

The two stop just beyond the entrance, beauty surrounding them, life shouting its emergence in calls of living creatures from the trees, from the ground—everywhere are sounds and scents and rebirth.

They walk in awe, this first couple. The woman pauses before a flower of remarkable beauty. She bends down, pressing her nose quietly among the petals, and takes in what these have to offer to her. Then she stands straight, realizing that nothing has changed—if anything the garden is more beautiful than at the beginning—yea, nothing has changed, except centuries of pain, of disease, of turmoil for the entire human race.

"And all because of me, and my man," she says out loud.

But I go to her, more like Stedfast than True, and I remind her that none of that matters, that she has been forgiven, that her man has shared in this forgiveness.

She smiles.

"Dear friend," she says, "I said that not in melancholy or regret any longer but in rejoicing that our Father can forgive so much, that He can welcome even us into His Kingdom.

She reaches out to touch the flower.

"And now we are back," she remarks softly. "Praise His holy name, He has allowed us to return."

I leave them to their walk along familiar paths amidst resurgent majesty. Soon they will come to the spot where the Tree of the Knowledge of Good and Evil once stood.

No longer.

It is gone. In its place stand angels at their station, angels who, like me, will be with them time without end.

"What now, Lord?" I ask as I stand outside.

"Be with them, True," He tells me. "Be by their side, but not as the guardian of this place."

"But as what, blessed Jesus?"

I hear a chorus then, a celebration among ten thousand upon ten thousand of my kind.

"Be with them, True . . . as their dear friend," Jesus the Christ proclaims.

Sin has been banished forever!

I think, for a moment, of my former comrade-in- Heaven, of Lucifer suffering amidst the flames for what he has done, that for which he has been judged. I think of his guilt, his shame. But nowhere is there his repentance. It never came. He clung to his abominations and could not, would not, did not let go.

Then I turn and enter Eden, and, in the midst of life as it was meant to be, I think of him no more.

finis

Fiction

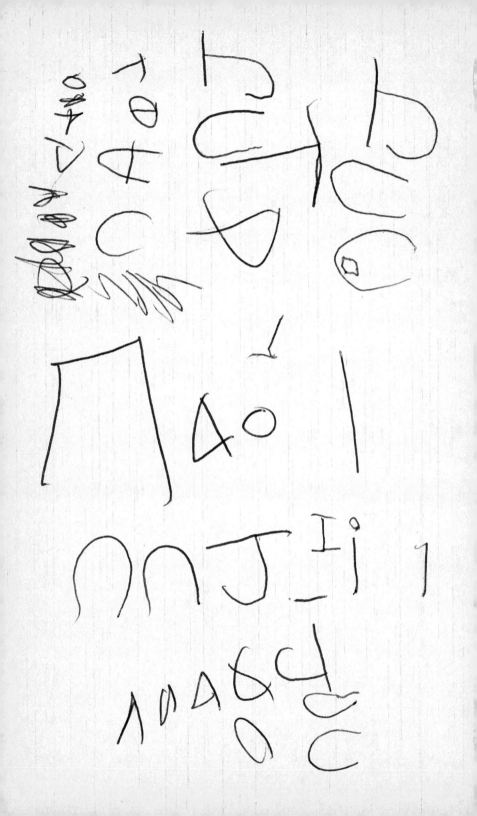